Sherlock Holmes and the Adventure of the Beer Barons

By Christopher James

Paperback ISBN 978-1-78705-558-2
ePub ISBN 978-1-78705-559-9
PDF ISBN 978-1-78705-560-5

Published by MX Publishing
335 Princess Park Manor, Royal Drive,
London, N11 3GX
www.mxpublishing.co.uk

Cover design by Brian Belanger

"He was a wise man who invented beer."
– Plato

"For a quart of ale is a dish for a king."
– William Shakespeare

For Claudia

ONE

The Cask

When I think back to the final autumn of the last century, I am reminded not of the russets and ambers of the lime trees in Regent's Park, but rather a glass of India pale ale. For those unfamiliar with this *elixir vitae*, for it has fallen out of favour of late, it is a highly hopped beer, brisk and bright in the glass. It slaked the thirst of men from Putney to the Punjab and brought fortunes to the enterprising men of the East Midlands; so much so that a new class was born: the beerage, which swept aside the contumacious descendants of the old knights loyal to their French king, William the Conqueror, and transformed the towns (one in particular) into new fiefdoms of wealth and fortune. What is more, this clear, delicious ale, brewed from those magical waters of Burton-upon-Trent, was responsible for a singular adventure that, until now, lay unread in my disordered manuscript volumes from the year 1899.

In the course of my adventures with Sherlock Holmes we were frequently drawn into new and unfamiliar worlds. These were often self-contained spheres that operated largely unseen, each with its own carefully calibrated hierarchy, its own codes and eccentricities. Such was the case with the "Adventure of the Beer Barons." It was a problem so disturbingly strange that even now I find it impossible to peer into a glass of pale ale without seeing the shadows that darkened the ominous autumn which closed a momentous century.

It was another baffling episode in an already perplexing year. Holmes, with his usual brusque efficiency, had already solved the cases known to the public as "The Adventure of Charles Augustus Milverton," not to speak of the harrowing tale of "The Retired Colourman." We had barely recovered from the macabre incidents described in "The African Horror," when the discovery was made. The services of my inestimable roommate were once again called upon and with them, by proxy, my own. As I shall relate, we also received some unexpected assistance in the resolution of this case. I am grateful for permission to include several extracts from a diary in this manuscript, which will illuminate this aspect of our adventure.

The day was slipping by as Holmes and I reclined in the lengthening shadows of our sitting room at 221b Baker Street. I lit the gas lamps then returned to my post opposite my friend. Between us a meagre fire burned, befitting the continuing beleaguered state of my finances. London, it seemed, had entered an unprecedented spate of good health. While beneficial, no doubt, to the capital's productivity and paying down the national debt, as a medical doctor, it had left me almost bereft. I survived by carefully rationing my already paltry army pension, substituting my beloved Laphroaig for a cheaper brand of Scotch whisky, and by subsisting, I am ashamed to say, on the generosity of my friend and the life-saving properties of Mrs. Hudson's cooking.

'I have been reflecting, Watson,' my friend remarked, 'on the folly of putting to sea in these floating steel islands.'

'You are referring,' I intimated, 'to the recent launch of the RMS Oceanic.' Lugubriously, I lifted *The Times* from where it lay on the coffee table and scanned the lead story. 'Over 17,000 tonnes,' I read.

'It is an act of the most astonishing hubris to expect these iron leviathans to roam the waters without expecting some disaster to befall them.' As if to illustrate the point, he produced a penny from between his fingers and dropped it into a glass of water that stood upon the table. It sunk at a slight angle to the bottom, sending a thin trail of bubbles to the surface. 'Once again,' he said, his brown eyes gleaming, 'it is man's unshakeable belief that he is the master of creation and that by sheer force of will he can conquer the very elements from which he is made.'

'You are an enemy of progress?' I challenged.

'Far from it,' he laughed, pressing his pipe into service. 'I only suggest that the progress is in the wrong direction. The future lies at an atomic level. It is the division of the molecule; the invisible work and interactions of the tiniest particles that will determine the future of mankind. These great beasts of the oceans are merely emblems of man's habitual delusion.'

As we spoke, I became aware of a set of heavy hooves in the street, drawing to a halt just below our window.

'A little late in the day for a delivery,' I remarked.

'The more singular detail,' my friend added, 'is that the cart is carrying barrels of ale. Did you not hear that distinctive knock of wood against wood? As far as I am aware, Mrs. Hudson has not responded to a new

6

calling to become a publican.' I rose and made my way to the window. 'Two horses, I fancy,' noted Holmes, without rising from his chair. 'The cart has larger wheels at the back; a smaller pair at the front.' 'You are perfectly correct,' I confirmed, glancing down. 'Anything else?'

'The driver has injured his left arm.'

'My dear Holmes!' I exclaimed. 'You have excelled yourself. You are right once again. It is held in a sling. An act of pure clairvoyance!'

'Flim flam!' scoffed Holmes. 'It is plain to anyone with ears that the horse nearest to us was slower to stop that the other.'

'But, surely,' I broke in, 'this man has the wrong address. What business do we have with barrels of ale?'

'We shall see,' opined Holmes as the knock came on the door. Mrs Hudson answered and presently requested that I join her at the entrance. I was greeted by the driver, an emaciated fellow with a permanent grin and protruding, jug-like ears. His small, porcine eyes, hooded with blonde lashes, were just visible below the brim of his bowler. He wore a tight-fitting overcoat, the left-arm sleeve empty and pinned to his coat. At his side was a lad of fifteen or so, who was sweating as he manhandled a barrel off the cart and rolled it to the door.

'Feeling thirsty, sir?' the driver enquired. 'A delivery for Mr. Sherlock Holmes.' I signed his delivery note and fished a couple of coins from my pocket, indicating that I required the barrel to be delivered *over*, rather than *to*, the threshold. He gestured to the lad to haul the barrel over the remaining hurdle.

Presently, I was left alone with the consignment, puzzling over this strange windfall. My thoughts turned once again to my financial predicament. If Holmes and I were to refrain from wine and hard liquor for a month or so, and switch our attention to beer, we would make a considerable saving in our housekeeping.

'I am partial to an ale on a warm summer's day,' remarked Holmes, whom I suddenly found at my side. 'Less so in the cold of an autumn evening. I find it has a soporific effect on the brain.'

'A pity,' I muttered. 'I believe this would have seen us through to the spring.' Holmes rapped the barrel with his knuckles then examined the sides with the utmost concentration, finally returning his fingers to his chin.

'As it transpires, Watson,' concluded Holmes, 'there is not enough beer in the barrel to even wet the bottom of a glass.'

'You are mistaken, Holmes,' I assured him. 'I saw the delivery boy exhaust himself simply wheeling the barrel to the door.'

'No doubt,' my friend agreed, 'but it was under the weight of something other than beer. Now be a good fellow and fetch the crowbar from beneath the stairs and we shall discover the contents for ourselves.'

Drawing on the remarkable reserves of strength he kept so well concealed within his wiry frame, my friend worked the crowbar beneath the rim of the lid. Then, with a sudden violence that would have startled the Ripper himself, he plunged down upon the implement and succeeded in springing the top from the barrel. I staggered back as the heavy wooden disk clattered to the floor and we took our first look inside. I was compelled to blink twice before assuring myself it was quite real.

Coiled, as a baby within a womb, we saw the form of a man. He was crouching, facing down, his skin horribly pale, evidently holding his knees, the pate of his balding head and the nape of his neck exposed to the light.

'Why, it is a man!' I cried. I examined him a moment and decided on the strength of the merest rise and fall of his shoulders, that he was alive.

'A blanket, Holmes, quickly,' I demanded, 'and fetch some brandy.' My friend leapt into action, bounded up the stairs and disappeared into our rooms. It was unusual for me to seize the initiative in such a way, but this was a medical matter and the crisis fell squarely within my purview. Holmes swiftly returned with the necessary items.

'Now, help me lift him, Holmes.' Gently, we eased our hands under his arms and, upon my signal, we took his not inconsiderable weight, raising him up and out of the barrel.

We hoisted him into the air, his legs tucked stiffly beneath him, as if rigor mortis had set in. A tin cup with a dented lid was all that remained at the bottom of the barrel. For a moment I doubted my original diagnosis that he was alive. He wore a pair of heavy work trousers and a thin white shirt that, though of good quality, hung loosely about his shoulders. He was perhaps forty-five years of age, barefoot, well built, with a thick neck and full moustache. As we laid him down and draped the blanket across his shoulders, he broke into a fit of the shakes, his teeth chattering so violently I feared he was in danger of shattering his molars.

'You must help me,' he stuttered.

'Drink this,' I ordered and pressed the brandy to his lips.

'Hennessy,' he whispered, swallowing the liquor, 'woody, with vanilla spice.' With that, he passed out. Holmes and I peered at each other.

'Invariably,' opined Holmes, 'it is the dullest days that deliver the most curious incidents.'

I awoke the next morning upon our velvet chaise longue, beneath a red woollen blanket we kept for such emergencies. Selflessly, I had given over my bedroom to our unexpected guest and for a moment struggled to orientate myself. A cloud of smoke drifted across my line of sight as if a cannon had recently been discharged on the field of battle.

'The year is 1899,' a familiar voice struck up. 'The date is the seventh of October and today, my dear Watson, a new adventure begins. Now I suggest that we rouse our visitor, make a start on the smoked Yarmouth bloaters Mrs. Hudson has exquisitely prepared, and see if we cannot extract some data to begin our case.'

Our guest ate ravenously at breakfast and we had few words out of him until his plate was picked clean. He soaked the juices from the plate with a slice of bread, consumed the remaining crumbs, then sat back with an air of satisfaction. Now washed, shaved except for his moustache, and wearing my second-best suit, it was as if my doppelganger had joined us at the table. Being prone to superstition, my heart sank at this, although I did not air my views for fear of incurring the wrath of Holmes, that logician and naysayer of fanciful notions.

'I am obliged to you for your kindness,' our guest said at length. The accent, I fancied, was Midlands, but it was not as flat as the Black Country.

'If you do not consider the questions too obvious,' I began, 'can you tell us who you are, and how you came to arrive at our front door in a barrel?' My friend laughed at this.

'Watson,' he cried. 'we can hardly trouble our visitor to respond to the first question when the answer is so plain.' I sent Holmes a puzzled look.

'My dear sir,' he said, addressing the man, 'please indulge my friend Dr. Watson and me, while we play our game. Note the discoloration of the fingernails, produced by the action of malt water on the pigmentation. Then there were the heavy trousers, worn only in this particular line of work, also impregnated with malt. Perhaps most tellingly, there was this pen I found in his pocket.

Our guest registered his surprise when he saw it and immediately held out his hand to reclaim it. Holmes obliged.

'Why, Holmes,' I said, 'it looks to be a perfectly ordinary writing implement.'

'And in some ways, it is,' he confirmed. 'Note the letters across the centre. 'BHC.' The callous on his right hand tells me he is a hockey player. That gives me Hockey Club. But the 'B' is suggestive of a place name. As you have detected from his accent, he is no native of Birmingham. No, this man is from the great beer town of Burton and a member of its newly formed Burton Hockey Club. Its secretary, I fancy. But the real clue is what's inside. For instead of ink, it is my belief that the ink channels contain a minute sample of a distinctive pale ale.'

'It is all true.' The man gazed at Holmes with something like wonder. He pressed a handkerchief to his lips, then peered around him. 'I can scarcely credit that I am alive.'

'There are,' my friend agreed with a thin smile, 'more straightforward routes to Baker Street.'

'On the strength of this, Mr. Holmes, you are as remarkable as your reputation suggests. My name is Harold Butterworth and I am, or rather, I was, the head brewer at Houghton's of Burton-upon-Trent. Until yesterday, I was second only to the mayor and the great beer barons themselves in importance. The town's folk would doff their caps to me as I walked down Shobnall Street. I own a fine house on the river, and men all over England knock at the door seeking my expertise. But today, I am a pariah. It is quite possible, that at any moment, a constable will appear at the door to arrest me.'

'No policeman knocks at the door of 221b Baker Street without seeking my assistance. You are as safe within these walls as you would be at a foreign embassy. Now, I suggest that after we retrieve our smoking apparatus, you begin at the beginning, sparing us no detail. Watson, I believe we have acquired a quantity of Mazawattee tea leaves. I suggest that we introduce them to some scalding water and then allow them to do their work. Shall we, gentlemen?'

10

Butterworth lit a cigar, inspected the smouldering end, then vigorously shook out the flame of the match. He reclined in his seat, and lifting the porcelain cup to his lips, sipped at his tea. For a few seconds he appeared to savour the taste, as if silently assessing its flavours.

'You will be aware no doubt,' he began, 'of the continuing popularity of the beverage known as India pale ale. For eighty years it has been the favoured drink of our countrymen in our adopted land. It is a highly hopped pale ale of the most supreme quality. It travels exceptionally well and each newly arrived batch is received with something close to rapture. Lord Curzon himself has gone on record to say that it is without peer as a drink to quench the dry throats of the Punjab.'

'As an advertisement for your beer,' sniffed Holmes, sending a plume of blue smoke towards the ceiling, 'your account has exceeded itself. As a statement of the problem however, it has told me nothing. Pray move to the nub of the matter.'

'Naturally, you are knowledgeable men. I shall limit myself to the appalling facts themselves. Fifty men of the Queen's Royal, West Surrey, Regiment have been taken gravely ill. At the last report, forty-eight lie in a high fever, and two have already lost their lives.'

'These are soldiers in a faraway land,' I put in. 'They know the risks they run. What part do you play in their misfortune?'

'They believe that my ale has poisoned them and a warrant has been issued for my arrest.'

'Spurious!' I declared, rising to my feet. 'There could be a hundred explanations. It is infinitely more likely to be caused by bacteria in the water than the beer. There is good reason why beer is drunk in favour of water in such places.'

'Be that as it may,' returned Butterworth, 'but a local scientist has analysed a sample of the batch and declared that it contains a toxin directly linked to the fatalities. Word has been communicated back and criminal charges have been brought.'

'You are man of good standing,' said Holmes. 'With your knowledge and reputation, you should have little trouble proving your innocence.'

'So you might think,' he agreed. 'But if you pardon my mixed metaphors, I have been thrown to the dogs, and they have me over a barrel. The Indian market is worth many hundreds of thousands of pounds to my employers. They can always acquire another head brewer, but their reputation is not so easily repaired. In our business, with competitors in every corner, reputation is everything. If they can prove that this is the work of one errant worker, then they are quite willing to make me the scapegoat and move on.'

'A formidable predicament,' mused Holmes. 'Goats, dogs *and* barrels. Now, speaking of which, tell us the circumstances of your escape.'

'By all means,' Butterworth agreed, sitting forward in his chair. 'Though it occurred not forty-eight hours ago, it seems the stuff of nightmares. It was three o'clock in the afternoon. I had just completed my inspection of the maltings, when I saw my assistant, Leonard Tolwood, dashing towards me, his apron flapping at his waist.

"Steady there," I told him, "you shall bowl us over like skittles." Yet his usual mirth was missing and his face was blanched white with fear.

"Mr. Butterworth," he gasped, "they mean to arrest you." I stared at him as if he were a wild man. I took him by the shoulders.

"What is the meaning of this, Tolwood?" I demanded.

"They are saying you have poisoned a regiment in India and they mean to take you in. Scientists have confirmed it. The police are at the front gates."

"We do not turn and run at the first sign of trouble," I assured him. "There will be a simple explanation and I am happy to help them discover it."

"But Mr. Butterworth,' he begged, with a look of desperation, "you do not very well understand. They have already handed you over. Your only hope is to run." I am not an impulsive man, Mr. Holmes,' he assured my friend. 'Brewing is not a business that rewards such behaviour. But even I registered that the situation was dire.'

"You cannot be complicit in this," I told him. "Do not throw away a promising career by covering my tracks." I could hear the thump of heavy boots tramping through the passage. "I will make my own arrangements," I assured him, "and prove my innocence. You go back and tell them I cannot be found. I shall be in contact. Look out for a letter from London. I shall sign it 'Wakefield.'"

"Very well," he assured me, clasping my hand in his and glancing behind him. "Good luck to you, sir."

'As soon as he left me, I sought out an old, trusted hand, Eli Arkham, our longest-serving cooper. He was old even when I was fresh-faced apprentice. But he could be trusted with the crown jewels

12

for the principal reason that he would have no use for them. His only passions are his work and his beer, which, in our fortunate case, are one and the same thing. I told him to do exactly as I said. It was he who imprisoned me within the barrel, providing one or two air holes, a tin cup, and instructions as to where I was to be delivered.'

'I had no idea,' I put in, 'that Mr. Holmes' fame had extended to your part of the world.'

'I am a distant relation of Eileen Butterworth,' he explained, 'whom Mr. Holmes assisted last spring in the strange business of The Silver Peacock.' Holmes remained impassive.

'I recall nothing of that case,' I said, turning to my friend, somewhat affronted.

'Some problems, you are aware, Watson, I pursue without your assistance. You are a busy man with your own matters to attend to. I shall impart the details of the case one evening when we have exhausted other avenues of conversation. It was not entirely without interest, particularly regarding the business of the feathered man. But we digress.' Holmes turned to Butterworth, fixing him with that disconcerting stare he employed when eliciting information.

'Naturally, I have some questions,' my friend continued.

'Then let me hear them.'

'This Mr. Tolwood,' he began, 'is he a man of some ability?'

'He has promise, certainly, but he has not yet shown originality in his methods. He is attentive however, and in time I believe will make a fine successor.'

'Do you have any evidence for the poisonings beyond Tolwood's account?'

'No,' Butterworth confessed. 'And it is not a matter the army or the brewery would share with the public.'

'Finally,' began Holmes, 'can you tell me, as a left-handed fellow, does Tolwood have any difficulty operating the brewing apparatus?'

Butterworth and I stared at Holmes in astonishment.

'How could you possibly know such a detail?' asked Butterworth, pitching forward in his chair.

'It is a guess, surely,' I scoffed. 'The odds are fifty-fifty are they not?'

'Incorrect,' said Holmes. 'In fact, the odds are ten-to-one. There is not an equal probability of left- and right-handedness in any new-born child. Forgive me, but I have the advantage in this area, having written a monograph upon the criminal history of the left-handed, with notations on the advantages and drawbacks accompanying this singular feature.

'Then, a very lucky guess,' I proposed.

'Luck, as you very well know, Watson, is the crutch of the superstitious, the feeble-minded and the naive. It is the philosophy of the fool. One may as well rely on luck as on a drunkard to deliver an important message.'

'Then explain your reasoning, Holmes,' I sighed.

'It is but the smallest feat of deduction,' he confessed, then reached inside his jacket. 'A letter arrived in the first post from Mr. Tolwood.'

'From Tolwood?' Butterworth repeated, much agitated. 'Then he knows I am here.'

'Apparently not,' said Holmes. 'It runs as follows.'

Dear Mr. Holmes,

I write on the most urgent and delicate business. A man's career, a company's reputation and a nation's army is at stake.

Yesterday a telegram was received at the offices of Houghton's brewery, from Lord Curzon himself in India:

Two men dead. STOP. Forty-eight incapacitated. STOP. Houghton's India pale ale tainted. STOP. Scotland Yard informed. STOP.

Within minutes of receipt of the telegram, the police were upon us. I had little time, but spent it warning our head brewer, Mr. Harold Butterworth, that his arrest was imminent. I advised him to flee and, although he was reluctant, I impressed upon him the gravity of the situation. Despite a thorough search of the yard, which is walled on four sides, he has vanished entirely.

Mr. Butterworth, I know, is a man of impeccable morals and scrupulous methods. I now believe I gave him poor council. I therefore seek your help finding him, proving his innocence, and discovering who or what has poisoned the casks of India pale ale sent to the Punjab.

If it is within your power, meet me at the Station Hotel, Burton-upon-Trent at 8 p.m. this evening. The landlord will be expecting you and your board and lodgings are arranged.

I have not advised my superiors of this correspondence and would be grateful if I could rely upon your discretion until such time you have made progress in this matter.

I have, I fear, cast aspersions on Mr. Butterworth's innocence. He has looked kindly upon my advancement and my conscience weighs heavily upon me.

I humbly beg your assistance and remain respectfully yours,
Leonard Tolwood
Assistant Brewer, Houghton's Brewery

Holmes leant forward and passed the letter to Butterworth. 'That is Tolwood's handwriting, is it not?' Butterworth nodded, as if in a daze. 'The tell-tale sign of a left-handed correspondent is the letter 't.' For a right-hander, there is invariably a sharp point at the left end of the 't' bar. For a left-handed person, the opposite is true. It will appear on the right. Once you are equipped with this knowledge, the identification of a left- or right-handed fellow is simplicity itself. Now gentlemen, if we are to arrive in Burton in good time, then I suggest we should catch the one twenty from St. Pancras. That will give us three hours.'

'Surely,' Butterworth began, 'you cannot expect me to return to Burton with you? Was my suffering inside that cask for nothing? As sure as night follows day, they will be waiting to arrest me at the station.'

'I agree there is a risk,' said Holmes, 'however I cannot help but feel that your presence is required if we are to make progress in this matter. We therefore need to mitigate this by finding you a suitable disguise. If you are able to travel incognito, then the threat will be significantly diminished.'

'A disguise?' he spluttered. 'I am no actor, I assure you, Mr. Holmes.'

'Yes, but, well, now let me see,' my friend mused, tapping his lip with a fingertip and scrutinising our client. 'You are a musician, I note.'

'How could you possibly know?'

'One violinist can easily recognise another. For example, a moment ago, you looked up when I hummed a bar of Mendelssohn's Violin Sonata in F Major. Then there are the well-developed calluses on your fingertips which indicate you are a player of a stringed instrument.'

'You are correct,' he admitted, 'but simply carrying a violin will hardly prevent my apprehension.'

15

'Ah,' said Holmes, 'I think we can do a little better than that. 'With an accent, a deliberate change in manner and movement, some eccentric clothing, and a day or two of whiskers upon your chin, we can conjure up a visiting member of the Prague Symphony Orchestra. You are journeying into the north to perform a special private concert in Edinburgh.' Butterworth appeared unconvinced, tapping his cigar on the edge of the ashtray, peering thoughtfully at my friend. 'Naturally,' added Holmes, 'I can provide a little tutelage along the way.'

Holmes then turned to me. 'Watson, can your practice spare you for a day or two? I do not believe it will take longer to resolve this matter and your assistance would be invaluable as always. If any further persuasion is required, it could give you an opportunity to sample Burton's excellent ale at its source.'

'Given the particulars of the case, Holmes,' I returned, 'it would seem sensible to abstain at the present time.' My friend appeared to take this as confirmation of my willingness to join him. The truth was, as in so many of these cases, that my curiosity was aroused. It was inevitable that having been present at its beginning, I would now need to be there at its dénouement.

'Very well,' I agreed. 'It will no doubt prove a story worth telling once the tangled skein is straightened.'

'Now, my first task is a scientific one,' said Holmes briskly. 'As I mentioned to my friend, Dr. Watson, only this morning, the great work of the world occurs at a micro rather than a macro level. A man of energy can believe himself a god by launching a great ship upon the sea, but a single microbe, invisible to the naked eye, can fell that man in a moment.' He turned to Butterworth. 'Am I correct in my assumption that within your fountain pen you have a sample of the beer in question?'

'Quite correct, Mr. Holmes,' he confirmed. 'In the few moments I had before effecting my escape, I took the opportunity to draw a small sample from the same batch of ale despatched to the Punjab. I felt it was my only chance to prove my innocence.'

'Quick thinking, Mr. Butterworth,' Holmes congratulated, clapping his hands together. 'I can see how you rose to your present station. Now, while you gentlemen prepare for the journey, I shall use my time to conduct a number of tests on the sample. I feel certain, part of the answer we seek lies therein.'

16

Butterworth rose to his feet and crossed to the low table, retrieving the tin cup that had accompanied him in the barrel. He turned it thoughtfully in his hands.

'Can I get you a glass of water?' I offered.

'Thank you, Doctor, but would you mind if I helped myself to another brandy?' I left him with his stiffener, which he took in the tin mug, then adjourned to my room to pack for our expedition.

I had barely retrieved my valise from beneath the bed when I became aware of a commotion at the top of the stairs. I ventured out to find Wiggins, that diminutive stalwart of the Baker Street Irregulars, attempting to twist his way out of Mrs. Hudson's vice-like grip.

'Please Doctor,' he implored. 'It's Mr. Holmes' brother. There's a ruckus up at Whitehall. They say he's off his onions, sir!' Holmes, mumchance, stared at the boy.

'Quickly, Watson,' he commanded, 'a carriage!'

TWO

The Family Weakness

The imposing figure of Tobias Gregson strode towards us as we approached the great stone palace of Whitehall, his thinning fair hair swept forward by the autumn breeze. Holmes leapt out of the carriage with an athletic bound.

'Where is he?' my friend demanded.

'In his office,' the inspector returned. 'The door is locked and barred. We have men with ladders attempting to gain access from the other side.'

'Tell them to stand down,' instructed Holmes. I hurried after the pair as they marched inside and flew up the staircase. I wheezed after them, clutching my leg.

Outside the door, red-faced officials were fretting, and glancing at their pocket watches. One of them, a plump Dickensian figure named Jellicoe, had a bulbous, plum-coloured nose, a shock of snow white hair and eyes so close together that they gave him an almost tarantula-like appearance.

'Mr. Holmes,' he cried, clasping his hands together in a desperate petition, 'not a moment too soon. There is a pressing matter of state. The War Office and the Treasury are tasked with the resourcing of our forces in the Transvaal. There are a thousand variables in the calculation and only Mycroft has the necessary data from each part of government relating to the cost per head. We simply must have his answer. Ships are waiting to disembark at Portsmouth and the Chancellor will not sign the warrants without the figure. The same calculation will take twenty men two weeks to complete. The situation is impossible!'

'How long has he been in there?' snapped Holmes.

'He arrived on the stroke of nine.'

'Anything out of the ordinary?' Jellicoe considered for a moment.

'There was an odd delivery waiting for him.'

'Define odd. The world is full of strange things. Am I expected to guess?'

'A barrel, Mr. Holmes.' My friend's eyed widened.

'A single drop of alcohol is enough to send him over the edge. We must gain immediate entrance.'

'Good God,' I shouted, then seized the doorknob, shaking it, my other hand pushing against the wood. Presently, I heard a snatch of singing from the other side.

> *'Oh Mister Porter, what shall I do?*
> *I want to go to Birmingham*
> *And they're taking me on to Crewe...'*

Sherlock tapped me on the shoulder and gestured for me to stand aside. 'Mycroft,' he said in a flat, commanding voice. 'It is your brother, Sherlock. Would you be so good as to open the door?' The singing ceased for a moment.

'I wish you all the joy of the worm!' Mycroft returned from the other side of the door, then burst into laughter. The singing resumed.

> *'Take me back to London, as quickly as you can,*
> *Oh Mister Porter, what a silly girl I am.'*

'Do you think it is possible,' I asked, 'he has the tainted batch?'

'There is every possibility,' muttered Holmes. 'But that is not something I can prove from this side of a solid oak door.' My friend considered for moment, then, raising a finger, leaned close to the door. 'Your lunch has arrived, Mycroft.' Once again, the singing abruptly ceased.

'Beef and horseradish sandwiches,' his brother elaborated. Some of the civil servants glanced around, as if they had missed the arrival of a luncheon trolley, but I had a fair sense of Holmes' strategy.

'Pah,' Mycroft scoffed. 'If a man had only a sandwich lunch to sustain him, he would be starved to death by three.'

'Well, he certainly doesn't sound too far out of sorts,' I suggested.

'I don't wish to sound pushy,' the oily mannered Jellicoe chipped in, 'but do you think you might ask him about the calculation?'

'We fear for a man's life,' I said. 'This is no time for arithmetic.'

'Surely,' the man remonstrated, 'he has merely overindulged. His head will be sore in the morning, but he will recover. Just a single question.'

'Do you feel unwell, Mycroft?' I asked. This time there was no answer.

'The number,' the man, pleaded, 'I must have the number.' We listened again, but there was nothing. My friend looked ashen-faced.

'There is nothing for it,' he declared. He unclipped his tie-pin, a white horse with a mane of amber feathers, a souvenir from that singular business of "The Jeweller of Florence." Unclipping the pin, he approached the lock and began to work the mechanism. I have recorded elsewhere that Holmes would have made a profitable career as a criminal and if he had chosen cracksman as his trade that would have certainly yielded a greater profit than that earned in the field of the private detective. There was an audible click and the door swung open.

If the Zulus themselves had rampaged through the room, they would have left it in a neater state. As it was, we were greeted by a scene of utter devastation. Two bookshelves lay face down like dead librarians, their respective contents littered across the floor. Chairs were upended and it appeared that Mycroft had turned his desk into some sort of rowing boat, the curtain rails serving as oars. Innumerable papers were strewn across the rug and a bust of Pitt the Younger was beheaded, as if by a deliberate act of vandalism. His head lay at my feet. The cask that had instigated this mischief stood in one corner of the room, its lid prised off and its volume reduced by approximately one quarter.

'By great Gordon's ghost, Holmes,' I spluttered. 'It appears he has drunk a gallon and a half of the stuff.' Mycroft himself lay spread-eagled, stripped to his undergarments, a paper hat upon his head that he appeared to have fashioned from a financial ledger. I knelt and felt for a pulse; miraculously, it was strong and regular. At intervals, he omitted a low, rumbling sound that made the floorboards quiver and the leaves of foolscap flutter momentarily above the ground.

'I believe him to be asleep,' I reported.

'Thank you, Watson,' said Holmes, a deeply troubled look across his face. 'Now, I will ask each of you gentlemen to take in this disconcerting spectacle, then dismiss it entirely from your mind. You will not mention it to your superiors, your friends at your clubs or even to your wives. When Mycroft returns to work in the morning, he will find his office as it was and nothing of what you have seen will be mentioned again. If, by the smallest chance, he does recall these events, you will peer at him as if he has taken leave of his senses. These are the conditions of his continued service. Do I have your word?' The assembled company said nothing and continued to stare at the sorry wreck of a man.

'There is,' Jellicoe began, in a sombre, yet somehow threatening tone, 'the outstanding matter of the calculation: the cost per head of the British Expeditionary Force. I will need to report to the Chancellor of the Exchequer that we do not have the figure he has requested. Knowing Mycroft's unimpeachable reputation for reliability and accuracy, he will surely ask the reason for the failure.'

'Then,' returned Holmes, insouciantly, 'there is no need to disappoint the Chancellor, for Mycroft has completed his morning's work.'

'I find that very hard to believe,' Jellicoe uttered, his eyelids half closed in studied disdain.

'Then, consider the figures for yourself,' my friend explained, extending a hand towards the ruins of his brother's office.'

'Gracious, Holmes,' I exclaimed, 'I believe I've got it. The coins on the table!' I rushed forward and examined several neat columns of coins, counting them for myself.

'One pound, three shillings and four pence,' I declared.

'It could merely be the loose change from his pocket,' the man dismissed. 'I am afraid that that alone does not give me confidence to go the Chancellor with an answer.'

'An enormous sum,' Holmes suggested, 'to carry around in one's pocket, would you not agree?' Without waiting for an answer, he put forward another theory. 'Perhaps, you would care to examine his fingers.' We immediately followed my friend's instructions. Mycroft's right hand was clenched into a fist. His left however showed three fingers: the first, third and fourth; with the second and thumb both folded in. 'One pound, three shillings and four pence,' Holmes repeated. 'Now, from the information you have relayed, I believe this information is urgently required. I suggest that you deliver it in person to Sir Michael Hicks Beach, who will receive it with gratitude.' The haughty administrator stared at Mycroft's corpulent frame, watching his chest rising and falling gently like a continent in the moments preceding an earthquake. He then returned his gaze to my friend with begrudging respect.

'An extraordinary pair,' he muttered. With this, he bustled away along the corridor. Holmes wrapped his knuckles upon the large mahogany

21

table top. 'Now, if you would be so kind gentlemen, perhaps you could assist us in transferring my brother onto this table.'

With enormous effort, we succeeded in rolling the beached brother onto this makeshift stretcher. Covering Mycroft's face with a large handkerchief to preserve his anonymity, we each took a corner. On the count of four we took the strain. It was like lifting the Great Sphinx of Giza. Lacking the Pharaoh's numberless hordes, the four of us staggered along the corridor and down the stairs to the courtyard where our four-wheeler awaited. Hoisting him to an upright position, we tipped him inside then set off for Baker Street.

'So,' Holmes declared, 'it appears the cask was delivered to the wrong Mr. Holmes.' He reached inside his jacket and withdrew a white envelope. Mycroft neglected to open the accompanying letter, he said, slicing it open. Unless I am very much mistaken in my thinking, this will be from the owner of Houghton's brewery requesting my services. There is still just enough time to collect Mr. Butterworth and make our way north.'

When we returned, Butterworth was unrecognisable. By selecting items from the nether regions of Holmes' wardrobe, he had mutated from an unremarkable journeyman into a rakish bohemian. A cerise cravat concealed his neck, while a harlequin waistcoat, green tweed-ish coat and purple trousers completed the transformation. His crumpled hat was of unknown providence but distinctly eastern European in taste, as if it had been swiped from the head of Slovakian farmer. In his hand, he clutched my friend's second-best violin, which, despite numerous scratches and scuff marks, still possessed a fine, clear tone.

'Splendid!' cried Holmes admiringly. 'But a disguise is as nothing without an accent. Let us hear you speak.' Butterworth paused, then addressed us in a slow, treacle-thick drawl:

'I prefer to let my music do the talking.'

'Capital!' my friend exclaimed. 'And you said you were no actor. Poppycock; you are first rate. Now let us not delay, gentlemen. Watson, if you would be so kind as to help me with the bags, our carriage awaits.'

We drew up outside George Gilbert Scott's magnificent Midland Grand Hotel, the gothic palace of red brick that stands in St. Pancras as the gateway to the industrial heartlands. The towers rose in triumph before us, demanding and receiving our attention. Perhaps because he was less familiar with it than ourselves, Butterworth stood gawping in its shadow, taking in its undeniable splendour.

'I find it unnecessarily florid, myself,' remarked Holmes, as if reading his mind. 'What's more, it's almost conceited. It is a building that looks unwholesomely pleased with itself.'

'It has good reason,' said Butterworth, admiringly, taking in its tall spires and chimneys, the intricate stonework and numerous window arches like a hundred raised eyebrows.

'It is a cathedral to commerce,' continued Holmes, 'but by rights it should reflect its vulgarity and functionality. Their mistake was to engage an artist.'

'A fascinating discussion, no doubt,' I broke in, 'but may I remind you we have a train to catch?'

'We have fifteen minutes,' my friend responded, glancing at his watch, 'which should allow us sufficient time for a short enquiry. Follow me, gentlemen.'

Holmes led us at pace beyond the hotel and deep into the station, his grey ulster flapping behind him. The crowds surged in and out of the great terminus, a thousand men and women preoccupied with their own thoughts, each furrowed brow in shadow beneath a bowler or flat cap.

We emerged at the end of a platform, stinking with soot and steam, along with the more appetising scent of hot eels, doused with butter and vinegar. It reminded me that we had neglected to take luncheon. The goods wagons lined up adjacent to smart carriages, and tradesfolk rubbed shoulders with the smart set just as readily. Shouts and curses, whistles and snatches of song filled the air, while the great mechanical beasts hissed and bellowed, impatient to stretch their steel limbs. Porters swung sacks, rolled casks and hoisted crates of every description, while commercial men weaved through the crowds, swinging their leather satchels, their minds on their next appointment.

'Over there,' commanded Holmes, and led us towards a strange mechanical device.

Tentatively, we stepped onto a steel platform at the northern end of the train shed.

'Is this entirely necessary, Holmes?' I enquired. My friend jammed a lever and suddenly the platform shuddered. By means of some hydraulic system we began to descend slowly below platform level to a nether kingdom of sweat and grime. We emerged in a dimly lit forest of steel pillars, each spaced an even distance apart. As far as the eye could see, there was barrel after barrel of ale.

'Welcome to the undercroft,' announced Holmes. 'As Mr. Butterworth is no doubt aware, each of the pillars is spaced precisely three beer barrels apart, ensuring maximum storage capacity. Ingenious ergonomics, wouldn't you agree?'

'Quite,' I said, peering around at the shadowy figures busy at their work, shifting the barrels hither and thither.

Presently, a giant of a man approached with black whiskers that obscured three quarters of his face. A flat cap was pulled tightly over his cranium and two gleaming amber eyes peered out. 'You there!' he called in a gruff, Cockney accent. 'What business do you have lurking down here?'

'An unfortunate error,' replied Holmes. 'We were awaiting our train when the ground gave way and here we are.'

'Well, you can go right back up then,' the man suggested. 'If you weren't dressed as gentlemen, I'd say you were bug hunting.'

'I assure you,' replied Holmes, 'we are not thieves.'

'That may be, but if you don't get yourselves on the fly, I'll call a crusher.'

'Of course,' stalled Holmes, 'but humour me for a moment. We are sporting men and it would be to your immense advantage if you could help on a small point of information. How many barrels come in and out of here each day?'

'Over three hundred each way,' he said.

'And does every barrel have its own unique marking?'

'Of course,' he added. 'You must think I'm sort of glock. If you aren't planning a flash bang job, I'm a monkey's uncle.'

'I assure you,' Holmes broke in, 'our interest is merely academic.'

'I think I've told you enough. Now how about a thick 'un for my trouble?'

While Holmes compensated the fellow, I took a final look at this modern Hades and the sallow-faced men who toiled there. The hoppy fug of fermenting ale hung in the air, while the rows of barrels stretched far into the distance; it seemed inconceivable that so much ale could be consumed by the inhabitants of a single city. However the evidence was before my very eyes; four million Londoners in the fish markets, the docks, factories and law courts could work up a quite a thirst.

Just as I turned to impress upon my companions the urgency of our departure, I caught a glimpse of a woman. It was the merest glimpse: the hem of a violet dress, a shock of short, dark hair and quick, intelligent features. I looked again but there was no trace. I stepped forward and craned my neck, but she appeared to have vanished entirely. It seemed impossible that a woman, especially one of her demeanour, could be roaming this godless underworld.

'You lost someone, sir?' asked the foreman, looking in the same direction.

'No, not at all,' I muttered. Then, to conceal my awkwardness, I retrieved my watch from my pocket. 'If we are to have any prospect whatsoever of making our train,' I urged, 'we must leave this instant.' As if to underline the point, a shrill whistle blew somewhere above our heads.

'Watson,' laughed Holmes, 'if I were travelling with my maiden aunt, there would be considerably less fussing and certainly more cream tea. Very well, let us ascend.' He threw the lever and we rose like angels.

We hurried along the platform beneath the great single-span roof, a miracle of iron and glass that loomed over us like a mechanical rainbow. Finally, we bundled aboard our carriage to the pantomime disapproval of the guard, who glared at us, his whistle gripped firmly between his teeth. Butterworth proceeded to third class with his violin case and haversack, while Holmes and I made ourselves comfortable in first. As Holmes shook out his paper and prepared his smoking paraphernalia, I stared down the length of the platform at the other late passengers, catching my breath and experiencing that familiar sensation of anticipation and trepidation one feels at the start of a new adventure. Just as I reached for my novel, Jerome K. Jerome's mildly disappointing *Three Men on the Bummel*, I saw the woman from the undercroft, standing perfectly still on the platform. I was alarmed to note that she was staring directly at me. Her chin was raised in a spirit of enquiry rather than superiority, and she fixed me with an almost amused expression. As the train began to slide away, I noticed a small, blue shield pinned to her hat.

'I say, Holmes,' I began, with the intention of pointing her out.

'Yes?' he answered at length, but the woman was already left far behind.

'Nothing,' I said. 'It was but a trifle.'

'You know my thoughts on trifles,' he muttered, 'there is nothing so important as trifles.' I relayed my observations, throughout which he nodded thoughtfully, while never for one moment shifting his primary attention from his pipe.

'So, what do you make of it, Holmes?'

'I suggest, Watson,' he declared, 'that you have an incorrigible eye for the ladies and are in thrall to yet another harpy singing from the rocks.'

I shook my head and laughed.

'Perhaps you are right,' I agreed. I found my page and did my best to put her out of my mind.

Slowly, but with the inexorable power of the industrial age, our train pulled out of the station. The pistons laboured and steam bellowed as if the locomotive were struggling against the gravitational pull of the capital itself. It was as if some great magnet buried in the heart of London drew in the money, the ideas and the very hearts and minds of England. But somewhere to the north, the other powerhouses lay: the brewers, the milliners, the shipbuilders; these were the great makers.

We ploughed through the parish of St. Pancras Old Church, the ghost of the young unfortunate Saint Pancras himself, roaming the churchyard, searching no doubt for his severed head. The spirits of the ancient burial ground seemed to impel us on: the actors, the poets, the composers and baronets returned to the earth, their memorials now jumbled, neglected or lost altogether. But instead of melancholy, I felt intensely alive. I thought of the extraordinary man sitting before me, his mind fizzing with a thousand thoughts. I could feel the very electricity of his presence. It seemed inconceivable he could ever die.

There was a reason I had tied my fate to Holmes; he gave me energy and purpose; once caught in his schemes, I could not fail to feel a frisson one might otherwise only feel on the field of battle, or in the throes of a new love affair.

Finally, we pulled free of London's clutches, leaving behind its dark brick warehouses and angular factories where grey lives slipped away. We were rewarded by the colours of the shires; the sunburst glory of ash and lime trees at the beginning of their autumnal death throes.

The fields were framed in russets and ochre; leaves lined the tracksides like tributes of gold.

Holmes had settled into his familiar travelling routine, pointedly ignoring anything Mother Nature could offer by way of distraction, instead scrutinising each of the papers in turn, no doubt searching for a detail that would elucidate an ongoing case.

Presently I found the ticket inspector standing at my side.

'A splendid afternoon,' I remarked as I patted my jacket pocket for my ticket. 'Are we making good time?'

'I'm afraid not, sir,' he apologised. 'Leaves on the line mean we'll be twenty minutes late coming into Derby. That's where I'll be leaving the train.'

'You must not forget to buy that hat for your wife,' Holmes remarked, without looking up. 'It is her birthday, is it not?'

'But,' the man stammered, 'how could you possibly know?'

'Simplicity itself!' my friend chuckled. 'There is still marzipan beneath your fingernails, no doubt from the cake you baked and decorated last night, not to discount the faint smell of vanilla about you. What's more, you have spent the last-minute studying each of the ladies' hats in this carriage, barely glancing at their tickets. If we handed you our betting stubs from the 3.15 at Aintree, you would happily put a hole through them and not noticed a thing.'

'Astonishing!' he cried.

'I confess there is one more detail. You have scrawled: "M's H" on your hand. Is it Mary or Margaret?'

'Margaret,' the man confirmed.

'Yes, I thought so,' my friend stated. 'Well, choose carefully. My friend Dr. Watson here is a fan of the draped turban.'

'Is that so? Well, now you can only be Mr. Holmes,' the inspector concluded.

'The same.'

'In which case, I have a message for you.' He dropped two fingers into his waistcoat pocket and fished out a small sheet of folded white paper. Holmes received it with interest, glanced at it, registering mild surprise, then scribbled a short note of his own.

'Would you be so good as to deliver this and return any reply?'

'Happy to oblige, sir,' said the inspector, still in some bemusement over

27

my friend's feat of deduction. The man moved on and Holmes and I were left alone once more.

'Autograph hunter?' I enquired, raising an eyebrow.

'Something like that,' my friend confirmed, then once more busied himself with his paper.

Great clouds began to gather in the skies to the north and presently the lamps were lit, glowing softy in the fading afternoon. Presently, Holmes retrieved a pencil and paper from his pocket, then leant forward in his seat.

'Allow me to show you the future.' He drew a long, undulating line on the page, then added what appeared to be three small boxes on the crest of one of the peaks. I peered at the sketch and frowned.

'A hilltop settlement?' I suggested.

'Look again, Watson!' My friend added two dots to the base of each boxes, creating what appeared to be three pairs of musical notes on a bending stave.

'Mark my words,' he said, pointing his long, pale finger at his handiwork, 'this will become the dominant leisure pursuit of the twentieth century. Millions will thrall to its very name.'

'I rather think,' I said, returning to my book, 'that I will stick to my snooker and whist.'

'From Brighton to New York, you will hear screams of delight from half a mile away. He continued the line, then, with a flourish, added a loop in the manner of an ampersand.

'It will make its creator a millionaire, and children everywhere will pester their parents for a penny to try it again.'

'Then, I take my hat off to this genie, whoever he is.'

'Edwin Prescott is his name, an American of great imagination. He is the inventor of the centrifugal railway.' I raised my eyebrows and looked again at the singular sketch.

'It is not a railway on which I intend to travel.' I placed a finger on the squiggle at the end of the line. 'And what, pray, is this?'

'Ah,' said Holmes. 'That is its very reason to be. In fact, I believe it is the name that will finally catch on. It is the Loop-the-Loop. The passengers climb aboard these carriages. They are transported along the railway, gaining momentum until they arrive at this stupendous obstacle. The carriages and their occupants will travel upside for a short period of time, before returning to the horizontal and slowing to a halt.'

'But the carriages will leave the track,' I protested, 'and the people will tumble to their deaths. It is the work of a madman!'

'You have not allowed for the action of an inertial force directed away from a rotating axis.' He laughed gently, as if explaining a simple sum to a child. 'The effect is such that both carriages and passengers remain quite firmly rooted to the rail and carriage. It is elemental Newtonian mechanics.'

'Of course it is,' I muttered, irritated by my friend's supercilious tone.

'In fact,' Holmes added thoughtfully, 'one might even credit Newton with the invention of this amusing contraption.'

'Enlightening,' I concluded. 'And if it catches on, I'll eat my hat.'

On Holmes' instruction, I set off to walk the length of the train to check on Butterworth in third and was grateful for the opportunity to stretch my legs. The passengers were a strange assortment of dour-looking commercial types, couples travelling together, and large, ruddy-faced industrial sorts, cradling bottles of claret as travelling companions. Small towns and villages swept past and I caught the occasional atavistic face of passing labourers, in drab threadbare jackets, treading the same path as their countless forebears, staring up as the mechanical wonder thundered towards the Midlands.

'Arriving in five minutes, sir,' the inspector muttered, tipping his cap. I had not yet reached Butterworth, but nevertheless felt that it might be prudent to return to my seat before we arrived. I had only just turned on my heel when I suddenly found myself flying backwards through the air, crashing onto the hard floor. The brakes screeched with the sound of a thousand knives being sharpened at once, and all about me I heard the oaths and cries of my fellow passengers, as they tumbled into each other's laps, burnt themselves on their cigarettes, or scalded themselves with spilt tea. My shoulder throbbed and I felt for a moment that I might have dislocated it.

I scrambled to my feet and pulled down the window. We had almost drawn to a halt and in the gloom, discerned some commotion up ahead. The fireman had already jumped down onto the line and a row of carriages lined up at the railway crossing. As we came to a stop, I opened the door and lowered myself onto the embankment. Four carriages down, I saw Holmes doing the same, and he quickly caught up with me.

'Look alive, Watson,' he cried. 'They may need a doctor.'

29

My first impression was that a ghastly accident had occurred, for I glimpsed a pair of white, stocking-clad legs lying stretched across the line. Then I noticed an encouraging sign of movement, followed by the indignant voice of a middle-aged woman. When I reached the scene, it was like something from a penny dreadful or comic strip. A woman of about fifty wearing a large bonnet bursting with small, trumpet-shaped, purple flowers, a voluminous, green dress and the steely look of a public school matron was lying across the line, her arm chained and padlocked to a railing. It appeared to be some sort of suicide attempt, but the woman's tone was entirely at odds with her predicament. Indeed, it seemed as if she had taken charge of the situation.

'For goodness sake, will you stop fussing!' she demanded. 'And does it really take ten men to break one small chain? If you're going to have me arrested, then please summon a policemen, or am I expected to do this myself.' Immediately I felt I was part of the problem and not the solution.

'I'm a doctor, madam,' I explained, crouching down. 'Are you injured?'

'No, of course I'm not injured,' she cried, swatting me away with her parasol. 'Can't you see the locomotive stopped a good twelve feet away?'

'Yes, but...' I stammered. A burly constable appeared, stumbling along the line, with one hand securing his custodian helmet and his whistle between his lips. He took one look at the woman on the line and appeared to sag visibly.

'All right, stand back there,' he instructed.

'Augustus?' the woman shrilled. 'Don't tell me they sent Augustus!' The policeman took a deep breath, as if this condescending form of address was not entirely unfamiliar to him.

'Now, Miss Bilton,' he warned, 'I would ask you to stay calm.'

'Stay calm?!' she cried. 'Little Augustus Jones is asking me to stay calm? These men were unable to murder a defenceless female. A simple piece of work, you might imagine, but they failed to accomplish that! It is small wonder the Roman Empire crumbled with men in charge. Mark my words, the British Empire will go the same way.'

'Virginia Bilton,' the constable continued in the face of this barrage, 'I am arresting you for the intentional disruption of Her Majesty's railways.'

'Well, about time too!' she cried. 'And will you inform the newspaper, or will I have to do that myself?'

'I'm sure we would wish to avoid that sort of publicity,' Augustus cautioned in a low voice.

'On the contrary!' she cried. 'Do you think I'm lying here for my own pleasure?' The driver returned to his cab then swiftly appeared with an iron lever. With little effort, he succeeded in freeing her from her bondage. Quickly she was on her feet, dusting down her skirts and shooing away any offers of assistance.

'Come along, then,' she declared, bustling ahead. 'Let us file the report. I expect you think I will help you write it too?'

Holmes, who had been watching this astonishing scene unfold, was smiling in an inscrutable way.

'What do you make of it?' I asked, shaking my head.

'A seventeen-minute delay,' he pronounced, then turned and headed back down the track to our carriage.

The fine, red-brick station at Burton finally hove into view, the splendid platform clock hanging over the newspaper vendors like the stolen pocket watch of a local giant. Even at this late hour, the station bustled with tremendous activity, the certain sign of the town's prosperity. On the skyline, bold lettering announced the names of the famous brewers and their pale ales. In the air hung that unmistakable smell of the mash tuns that had made the town its fortune.

'A remarkably pungent odour, Holmes,' I remarked as we stepped onto the platform, 'and not entirely unpleasant.'

'Only perhaps to a lover of beer,' my friend returned, peering up at the sky, as if we would be able to see the scent hanging there. 'To the nose of a sommelier this place would be unsavoury.'

We watched Butterworth step out of his carriage, first testing the air with an open palm for signs of rain. Barely glancing in our direction he strode across the platform and out into the street. This hardly came as a surprise; he had agreed to find lodgings in a cheap boarding house well away from the old coaching inn where Holmes and I had secured our rooms. Notwithstanding his disguise, he did not dare visit a pub or hotel for fear of being recognised by the publican.

'Now, how about a drink before we head to the hotel, Holmes?'

'It feels,' he concurred, 'like a logical course of action.' Holmes tapped the end of his cane against the cobbles, as if to check they were not figments of his imagination.

'The Cooper's Tavern, I have heard,' I continued, 'serves an excellent pint. The beer barely travels a hundred yards from the place it was brewed. It continues to ferment in the barrel.'

'My dear Watson,' my friend smiled. 'I was sold at the word drink.'

We hurried through the narrow streets as a thin rain began to fall and the sky turned the colour of a velvety porter. The public house was a squat, rectangular-shaped, red-brick building, singularly unpretentious in its design, and tied to one of the biggest brewers. A welcoming glow radiated from its four evenly spaced windows and a convivial hubbub could be heard from within.

Squeezing through the narrow entrance, we emerged into a welcoming grotto, with red- and yellow-painted walls discernible behind a thick veil of smoke. Casks lined the bar; rows of bottles filled the shelves and the queue at the bar was three deep as we approached. The clientele was almost exclusively male, dressed in dirty work clothes, stained and smeared with the detritus of the brewing process. The smell of beer from both pump and customer was almost overwhelming.

Holmes tapped a fellow on the shoulder, who turned with a look of mild irritation.

'Mr Arkham, I presume?'

'Who's asking?' He was a straight-backed, silver-haired man of about sixty, with prominent ears, rubbery features and a permanent air of amused cynicism. He wore a white shirt, black waistcoat and a tie with a knot so thin, it is a wonder he was able to untangle it at the end of the day.

'A friend of Butterworth's.' Arkham peered intently at my friend, then eyed me with suspicion. He beckoned for us to join him at a table in the corner. As he approached, the two drinkers happily vacated it without saying a word.

'What did you say your name was?'

'I didn't,' my friend reminded him, 'but I'll happily volunteer it. Sherlock Holmes. This is my friend, Dr. Watson.'

'Don't worry, I've heard of you,' he muttered. 'Who hasn't? But how did you know who I was? I wasn't aware my fame extended as far as London.'

'Simplicity itself,' he laughed. 'There is a callous on your right hand associated with the hand adze, the indispensable tool of the cooper.'

'But I could be any jobbing cooper,' he challenged.

'There was a circle of coopers formed around you that suggested a measure of deference and respect. It was clear to me who held seniority in that company.'

'So,' he said with begrudging admiration, 'you have a bit of a knack for these things. Now, what do you know of Butterworth? Is he safe?'

'As safe as a man can be who has spent the night in a barrel.'

I supped at my ale, a bright, golden brew of almost miraculous clarity. It tasted of Seville oranges, butter biscuits and bitter hops. Arkham observed my startled reaction as each of these distinct tastes announced themselves on my palette.

'Not a bad pint, is it?' he put in. 'That's Butterworth's work, is that. We call him 'The Alchemist.' Now, don't tell me where he is. I don't want to know.'

'Why is that?' I asked.

'Because they'll have it out of me,' he confessed, raising his pipe to his lips. 'They've already put the thumbscrews on me. It'll be better that I don't know. But there's a thing or two you might find educational if you mean to get to the bottom of things.'

'Go on,' my friend instructed, sipping cautiously at his ale. I considered for a moment the allusion Holmes had made to 'the family weakness.' He had so many vices that I felt it impossible to pinpoint any single one. Arkham drank deep of his pint, then lowered it with deliberate care onto the table.

'Butterworth was to become a part owner of the business.' Holmes shot me a glance.

'Indeed,' my friend nodded.

'In view of his years of loyalty and prodigious talent, he has no reason to destroy Houghton's reputation. He loves that brewery and he loves this bloody town.'

The next morning, I woke to a commotion in the street below: a blowing of whistles, the whinnying of horses, shouts and cat calls. I stumbled to the window, bleary-eyed and pulled open the curtains.

'Upon my word!' I cried.

'Quickly, Holmes, you must see this.'

Holmes folded his newspaper and frowned. 'I have always felt you are prone to distraction, Watson. He who shouts loudest, rarely has much to say. Empty vessels make the most noise.'

'I promise this is worth seeing.' My friend tapped the remaining ash from his pipe bowl, then rose to join me.

'Well, well, Watson,' he concurred, 'a singular sight and no mistake.'

There must have been two hundred women lying prone in the street. In front of shops and businesses, even the police station, women lying on their backs, their hands folded neatly on their stomachs. I counted half a dozen who were expecting. Beside them was their shopping, their luggage, their parcels, and in some cases even their prams. Before the great gates of Houghton's brewery itself, lay a plump, middle-aged woman, her bonnet still secured to her head. Beside her stood a sandwich board bearing a slogan.

'Do you have your opera glasses, Watson,' Holmes enquired. I opened my valise and tossed them across to him. He pressed them to his eyes then smiled.

'Why, if it's not Miss Virginia Bilton! You remember the woman on the railway line?' I nodded. 'It appears she has orchestrated another public relations coup.'

'To what end?'

'Emancipation, Watson! What else?' I took the opera glasses from Holmes and trained them on the sandwich board. I read the words.

'WE WILL NOT TAKE THIS LYING DOWN!'

'She has made her point most forcibly, wouldn't you agree, Watson?'

From the diary of Miss Gertrude Cresswell, 8th October, 1899

Burton is a perfect wonder. The town seems to me like a sort of beehive. But instead of honey, they produce their prized amber ale. I confess I have developed something of a taste for it since my arrival. It not only serves as remarkable refreshment but gives me great lucidity. They say Catherine the Great of Russia prized its great clarity and considerable strength. On this, we are as one. I have not touched the three bottles of ginger wine and Norwegian glass tumbler that I brought with me from London to tide me over for the duration.

But Burton. Yes, it is a veritable hive. Everyone knows their place. The lowly worker bee does not regard itself as inferior. It simply has a function and pursues it without question. In a similar way, those in the upper stratum do not consider themselves privileged. It is simply the way things are. Naturally, there is a place where my analogy falls down. There is no woman in a position of senior responsibility. The only exception to this, I have observed, is the formidable Miss Bilton, a recently retired schoolmistress. A woman of commanding stature with dresses that belonged to the 70s, and a brusque manner that could have belonged to Elizabeth I. I shadowed her for an afternoon and was left exhausted from her diary of appointments. Unable to face another afternoon of subterfuge, I resolved simply to take her to tea. The opportunity arose at a quarter to five this afternoon as she emerged from a solicitor's office.

'I say, Miss Bilton?' She swept around, her bustling skirts following her at a half-second delay.

'And you are?'

'Miss Gertrude Cresswell.' She narrowed her eyes.

'Were you one of my girls?' At close quarters, I noticed her skin was plastered with some ancient whitening agent, which I sincerely hoped was not lead-based.

'No, I don't think so.'

'What, in heaven's name, are you doing with that absurd umbrella? There is not the slightest chance of rain.'

'Is a lady not entitled to her accessories?'

'Not if they are absurd. Yellow is a most unsuitable colour for an umbrella. You should have chosen blue.'

'I see.'

'No, I'm afraid you do not see,' she answered, eying me like a hawk. 'For as long as mothers put their sons in blue shorts and dress their pretty daughters as bright flowers, there will be no equality. It is nothing short of conditioning. We are doomed almost from birth to be ornamental.' She looked me up and down, silently registering her disapproval for my hair and clothes. 'You are a tutor, no doubt.'

'No, madam,' I replied with a small smile, 'I am a private detective.' Miss Bilton almost dropped her handbag.

'A revolveress?'

'Hardly,' I laughed. 'The most dangerous item I carry is my notebook.'

'And what business do you have with me?' She glanced up and down the road. 'I may lie in the street and chain myself to train tracks, but I am a respectable woman.'

'I am here to investigate a double murder. Two soldiers in India are dead from drinking contaminated beer and the head brewer has vanished into thin air.'

'And?' she challenged.

'And what?'

'Do you believe I am harbouring a murderer in my back bedroom?'

'What an astonishing assertion.' Miss Bilton appeared to inflate with indignation. She tilted her head back, gathered up her skirts and bustled off in the direction of the town hall.

'Good day, Miss Cresswell,' she called back without turning, 'and I wish you well with your murdering.'

THREE

The Barons

Holmes was sitting, folded into his customary figure of eight, his arms and legs crossed, deep in contemplation. Presently, he leant over the table, picked up a pencil and sketched a triangle on a piece of paper. He slid this towards me then awaited my reaction with a thin, mischievous smile.

'Is this some sort of parlour game?' I frowned, examining the design, without going so far as to pick it up.

'Far from it!' he declared. 'This simple shape has earned millions of pounds for its owner. Can you explain why?'

'I'm afraid not.'

'Don't be afraid, just tell me what you see.'

'One of the great pyramids of Giza?'

'Nothing of the kind.'

'Then, a poor drawing of some remote mountain?'

'Wrong again.'

'Then, explain yourself!'

'It is recognised from Walsall to Waziribad.'

'Well, I can only speak for myself. I recognise it only in as much as it looks like a triangle drawn by a schoolboy.' Holmes winced.

'Without this, the firm would earn a fraction of its profits.' I scrutinised it again, but drew a perfect blank.

'I am being unfair, Watson,' my friend conceded. He rose briskly, crossed the room and fetched a pot of red ink and a pen. Returning, he swiftly filled the shape with a wash of red ink.

'What about now?' There was a stirring of recognition.

'Perhaps this will help,' he said, then scribbled the word, 'Bass,' beneath the triangle.

'Of course!' I cried. 'The brewer. How could I be so slow? But what is your meaning?'

'My meaning is that symbols possess immense power. Think of Christianity. There was no patent office extant in the first century, but the crucifix has been registered with a higher authority and is recognised across the planet. Were you aware that this simple triangle was the first-ever trademark? It was registered in 1876. Some poor clerk was tasked with queuing up all night outside the office to ensure it had priority. The brewer uses it to differentiate its casks and bottles. It is the instant assurance of quality.'

'Holmes,' I said, 'this is an education and I am grateful for it, yet I hardly believe you are imparting this information apropos of nothing. You have a point to make, so please be so good as to throw the spear.'

'It crossed my mind, Watson,' he said, 'that I should produce a similar emblem for my consulting work.'

'A triangle?'

'No!' he cried. 'Something unique. Instantly relatable to me.'

'Your pipe?'

'Too common.'

'Your hat?'

'My hat is no different from that worn by a hundred thousand men across London and I assume you do not mean the spurious and wholly misleading deerstalker your illustrator created for me to accompany your fiction.' I ignored this sleight and pressed ahead.

'A magnifying glass then?'

'When was the last time you saw me use one?'

'Then, what is your suggestion?'

'221b.'

'Our address?'

'It would save having to repeat it on our stationery.'

'Well,' I admitted, 'I can see the advantage, but do you really think a trademark would benefit you?'

'Mine is no longer the only consulting agency in London,' he explained. 'Only the other day did I see an advertisement bearing the legend: "We solve it like Sherlock!"'

'You should take it as a compliment,' I suggested. 'What defines you is not a trademark, but your results.'

Holmes settled back in his chair, joining his fingers together in satisfaction. It seemed conceivable this entire discussion was a circuitous route to soliciting my approval.

'You are the finest consulting detective in England,' I added, shaking out my paper. 'Let the also-rans fight it out amongst themselves.' I could not be sure, but I believe I heard a sigh of satisfaction as Holmes lit his pipe and sent a plume of blue smoke into the air.

Holmes and I returned to the Three Queens Hotel. Fatigued from our day's enquiries, we retired directly to our rooms, requesting a supper of cold meat and beer to be sent up. I had barely loosened my collar when a plate of dismally plain fare duly arrived, which Holmes eyed with distaste.

'Food is a chore at the best of times,' he remarked, pulling a face at his first mouthful, 'but at least Mrs. Hudson's dishes have the benefit of seasoning.'

'Come now, Holmes,' I chided. 'You would never survive in the army. Three weeks of bully beef and you would dream of grub such as this.'

'Give me an orange and a pound of tobacco,' he returned, 'and I could live for three days without the least discomfort.'

Presently, there came a knock at the door.

'Our needs are adequately met, thank you,' I declared, anticipating the fussing of our over-attentive landlady. There followed a second knock. I sighed and laid my tray to one side, crossing the room to open the door.

'As I said,' I began, before trailing off. Standing there was quite the most arrestingly beautiful woman I had ever seen. Her eyes were kingfisher blue; her skin pale and face framed with square cheekbones; the kind you only see in pre-Raphaelite paintings. She wore a matching shawl of electric blue.

'Have you come for the plates?' I stammered.

'I have come for my husband,' she answered.

We deposited the remains of our supper outside the door and cleared a chair for our guest.

'We were not expecting visitors,' I apologised. 'In fact, I was unaware that our arrival had been advertised.'

'No doubt, Mrs. Butterworth,' said Holmes, showing her to a chair, 'you are already aware that your husband is perfectly safe.' She hesitated as if uncertain whether to confirm this assertion. 'He left word, did he not, with Arkham to inform you that he was to be delivered to 221b Baker Street? She nodded imperceptibly. 'And it was Dr. Watson here who sent you the coded telegram to confirm that he had indeed survived his unusual voyage.'

'Ah, yes,' I replied, recalling the line: 'The flowers have arrived unspoilt.' She appeared to relax a little and accepted the glass of water I offered.

'But what now?' she asked.

'Well, it's all perfectly straightforward,' I assured her. 'My friend Holmes here will straighten out this small misunderstanding and your husband will return to his position on Monday morning.'

'Thank you, Watson,' Holmes said tersely. I sensed a note of disapproval.

'Now, Mrs. Butterworth,' he resumed, briskly checking his pocket watch, 'I am going to ask you three questions. If you answer them as fully as you are able, I assure you I will not detain you longer than is absolutely necessary.' She swallowed a mouthful of water, and unconsciously reached for her wedding ring, twisting it on her finger.

'Over the last six months,' he began, 'has your husband had cause to leave the country on business?'

'Yes,' she replied, 'a week in May, three weeks in June and two weeks in July.'

'And did he explain the purpose of these visits?'

'Yes, of course. They were to breweries in Norway, Russia and Poland. He was inspecting their facilities and studying their methods in preparation for an expansion at Houghton's. It was all quite above board.' Holmes nodded slowly and made a small entry in his notebook. He snapped the book shut and stared directly at Mrs. Butterworth. 'Would it surprise you to learn that your husband was signed off sick for these spells of absence?' Mrs. Butterworth's eyes watered a little at this, but the remarkable woman held her nerve.

'What is your inference, Mr. Holmes?' she asked coolly. 'Are you suggesting my husband has been conducting an affair?'

'That would seem an absurd notion.'

'I'm glad you think so.' My friend rose to his feet, walked to the window, pushed open the curtain with a finger, then peered down into the street.

'And now for my third question. On any of these visits away, did he bring back a gift for you?' Mrs. Butterworth looked puzzled. 'Why, yes,' she said after some thought, 'a new hat, a brass mug and a nasty bout of Spanish flu. I can't say I was delighted with any of them.' Holmes handed her a handkerchief. 'In fact, I can't say I'm delighted with him. May I speak to him?'

'That would be unwise,' cautioned Holmes. 'However, I may be able to relay a message.'

'Then give him this.' She took off her wedding ring and placed it emphatically on the table, rather like a gambler placing their last chip at the casino. 'If a man cannot speak truthfully to his own wife, then...' she trailed off. 'Tell him he must have good cause for his behaviour. Tell him I will wait.' She collected her umbrella and made for the door, pausing.

'Please help us, Mr. Holmes,' she said. 'We have five children. The police are watching our house, my husband has been labelled a murderer and we have no means to pay next month's bills.' Holmes gave a low neck bow as Mrs. Butterworth swept through the doorway.

I closed the door behind her and waited until her footsteps receded down the stairs.

'My dear Holmes!'

'Yes?' He busied himself, stoking his pipe.

'When did we learn all this?'

'*We* didn't learn all this. *I* learned all this from Arkham in The Cooper's Arms. Meanwhile you were playing skittles with your new friends.'

'And would you care to elucidate me?'

'Not just at present,' he said, pocketing his pipe and taking up his cane. 'We have a meeting in a quarter of an hour with our client, Mr. Michael Houghton, the richest man for a hundred miles in any direction. I suggest we do not keep him waiting.'

The Houghton Head Office was set a little way back from the main road: a fine, red-brick construction with high roofs and tall chimneys in the Tudor style. A single knock sufficed to announce our presence and the mahogany door swung open. A manservant of short stature but enormous whiskers greeted us in dignified silence and gestured for us to enter. Inside, the building resembled more closely the house of a foreign ambassador than the headquarters of a brewing empire, with marble pillars and ornately carved stonework. A magnificent stairway led up to a mighty window that afforded views of the brewery beyond before dividing to the left and right. A chandelier hung on an extended chain like a growth of bright mistletoe.

Michael Houghton sat at the far end of the boardroom with a sheaf of papers laid out before him. His face was perfectly smooth and round, almost as if it had been pumped by some pneumatic means. His hair was oiled and combed neatly to one side; a luxuriant handlebar moustache was his single flamboyance. He glanced up as we were

41

shown in, his head to one side, his eyes both wary and inquisitive, as if interrogating our characters.

'Gentlemen,' he said. 'Good of you to come. Do sit down.' He signalled for the hirsute aide to leave us. 'I was just reviewing the plans for an extension to our facilities. Our business continues to grow exponentially. I rather fear that we are victims of our own success.'

'I congratulate you,' remarked Holmes. 'Tell me, by how many tricks did you let the Prince of Wales win?'

'I beg your pardon?'

'You recently played bridge with the Prince of Wales, I note. Three days ago.' Houghton rose to his feet and crumpled his hitherto smooth brow. He planted his knuckles on the table and leant his substantial frame forward in a most intimidating manner. 'The Prince's visit to Ingleforth was conducted in the greatest secrecy. How could you possibly be aware of the arrangements?'

'Simplicity itself,' smiled Holmes. 'Your gold tie-pin bears his crest and the motto *'Ich Dien,'* "I Serve." I happen to know that such an accessory can only be acquired as a personal gift.'

'That is easily enough explained,' he agreed. 'But what of our choice of after-dinner entertainment?'

'You have a paper cut on your right thumb, quite common with card players.'

'So that gives us the playing cards. But what is to say we did not play poker?'

'It is true that a portion of your party played poker. However it is well known that his companion, Mrs. Keppel, insists on bridge, and that the Prince always obliges her. Besides, the tip of your scorecard is visible in your jacket pocket and bears a trace of ladies' rouge. No doubt you kept it as a souvenir of your royal opponent. My supposition is that you made up a four at bridge with your brother, the Prince and his companion.'

'Remarkable!' said Houghton, gazing at my friend.

'Is it not also true that the Prince emerged the victor?'

'Once again, you are perfectly correct,' Houghton marvelled.

'He is a notoriously sore loser. It is inconceivable that he would have left you with such a prized memento if you had humiliated him at the bridge table.'

'It is an act of pure clairvoyance,' the brewer said, shaking his head.

'Merely observation and deduction,' corrected Holmes. 'Now let us attend to the matter at hand.'

'Let me speak plainly, Mr. Holmes.'

'By all means,' my friend assured him.

Houghton rose to his feet, his face darkening with purpose. 'Something or someone means to destroy me. Not just me, but this great business too. Think of the countless men who rely on me for their livelihoods. Think of their children playing in the street, and of their wives gossiping on the corners. Their prosperity is linked to mine. We make beer, sir, but that is almost ancillary to the workings of this town. We are a community. This smear on our reputation is enough to bring us all down and smash this utopia we have created together.' He paced the length of the room, his hands fixed behind his back.

'The golden age of the Burton Pale Ale, I fear, is behind us. Our methods are replicated from Bristol to Birmingham. Goodness knows, there are scientists in London who can recreate the very waters of Burton itself: a pinch of magnesium here, a little potassium there - you cannot tell it apart! Gone are the days when the shoes came from Northampton, the coal from Newcastle, and the beer from Burton. The market is wide open. All we have is our expertise and our reputation. With Butterworth vanished, a regiment poisoned and our name in the mire, I fear we have lost both in one foul swoop.' Holmes nodded gravely.

'You make your point, most forcefully,' he asserted. 'Do you have your suspicions?' Houghton tapped the table with the end of a sturdy finger.

'I cannot believe Butterworth would do such a thing. To sully his own beer would be akin to Mr. John Constable wilfully defacing his own painting. Mr. Butterworth is an artist. It is unthinkable! He collapsed into his chair and stared up at the ceiling. 'I am a man of great forbearance, Mr. Holmes,' he said, 'but even I have my limits. I will pay you handsomely if you find the culprit. But if by the end of a month we are no closer, I will pursue my own lines of enquiry, exercising all necessary force.'

'You will take the law into your own hands?'

'Mr. Holmes, be under no illusion; in this part of the world we brewers are the ultimate authority. We are the magistrates, the landowners, the employers. The police do their work well enough, but we hold the balance of power. Inspector Hubble, an able man, is making steady progress, but this particular case I believe requires more than competence. It must be resolved quickly and conclusively. That is why I have invited you here, Mr. Holmes.'

'As I indicated in my telegram, Mr. Houghton, I am most willing to apply my methods to this singular matter. My discretion, and that of my companion, Dr. Watson, is assured. However my success will depend entirely on data. In the absence of data I will reveal nothing. I therefore require full access to your premises and the mechanisms by which you prepare your ale. I am an amateur chemist and have a basic understanding of your processes. I will seek the unusual, the telling detail. But answer me this: Who do you think poisoned your beer?'

Houghton sighed deeply, his stature visibly diminishing as the air escaped from his chest.

'Evercreech,' he muttered, his knuckles pressed to the table. 'It can only be Evercreech!'

'Nathanial Evercreech,' repeated Holmes. 'Your fellow Burtonian and brewer? What of this great utopia you speak of?'

'It is painful to admit,' he confessed, 'for we present a united front to the world, but the reality is that he is the bane of my life. He is cutting in on our trade and luring away my workers with promises of long holidays and inflated wages. A disaster at Houghton would serve him handsomely.'

'What of Butterworth?' I asked. 'Is it possible Evercreech has some power over him?

'All these things are possible,' remarked Holmes. 'However, we must support this conjecture with fact.'

'Mr. Holmes,' stated Houghton, 'you will have all possible access and assistance. You may tour the brewery this very afternoon. I will ask Butterworth's deputy, Leonard Tolwood, to be your guide. Then there is a further opportunity. Tomorrow evening, I am hosting the four great barons. I will invite you as a guest on some suitable pretence, so that you may observe them at close quarters. If your powers are as great as they say, I have no doubt you will have identified the culprit by the time the coffee is drained and the cigars are smoked.'

My case notes from the year 1899 are by no means exhaustive. Such was Holmes' frenetic level of activity, it was not always possible to keep a perfect record of our adventures. Consequently, certain nuances of the more mundane affairs are now lost to posterity.

However, when I look at the thick sheaf of notes laid out before me, I am gratified that I took care to document in some detail our visit to Houghton's brewery, for it gave rise to several of those brilliant moments of deduction upon which my friend has built his reputation.

We journeyed the short distance on foot from Houghton's office to the brewery, Holmes tapping his cane every two yards or so to keep a measure of the distance. As we approached the building, we had cause to negotiate the lattice of railway tracks that terminated in the yard and which gave the site the appearance of a railway terminus, rather than a place of work. The brewery itself was a towering brick construction that was a cross between a factory and warehouse. On the exterior were a series of attractive architectural embellishments: ornate lantern and intricate brick patterns that rendered the whole not entirely unpleasing to the eye.

Tolwood was waiting in a small side doorway, a nervous, handsome young man with fair hair, neatly parted, and clear, dark eyes. His chin was raised and his tightly pressed lips suggested a certain firmness of purpose. He shook our hands with great solemnity and thanked us quietly for visiting. 'We are, I admit, most sorely missing Mr. Butterworth's guiding spirit,' he whispered. 'It is so very good of you to come.'

Stepping inside, we entered an alien world of pipes and basins, ducts and gantries. It was as if a five-storey hotel had been gutted, its floors torn away, and the space given over to the construction of a moon rocket. I gazed in wonder at the apparatus and breathed in the stupendously rich odour, a giddy blend of coconut, wheat and hops that was almost overpowering.

'After a while,' Tolwood remarked, 'it is fresh air that becomes the novelty. This way gentlemen, please.' He led us at a brisk pace down two steep flights of wooden stairs, descending with the speed of a sailor into the hold of his ship. We emerged into an enormous open room, with glazed, white-brick walls and a ceiling that rose to an impressive height. At intervals were great oak tubs, covered with flat wooden lids, each supplied by a metal dispenser of some description.

'The mash tuns,' he declared. 'This is where we convert the crushed grain into the sugars we need for fermentation.'

'I thank you for your explanation,' Holmes interjected, 'however, I am well acquainted with the principles of brewing. I see you employ the modern method by which there is an opening at the bottom to allow the grain to exit.'

'In earlier days our predecessors climbed inside and shovelled it out by hand.'

'Indeed.'

'What we are left with,' said Tolwood, continuing with his lecture, 'is the wort, the precious sugary liquid that will be fermented into alcohol. This is then transported into the boiling coppers where hops are added. If you would be so good as to follow me to the boiler room.'

By means of a smaller set of steps, we proceeded to a room of equally impressive size, dominated by two enormous boiling coppers, like futuristic submarines from the imagination of H.G. Wells. My friend studied these at length.

'Tell me,' enquired Holmes, 'how many visitors have you received in the last week?'

'Besides the local inspector,' Tolwood recalled, 'and two constables, you are the first.' My friend seemed much taken by this mundane piece of information.

'The gangways beside the vessels are remarkably wide,' I noted.

'With good reason,' Tolwood returned. 'These coppers would scald a man if he brushed against them. We prefer to give them a wide berth.'

'In which case,' I put in, 'it feels remarkably dangerous to have these sacks lying about in the passageway. One stumble could spell disaster.'

'That,' our guide informed us, 'is unavoidable. They contain the hops with which we supply the copper. As I'm sure you are aware, the hops provide the beer's essential bitterness. Beer with no hops would be akin to an opera with no singing.'

'A vivid analogy,' I remarked, stepping gingerly over one of the sacks.

'Now, gentlemen, only a little way to go,' Tolwood assured us, trotting up a few more steps. 'We find ourselves in the hop back room. It is from here that the wort is pumped upwards, defying gravity, and, naturally, we shall follow it.'

We felt some empathy for the liquor on its weary journey north; we ascended flight after flight of stairs. I chatted amiably with Tolwood; however, my friend seemed utterly preoccupied. He appeared to be in a kind of trance, barely registering the running commentary from our obliging guide.

'Now,' said Tolwood, 'I believe you have seen enough. It is time for a tasting.' The brewer carefully poured a measure of golden ale into a glass, then held it up to the light.

'Mr. Tolwood,' I put in, glancing at my pocket watch. 'It will not surprise you to learn that we have tasted ale before.'

'Not like this,' he said. 'Now gentlemen, please inspect it closely.' I confess that it gleamed with a quality that seemed almost ethereal. I frowned.

'Have you done something to it?'

'I brewed it!' he laughed, adding quickly: 'with my friend, Mr. Butterworth. But in reality it has little to do with us. It is the water. You could travel the world and find no water better suited to brewing than the waters of Burton. For fifty thousand years, the waters have seeped through the sandstone and gravel of the river valley, infusing them with a miraculous combination of minerals.' He glanced across at my friend. 'Mr. Holmes, you are a man of science. You will appreciate the natural alchemy that that has led to this happy accident.'

My friend lifted the glass and held it closer to the light. Narrowing his eyes, he lifted it to his lips and took a draught.

'High in sulphate, calcium and magnesium,' he declared. 'Low in bicarbonate and soda.'

'Upon my word, Mr. Holmes,' Tolwood said admiringly, 'all that from a single tasting?' Holmes smiled and returned the glass to the table. I suspected my friend had some prior knowledge, but for the sake of his vanity, I held my tongue.

'It has made Burton the world capital of beer,' he continued, a misty look in his eyes. 'Our waters are the envy of brewers the world over. None more so than in London. Go into any pub you like. You will see for yourself that porter has fallen out of favour. They drink nothing but pale ale and it is the Burton ales that outsell the others, ten to one. And for our men overseas it is the same. Without their supply of pale ale, our armies in India would mutiny.'

'No doubt,' Holmes concurred.

'But our dominance is threatened.' He glared darkly at the glass. 'We have elicited not only the envy, but the fury of the London brewers. They will not stand idly and watch their businesses fall into ruin. They have made alliances, pooled their learning and are bearing down on us. They are converting their systems, dismantling their porter operations

47

and switching lock, stock, and dare I say barrel, to the production of pale ale.

'But,' I pointed out, 'you hold the trump card. They do not possess your miraculous waters.'

'Precisely. They knew their waters could not compare. So the London brewers have set up in Burton. They are using our waters and returning them to London as their own. And, if that's not bad enough, now there is a new threat.'

'Wine!' I declared. Tolwood winced, as if I had sworn in front of his mother.

'No, it is called Burtonisation, Doctor. Their scientists have studied our water. They have broken it down and recreated it in their laboratories. What took millennia to evolve in our river valley, they have synthesised in a matter of months. Now their ale is...' He hesitated while searching for the *mot juste,* glancing around the room as if he might find it pinned to the wall, 'passable.'

Just as we were about to resume our tour, Holmes stopped in his tracks. His eyes lit upon a small object partially concealed beneath one of the iron-grey tanks. Stooping, he retrieved it from the shadows and held it up to the light.

'A religious medallion,' he noted. 'What do you make of that, Watson?'

'A St Christopher medal?'

'No, I don't think so. A more obscure figure it seems. Clearly, I did not spend enough time with Butler's *Lives of the Saints* as I might have. Tolwood, do you have any ideas?'

'Beer is my religion,' he confessed.

'Then we must seek specialist help.' He pressed a finger to his lips, lost in thought. It was a look I recognised.

'Something is troubling you, Holmes?'

'A singular object,' he noted, 'and yet it is strangely familiar. Pray, let us continue.'

We stepped out into the yard, blinking in the light. A smooth, white mist, as fine as a veil of woven silk hung low over us. The breweries' chimneys vanished, as if they were beanstalks disappearing into the heavens. Holmes and I were pacing the yard, barrels stacked ten-high on each side, following Tolwood, who walked briskly ahead. Holmes came to an abrupt halt. 'These barrels,' he said, to no one in particular, 'they are numbered are they not?' I glanced over at the nearest one.

'I have no idea,' I replied.

'Then, let us see for ourselves.' Tolwood, glanced behind him.

'For pity's sake, Mr. Holmes,' he cried, raising his hand in warning, 'leave that alone.' My friend paused and looked up.

'Dislodge one barrel,' Tolwood said, 'and the whole lot will come crashing down. Every one of us will be as flat as a beaten farthing.'

'I have no intention of dislodging anything,' remarked Holmes, 'except the truth.'

'Well, I can tell you that the barrels are indeed numbered. There is a small branded numeral on both the lid and the side of each barrel. Look here, can you see?'

'Splendid,' exclaimed Holmes, 'then we should know the number of the barrel which contained the beer that poisoned the regiment.'

Tolwood shook his head. 'We send hundreds of barrels to India. How would we know which one?'

'I assume the offending consignment was retained?'

'I wouldn't know,' Tolwood returned.

'Then, let us send a telegram to the regimental headquarters and find out.'

'To what possible end?'

'Would it not be possible, even likely,' Holmes postulated, 'that our poisoner would contaminate more than one barrel?' Tolwood nodded slowly. 'And if he were to do so, would it not stand to reason, given no doubt, that he would have acted in haste, that he would tamper with those barrels closest to the first? If we discover the number of the barrel, we will know the numbers of those that were stored on either side. Each of those could contain the same toxin.'

Holmes paced the yard, as restless as a man who had staked his fortune on a single horse.

'Surely,' I reasoned, 'the sequential barrels would have all travelled to India as part of the same consignment?'

'It's possible,' said Tolwood evenly, 'but I couldn't say for sure. Some are sent to the next street, others to the next continent.' Nonetheless, I could see concern writ large across his brow. Whether it was genuine concern for his fellow Burtonians, or concern for his own career, it was impossible to say.

'But you keep a record of which barrels are sent where?'

'Yes, of course.'

'But this incident. It took place well over a week ago. The beer brewed with it could have been sent anywhere in the world by now. It could be stowed under the platform at St. Pancras Station, on a barge on the Manchester canals, or off the coast of Africa.'

Tolwood clicked his fingers and a boy, with a densely freckled face and a striking shock of red hair appeared as if from nowhere. The brewer scribbled a note, then pressed it into the boy's hand. 'Send this straightaway and bring me the reply the moment it arrives.'

'Is it beyond hope, Watson,' Holmes muttered darkly, 'that the police can make even the most rudimentary enquiries?' We found a step with a fine view of the yard. Holmes smoked his pipe, keeping his own counsel, while turning the medallion over thoughtfully in his long, pale fingers.

Half an hour passed, by which time I believed I was beginning to develop a chill. Presently, the boy came sprinting into the yard, his shoes slipping on the cobbles, his cap flying off as he rounded the final corner. He waved a telegram above his head.

'14,793!' he cried. '14,793!' Tolwood turned to us. 'This way, gentlemen,' he beckoned, then paced purposefully towards the office. The room was a dimly lit mausoleum of papers and administrators. There, we found a score of identical desks, each piled high with ledgers, papers, ink wells. Each desk was attended by a diligent looking clerk, his jacket hung up behind him. The clerks varied in height and age but seemed to share the same industrious air.

'Quickly, Barniston,' snapped Tolwood, ambushing one of these men toiling there, 'fetch me the prime register.' A small, owlish-looking fellow, with tightly coiled, grey hair sprang to his feet. He wore an expression of utter astonishment, his eyes wide open, his silvery eyebrows raised high on his brow. Could the request be unusual? The man's singular countenance, Tolwood later revealed, was the result of an incident he had witnessed many years ago. It had proved so traumatic that his reaction was stamped permanently on his features. Barniston went to a small cabinet and retrieved a key. We then followed him down a narrow corridor that led into another room, identical in every way to the first. He advanced on a large cabinet and retrieved a volume as stout as the King James Bible. With some considerable exertion, he swung it onto the desk top, opening it at a previously marked page.

The clerk placed a finger on the ledger and traced a line down the page. He paused halfway down then turned to me, wearing a look of astonishment.

'What is it?' I gasped?

'Nothing,' he stated. 'I have not yet located the entry.' I had momentarily forgotten his affliction.

He continued his search, finally turning the page. This continued for a second and a third page.

'Yes,' he announced at last, 'here it is. It appears that barrels 14,792 and 14,794 were local deliveries: to the The Fox and Goose on Burton Bridge.'

'And when,' demanded Holmes, 'were those barrels dispatched?'

'Only yesterday it seems.'

'Come Tolwood,' my friend cried, 'they could be pouring the beer as we speak.'

Leaving the clerks to their fudgelling, we sprinted to the gates, almost colliding with Houghton as we left.

'Why the haste?' he asked gruffly. 'We believe a second and a third barrel may be contaminated,' Tolwood explained. 'Over at The Fox and Goose.'

'Then, waste no time,' he said. 'Go to it.'

Dodging a pram, three newspaper vendors and an umbrella man, we darted along the road in the direction of the bridge.

'Can we not hail a hackney?' I cried, leapfrogging two boys playing marbles in the gutter.

'Quicker on foot,' Tolwood called back.

We rounded a corner, then almost at once discovered we had arrived. It was a homely establishment, the inviting, yellowish gaslight seeping into the grey afternoon. Holmes connected with the front door at a rate of knots and we burst into the public bar. Five men were seated on stools, each cradling a glass of amber ale. The drinker nearest to us was a portly fellow, with a head of golden ringlets and cheeks as ruddy as a pair of beef tomatoes. He inspected us with an air of some amusement.

'Someone's thirsty,' he remarked.

At once Holmes shot out a hand and pushed the glass from his hands. It shattered against a tap and a glistening pool of beer and froth formed

51

in front of the men. The golden-haired fellow peered at the remains of his pint, then back at Holmes.

'I was looking forward to that.' A bull-necked fellow to his right delivered a well-aimed jab at my friend. With the instincts of one who had applied himself to both the theory and practice of the fancy, Holmes deftly side-stepped it and swerved his head to avoid the follow-up.

'A dancer, then, are you?!' the fellow warned. 'Why don't you put up like a man?'

'I assure you,' a sonorous voice piped up from the other side of the bar, 'he has your very best interests at heart. College boxing champion three years on the trot.'

'And you are?' the drinker growled.

'His brother.' The gigantic figure of Mycroft Holmes turned to face us from his window seat. He folded his great, fleshy fingers and peered at us with that look of weary resignation. It seemed to imply that not only that had he foreseen the outcome of our investigation, but, to explain his reasoning would as tedious as it would be exhausting.

'Mycroft!' I called. 'What in heaven's name…?'

'I have already taken the liberty of securing barrels 14,792 and 14,794. I had a quiet word with our publican, Mr. Todder, and purchased them outright.'

'But how…?'

'When you have connections such as mine, securing a small favour in the office of a large brewery is no great feat.' He peered at his brother and frowned. 'Sherlock, I am surprised that it took you so long to identify this danger.'

'My mind was occupied with other matters,' he explained dryly. 'Notably, which of the Houghton's competitors, employees, or as yet unidentified miscreants were responsible for the poisoning. It takes time to conduct enquiries.'

'You will know,' Mycroft yawned, 'I have no energy for such things. But neither could I sit idly by and wait for another man to die. It was immediately clear to me that the poisoner could have tainted three barrels as easily as he could have one.'

The bull-necked fellow still stood poised to bludgeon my friend, his hand formed into a fist, yet he now appeared less certain. His eyes moved from one Holmes brother to the next.

'Your ale is perfectly safe,' Mycroft assured him. 'It is from barrel 11,539. Perhaps, Mr. Todder, you would be so good as to fetch this gentleman a new glass and charge it with Houghton's Best Bolter IPA.' He placed a guinea on the counter. 'In fact, why not pour us all a glass and we can recover from these exertions.' Silently, we supped the amber ale, savouring its bitterness and slightly citrus aroma.

'The colour of sherry,' Tolwood remarked proudly, 'and the condition of champagne.'

From the diary of Miss Gertrude Cresswell, 9th October 1899

Breakfasted on some kippers, which were almost certainly off. I informed my landlady who inspected them but did not contradict my diagnosis or offer any defence as she removed them, presumably to palm off on some other unsuspecting guest.

Dressed in a plain shawl and chose a dull umbrella: necessary, though painful precautions. Decided to focus today's attentions on Mr. Tolwood as a person of interest. Having extracted his address from a dim-witted yardman, I contrived to be opposite his front gate at eight o'clock as he left for work. It appears he still lives with his mother, who saw him off at the door with a packet of sandwiches. Followed him for two minutes, whereupon I saw him deposit the sandwiches into a bin.

Feeling a little sorry for his mother, I fetched them out and handed them to a hungry-looking urchin on the street corner. He seemed grateful enough. A quarter of a mile on and Tolwood stopped abruptly and looked directly behind him, forcing me to duck into an alley. When I emerged he had disappeared. Felt a total fool.

Am I losing my touch? Suddenly felt queasy as the kippers repeated on me, but managed to hold my nerve. Found a café across the street and ordered a hot water and lemon. The plump woman at the counter, who called me 'duck' (as in 'yes, me duck'), appeared never to have received such a request before. However, much rummaging behind the scenes produced some lemon and soon I was sipping calmly in the window, watching the property across the street.

Not five minutes later and I saw his face in the upper window. Not Tolwood, but Butterworth! So he is here – how brazen! Surely he knows that he is England's most wanted man? All the rumours are that he has fled the country.

My employers, Evercreech, would hand over a handsome fee simply for this information. So far as the London brewer is concerned, if Butterworth were to be found and convicted for the poisoning, then that would constitute an entirely satisfactory conclusion to the case. I do not think they much care whether he is guilty or not. While there are stories circulating of poisoned ale, it hurts every brewer. And besides, if Houghton's are deprived of their greatest talent, then the quality can only go down, which spells more good news for Evercreech.

But there is more to this. I am a servant of the truth, not a mere fee. Besides, I find it impossible to believe that Holmes has not discovered that Butterworth is under his nose. And if he knows that, what else has he discovered? Nor do I know yet who has engaged Holmes' services. Is it Houghton's? Have both brewers abandoned all faith in the police and engaged the services of private agencies? I have a troubling dilemma. Do I throw in my lot with Holmes and pool resources, keep a watch on him, or simply hand over Butterworth? Too many decisions for so early in the morning.

The shop doorbell rings. Tolwood! He glances around the café, steps up to the counter and orders bread and dripping. A repulsive dish, but one he clearly prefers to his mother's sandwiches. He takes his tea, scans the shop, then marches directly to my table.

'*May I join you?*' *he asks.*

'*By all means,*' *I blurt in my best Chelsea without thinking to affect a local accent.*

'*Not local then,*' *he says.*

'*Just up from London.*'

'*Oh, I see. Looking for work?*'

'*Yes, as a matter of fact.*'

'*What is it you do?*'

'*Tutoring.*'

'*Really?*'

'*Yes, music.*'

'*What's your line?*'

'*A little of everything, but ukulele is my main instrument. Music hall.*'

He expressed mild surprise, but not suspicion I didn't think.

'*I'd have you down as the classical type.*'

'*Well, you have me down wrong, Mr...*'

'*Tolwood.*'

'*Gertie,*' *I said, and extended a gloved hand in greeting. He had a firm handshake, no wedding ring and a broken knuckle on the index finger of his right hand.*

His breakfast arrived and he glanced up at the waiter in acknowledgement, at the same time stuffing a napkin into his shirt collar. He was young, but not without that certain confidence and self-possession a growing mastery of his craft no doubt had lent him.

'I wouldn't have thought,' he said, forking in a mouthful, 'there was much call for a ukulele teacher around here.' He tucked in with some enthusiasm.

'You would be surprised,' I informed him. 'Lots of new money means time for leisure; time for hobbies.' I was warming to my subject. 'In fact, I have been meaning to leave my card with Mrs. Michael Houghton. I've heard she is very partial to music.' His face brightened.

'Mrs. Houghton? I know her very well.'

'You do?' I managed to sound suitably surprised and for a moment thought I'd over-egged it.

'Yes. I work at the brewery.'

'In what capacity?' He blushed a little.

'Well,' he said, with no small degree of pride. 'I'm the acting head brewer.' He patted his pockets for his cigarettes.

'Goodness!' I exclaimed.

'I suppose you've heard about the poisoning?'

'Yes, I did read something. The former head brewer wasn't it? What was his name, Buttermere?'

'Butterworth,' he corrected. 'No truth in it if you ask me. Butterworth loves the company. He lives for it. It wasn't him in a million years. But try telling that to the police, or Sherlock Holmes.'

'Sherlock Holmes? In Burton? He never is!'

'It's perfectly true. It's the talk of the town. The paper's having a field day. People are writing in with cases for him to solve. Missing relatives and haunted houses.'

'Gosh, wouldn't it be wonderful to meet him, such a fine mind!'

'I spent most of the day with him yesterday.'

'No!'

'No word of a lie.'

'And what's he like?' Tolwood paused for a moment. 'Quite thorough,' he replied.

'All this,' I suggested, 'is bad for business?'

'We've seen some downturn, that's true,' he admitted, 'but as long as men walk on two legs they'll drink beer. We just hope it continues to be ours.' He let his fork fall onto his empty plate, then dabbed his lips with a napkin.

'Here,' he said, handing over his card, 'call me at the office and let's see if we can't arrange an introduction to Mrs. Houghton. I think she'll like you.'

'Really,' I said. 'Mr. Tolwood, that would be too much to ask.'

'Not at all,' he said. 'I'm from a musical family myself. My sister arranges the programme for the opera at Buxton. No aptitude for it myself, alas. Cloth-eared, she calls me.'

'I don't believe it,' I broke in. 'You have a melodious voice. I suspect there's a baritone hiding in there somewhere.' He stared at me for a moment, wary perhaps of the flattery. Was I making an advance?

'Well...' he said at length, blushing slightly again, 'you'd have to look hard to find it.' He rose to his feet. 'I must be getting on. But do call in at the office.' I extended my hand again.

'I shall,' I agreed. 'What a fortuitous meeting.'

'Yes, indeed. Good day, Miss...?'

'Just Gertie.' He straightened his hat with a trace of amusement, wondering perhaps whether I wasn't a professional of a different sort.

'Well, good day, Miss... Gertie.'

FOUR

The Astronomer

I leapt from my bed. Against the opposite wall dangled a burning rope, its entire length consumed in flame. Only as my brain shook off the stupor of sleep did I see that it was nothing more than a strip of sunlight streaming through the curtains. Wincing a little from the combined effect of the India pale ale and the bright light, I slipped from my cot and drank a glass of water.

I was still knotting my tie as I made my way into the sitting room, seduced by the powerful aroma of freshly brewed coffee and less palatable reek of tobacco smoke. Holmes sat with his first pipe of the day, peering intently at a letter before him on the coffee table.

'Well, Watson,' he declared, 'it appears someone else has discovered our whereabouts. We may as well have advertised our address in *The Times*. The letter was slipped under the door during the night.'

'Perhaps,' I suggested, 'it is just our bill.'

'I think not,' replied Holmes tersely. 'It is stationery of a singular quality. Do you see this crest? He tapped the reverse of the envelope with his fingernail. I peered closely at the embossed design.

'A fire-breathing horse,' I remarked with no little surprise.

'I concur. A remarkable flourish for an hotelier, don't you agree? Now my knowledge of the classics does not rival Mycroft's,' Holmes confessed, 'but I would not be at all surprised if that is not Aethon, one of the immortal fire-breathing steeds of the gods.'

'If you say so, Holmes. Speaking of Mycroft, do you think it was wise for us to put him on a train back to London?'

'What was the alternative?'

'To accompany him.'

'He is his own man.'

'And what of the temptations of the buffet car, or the wine list?'

'I instructed the guard not to allow him anything stronger than ginger beer.'

'And what about when he leaves the train?'

'I cannot live his life for him,' Holmes sighed, then instinctively ran his hand along the inside of his sleeve. 'We must all wrestle our own demons.' I gave silent thanks for the fact that as of late, I had not witnessed my friend succumb to the seven percent solution.

'Well,' added Holmes more cheerfully, glancing at the letter, 'let us not delay any longer.'

My friend slit open the envelope with his pocket knife and shook out the contents. A single slip of card tumbled onto the desk. Holmes scanned the message and furrowed his brow.

'It appears,' he said tossing the card in my direction, 'that we have been summoned.'

'Anaxagoras Houghton,' I read with some difficulty, 'requests the pleasure of your company at the summit of Waterloo Clump, Winshill, this evening at nine o'clock. He has information which will be to your advantage.' I placed the invitation on the table and poured myself some hot coffee. 'An extraordinary moniker,' I suggested. 'Any idea who he is?'

'One of the dynasty, I surmise,' mused Holmes, joining his fingers. 'Something of a black sheep by all accounts. I know only that he is a man of mathematical gifts, prefers wine to ale, and has a small injury to his left wrist. He is also a man who has recently lost a good deal of money. His education exceeds his station and he has a score to settle.'

'You know all this from two lines of handwriting?'

'It is as revealing,' Holmes laughed, 'as a three-volume biography. Now, our appointment is some hours off. Would you indulge me with a stroll into town so that I may replenish my supply of tobacco?'

A quarter of an hour later, Holmes and I were trussed up against the cold, our ulsters drawn tightly around our shoulders.

'An autumn in the north,' I grumbled, 'is a winter in the south. Let us resolve this case with all speed and return to the balmy climes of Baker Street.'

'Come now, Watson,' my friend retorted, 'where is your pluck? Where is your guile?'

'Where I left it,' I muttered gloomily, 'in Maiwand.' A blizzard of leaves blew belligerently in our faces. Presently Holmes stopped in his tracks.

'Do you smell that, Watson?' An expression of great delight spread across Holmes' face. 'Chestnuts!' he cried.

Lengthening his stride, Holmes hurried towards a street vendor plying his trade in the far distance. I struggled after, and had almost drawn level by the time we reached the stall. But it was no ordinary concession.

'Extraordinary!' I marvelled. 'But what is it?' Before me stood a great whirling machine, painted in a livery of crimson and gold. Steam billowed from valves and trumpets; wheels turned and levers elevated in synchronicity. Most astonishing of all, a great lizard-like head nodded menacingly, yet more steam billowing from its nostrils, while a pair of red wings rose and fell at each side. And in its fiery belly was a furnace where the chestnuts slowly roasted.

'A mechanical dragon,' I cried.

'You like it, then?'

'Crabtree!' I exclaimed.

'My dear fellow,' Holmes re-joined.

Those familiar with my accounts of Holmes' exploits, will remember the diminutive monocle seller we first encountered in 'The Adventure of the Ruby Elephants.' What he lacked in stature, he more than made up for in gumption. We owed him our very lives.

'What, in heaven's name,' I demanded, 'are you doing here?'

'You must allow a man the capacity for change,' he declared, proudly tapping the flanks of the iron dragon.

'You engineered this monster?'

'Of course,' he said, barely concealing his pride. Holmes and I were soon enjoying the piping-hot chestnuts.

'You are as fine a gourmand,' declared Holmes, 'as you are a fabricator.' Crabtree busied himself, serving customers or feeding the beast oil and water. Children ran to the dragon's head, then hared off, waving their arms with squeals of terror and delight. Finally, after the hubbub had subsided, we found a moment to speak.

'I tired of the monocle business,' Crabtree confessed, wiping each of his eyeglasses on an oily rag. 'It had become a chore; it was time to indulge my vocation as an inventor.'

'An inventor you say?' questioned Holmes.

'I was not,' he admitted, 'an immediate success. 'My mechanical scarecrows caught fire and my patent submarine lies at the bottom of the Thames, just off Eel Pie Island. Herbert here, was my first triumph. To fund my next project, a mechanical elephant, I have taken Herbert on a tour of the kingdom. My grandfather was in the chestnut trade. I revived the family tradition and am doing steady business.'

'A capital effort,' said Holmes clapping him on the back. With a conspiratorial glance left and right, Crabtree drew closer to Holmes. 'I heard you were here,' he whispered. 'If you want my view, you will already be well-acquainted with the murder. Never trust the quiet ones.' Holmes nodded, showing no signs of mockery or condescension. 'I shall most certainly bear that in mind.' We left Crabtree with an invitation to call upon us at Baker Street when he returned to London. 'Fancy!' I marvelled as we walked away. 'Dear old Crabtree, here in Burton.'

That evening, the moon was like a brilliant pearl in the sky. Holmes and I collected our canes, stuffed flasks of brandy into our pockets, then ventured out into the night. We had elected to walk the short distance to Winshill and found ourselves in a clear, cold night, crossing the long bridge that spanned the Trent. The moon slid across the slowly undulating surface of the river, as if attempting to return to find the oyster from which it sprang.

'The local saint, Modwen,' muttered Holmes, 'founded an abbey here on an island.' He gestured into the darkness. 'She was, I believe, a nun who performed miracles when the whim took her. However, the greatest marvel of all, we now know, is the water itself which flows up from the rocks. It has, as we are so often reminded, a miraculous purity.' I stared out into the night, the mists that gathered on the riverbanks, and fancied I could see an apparition of a nun gliding across the river. I reached for my flask and took a swig. 'On nights such as this, Holmes,' I confessed, 'I have little use for water.'

'I believe, Watson,' smiled Holmes, 'that you are a more superstitious fellow than you care to admit. But you have seen ghosts more malevolent than this. Why, there are a hundred of them within the square mile that encloses Baker Street, if only you cared to look.'

We strode onwards, the road growing ever steeper, past handsome stone houses on either side. They belonged, I presumed, to the wealthy directors and investors in the brewing corporations. I peered in at warmly lit sitting rooms, where children in sailor suits and pretty dresses played the piano or sat with their crochet under the tutelage of their mothers, while the man of the house sat in the corner with his pipe and paper. It occurred to me that there was something appallingly dull in this vision of domestic tranquillity.

'The poor have more fun, wouldn't you say?' remarked Holmes, as if reading my thoughts.

'So long,' I replied, 'as there are shoes for the children and bread on the table.'

'So long as there is beer in the glass,' parried my friend, 'the working man's lot is a happy one.'

'You are a reductionist, Holmes,' I accused.

'On the contrary Watson,' he returned, 'my business is deduction, not reduction.'

We found ourselves on the edge of an argument and I thought it prudent to curtail our discussion. For a while, I followed the red glow of his pipe and our footsteps were the only sound. Presently, Holmes pointed at the outline of yet another hill. 'Waterloo Clump,' he declared.

'Waterloo Clump?' I repeated.

'A wood planted to commemorate the disquiet Sunday,' he explained, 'when Wellington advanced the retirement of a certain diminutive Frenchman.'

'I'm not unaware of the battle,' I muttered with some irritation.

'A great British victory,' continued Holmes, 'with hardly a Briton on the field of battle as it happens. Most were busy, you remember, sporting with the Americans.'

'I may be drawing my army pension, Holmes,' I warned him, 'but I still retain a vestige of regimental pride.'

'And so you should, Watson!'

My friend directed me off to the left and we advanced up a track. Soon we were in open field, the long, wet grass licking the toes of our boots. The yellow lights of the town shone in a rain-blurred glow below us, while beyond lay the peaks and dales hidden somewhere in the vast, dark vestiges of night.

'I believe,' said Holmes coming to a sudden halt, and glancing about us, 'that we have reached the top.'

'I see,' I remarked, when in fact I could see very little.

'There it is!' We heard a man's voice cry out in the dark. It belonged to this man, Anaxagoras, and was filled with a kind of wild delight. 'Just there,' he directed us. 'It has a beguiling beauty all of its own, would you not agree? You may see for yourselves!'

Presently, I discerned a figure in the dark, clutching a gleaming implement that could only be a telescope. It was copper-gold in the moonlight.

'Surely,' I said, peering up, 'you are referring to Jupiter.'

'I do not speak of Jupiter!' the man laughed. 'One grows tired of his cheap pyrotechnics, not to speak of his tantrums. Just think of the storm that has raged for centuries. Let him rage at the heavens. No, I speak of Ganymede, the most beautiful of the mortals and cup-bearer to the gods.'

'Ganymede?' I questioned. 'Holmes, are you familiar with such a planet?'

'I am barely conscious of the one beneath our feet,' he dismissed. 'You forget, Watson, I have little interest in the celestial bodies. Only the bodies that lie unidentified in the morgues of Scotland Yard.

'Not a planet, my friend,' the man corrected, 'but a moon. It was discovered by Galileo himself some three hundred years ago. Ganymede was swept up by an eagle and transported to Olympus to pour wine for Zeus and now we have found him. See for yourself.'

We approached the man who gambolled towards us, almost as if he were dancing. He had a long, grizzled beard in the manner of W.G. Grace, contrasted with immaculately coiffed hair. A long, white shirt protruded beneath a full-length black cape. He was perhaps forty-five, but had the eyes and mannerisms of a much older man. He struck me as a sort of mad prophet.

I accepted his invitation and put my eye to the telescope, observing three pinpricks of light adjacent to the bright orb of Jupiter itself.

'Remarkable,' I said.' Which is Ganymede?'

'It is the third moon from the planet, but the largest of them all.'

'You have a special affinity for it,' remarked Holmes coolly, in that you were the oldest of your father's sons, but the third in his affections.'

All mirth disappeared at once from the man's face, who instead stared directly at my friend.

'It pains me to admit it, Mr. Holmes, but you speak the truth. If you know this much, then you will know that I am the eldest son of Sir Edwin Houghton, the son who was passed over in favour of his two brothers, Michael and Samuel.'

'My enquiries,' my friend confirmed, 'provided the same intelligence.'

'And no doubt you will also be aware of the incident that led to my fall from grace?'

'Not two months into your stewardship of the firm, you lost a king's ransom at the Doncaster Races.'

'Quite,' he mused, his eyes misting over at the memory. 'Surefoot was the name of the horse and a sure-fire winner too, I was told. But never was there a horse in the history of racing so poorly named. He crashed out at the first corner, unseating his rider. At the time horses were my life. The business was merely a means to fuel my despicable habit. Yet on this occasion I had over-reached myself. The losses were catastrophic. Even though my father was aged, he had enough breath left in him to instruct that the business be handed over to my two younger brothers.'

I felt the wind nip at my face and my body began to freeze at its core. It was remiss of me not to have donned an extra layer beneath my ulster.

'I can see you are feeling the cold,' remarked Anaxagoras, his beard tugged sideways by the wind. Can I interest either of you two gentlemen in a glass of 1895 Chateau Montrose?'

'You must certainly can,' I affirmed.

The extraordinary fellow produced a pair of folding, wooden chairs, relics I surmised from years spent on the racecourse, and invited us to sit with him while he poured the wine. From a large carpet bag, he also produced blankets, which he offered as insulation from the cold. The combination of this and the wine made our moonlit picnic somewhat more bearable.

'You asked to see us,' Holmes reminded him. 'I assume it was not solely for the purpose of expanding our knowledge of the solar system.'

'If I have increased your appreciation for our place in the universe, then that alone, I hope, was well worth your trouble. But no, there is another reason.'

'We are busy men,' my friend said.

'Quite,' agreed Houghton. 'As busy as ants building their colonies. To them their nest is their world, while of course to us their work is of little significance. We are nothing but the ants of the universe – utterly insignificant. We are but motes of dust passing through a beam of sunlight.'

64

'If we think too much on these things,' I countered, 'we may as well lay down and die.'

'Pray come to your point,' urged Holmes.

'I believe,' said Houghton, 'I know your poisoner.' I was taken aback, but Holmes himself looked unperturbed.

'It is my brother, Samuel.'

'On what grounds?'

'An argument over a fish.'

'A fish?' I repeated.

'A barbell to be precise,' Houghton elucidated. 'A ten-pounder.' He put his nose to his wine and breathed in the vapours. 'There's plum there,' he said, swirling the glass, 'and spices. But there's something else too. Almost a minty note. Have you detected it?'

'Please return to the fish,' instructed Holmes.

'Yes, of course,' he said. 'I am easily distracted by pleasure. It is a vendetta between Samuel and Michael that goes back thirty years. What is more, I can pinpoint the precise moment it began. It was a slow, balmy afternoon in July, just at the start of the school holidays. The three of us were lined up on the bank, our fishing rods arched over the brown waters of the Trent, the lines sunk deep. We talked of idle things and watched the smoke billow from the chimneys on the skyline. This was when Samuel had a bite.'

The rod plunged deep into the water as the fish fought valiantly for its life. Samuel was on his feet, wrestling with the line. He demanded our help and immediately I leapt to my feet and seized the rod. But even the two of us were no match for this leviathan. "Michael!" my brother shouted, but he refused to be moved. He had a bite of his own and was not willing to jeopardise his own catch. "Michael!" he called again, but still he ignored him. Suddenly, the fish leapt up into the air and for a moment we caught a glimpse of it, flashing silver in the light. Then it broke free and was gone. Samuel was inconsolable. To this day he has not forgiven our brother for his recalcitrance.

'A childhood squabble,' I suggested. 'Surely, this is something to laugh about as grown men.'

'Do not be so sure,' said Houghton.

'What evidence do you have?' challenged Holmes.

'Perhaps not yet enough for a court of law. But mark my words, Samuel is behind this. Besides he has everything to gain. Michael will be discredited by the scandal and his resignation is sure to follow. Despite the damage to Houghton's reputation, Samuel will find himself in sole charge of the company.'

'A fascinating theory,' remarked Holmes. 'Yet one thing puzzles me. You suggest bad blood between Michael and Samuel, but you made no mention of a quarrel between you and Michael. Will you be happy to see your own brother disgraced?'

'I am merely a believer in the natural order of things. To my sorrow, I speak to neither of them and I have no wish to be involved or named as a source. It is up to you to furnish the courts with the necessary evidence.' He jumped suddenly to his feet and peered at a streak of light in the sky.

'A falling star, gentlemen!' he cried. 'Auspicious. Most auspicious! But drink up, the night grows cold. I should detain you no longer.'

'Where can we find you?' I asked.

'If you need me,' he advised, 'leave a message at the grave of John Henry Carr in St. Peter's Churchyard.'

'You do not have an address?'

'I am a citizen of the world,' he muttered.

We marched briskly down the hill towards the town, trying to put some heat back into our limbs.

'A singular fellow,' Holmes remarked.

'Do you believe his story?'

'Of course,' he said. 'However, it is hardly a solution in and of itself. This problem, Watson, has assumed an appealing complexity. I confess that I was not expecting to be taxed in any significant fashion, but with each passing minute the case takes on new light and shade. It may well yet graduate to one of those adventures you deem of sufficient novelty to present to the public.'

I stamped my boots, heavy with mud from Waterloo Clump. The swollen moon rose slowly through the trees and a bird swept across it in silhouette, as if it were a giant creature whose origins lay somewhere deep in space. Blue clouds swept across the sky, and the invisible scurrying of nocturnal animals could be heard all around us. Below, the river flowed in a silver slick in the valley and the floodlands lay beyond as a marshy no man's land that kept civilisation away from the river itself.

'Look there, Holmes,' I cried. I pointed ahead to an ethereal figure in white, standing on the island in the river. 'Do you see her?'

'Great heavens, Watson,' he smiled, 'I do.'

'Surely, it is the ghost of St. Modwen herself!'

'A fanciful notion, Watson. The supernatural, as you well know, plays no part in my view of the world. Need I remind you of the outlandish suggestions made during that remarkable business with the Baskervilles? They proved as unfounded as the curse itself. There is rarely an instance where the seemingly extraordinary does not have a perfectly ordinary explanation.

'Then, what,' I cried, staring at the apparition, 'do I see before my own eyes: a swan; a Great White Egret?'

'More than likely you have provided your own explanation,' muttered Holmes.

We watched the spectre drift across the island, her white robes flowing behind her. Presently, I saw her turn to look at us, before continuing on her way. 'By heavens, Holmes,' I murmured, quite spellbound, 'it is the Lady of the Lake!'

'I would caution against such speculation,' urged Holmes, 'but seeing that the phenomenon has gripped your imagination, I am happy to indulge some further investigation. Let us hurry down to the river and see if we cannot solicit an interview with your apparition.'

We marched together, beneath the heavy skies, to the riverbank, our boot heels counting the minutes along the deserted path. Arriving at the spot, we cast about for signs of our ghost. We saw nothing but a fox, staring back from the opposite bank.

'Whoever she is,' remarked Holmes, bringing a match to his pipe, 'she is playing coy.' I shook my head, unable to shake the vision from my mind.

'Come now, Watson, let us discover whether beef tea is available in these parts and blame this vision on the tricks of the moon and the shadows of the night.'

Just as we turned to leave, I saw Holmes suddenly glance back. He crouched, tested the earth with the end of a finger, and frowned.

'What is it Holmes?' I asked. He glanced up and peered gravely. His emaciated face caught the moonlight and for a moment he assumed the aspect of a ghoul. 'Either someone is playing games, or I have just discovered the footprints of a three-legged man.'

I stared at him, quite unable to speak. Finally I found my voice.

'Surely, you are tooling with me, Holmes.'

'I assure you,' returned my friend, 'I am pulling neither *your* leg, nor any other. Now, for once, I believe we ought to summon the local constabulary. I would be curious of their view of the matter.'

Half an hour later we were stood again at the scene, this time accompanied by Inspector Hubble, whom we had once again fetched from his home.

'Well,' concluded the inspector, his lantern held close to the prints, 'it appears I have been roused from my bed to find that it is Hallowe'en. You are quite sure that one of you gentlemen did not mistakenly add a footprint of your own to an existing pair?'

'Quite sure,' I put in, glancing at Holmes, and then back at the imprints.

'You will note,' my friend remarked, a little impatiently, 'even at a glance, that the prints do not correspond with either the size or style of Dr. Watson's or my shoes.' The inspector considered this, then moved his lantern closer still.

'We can see quite well by the full moon,' observed my friend, Sherlock Holmes. 'You can put your lantern away.'

Hubble was a wire-thin student of the law, with a countenance of permanent suspicion, his brow creased like a folded note. He snuffed out the light. Indeed, the moon shone with a preternatural brightness that evening, appearing to fill the footprints with quicksilver.

'They are a size eight, and six hours old.'

'I put them nearer four,' the inspector parried.

'Which puts you at odds with the truth,' Holmes returned. 'You will observe the depth of the toe, which is the last part of the imprint to dry.' Holmes stood up and straightened his back, wincing a little, before surveying the lights of the town below us. 'What we can all agree on is the singular nature of these footprints. Or rather, the singularity of such a sighting. Perhaps Dr. Watson can confirm, as the keeper of our chronicles, but my feeling is that it is the first time we have been set on the trail of a three-legged man.'

***

'A little chess, Watson?' Holmes appeared at the door, tied into his dressing gown, pipe in his hands. I glanced at my watch. It was not yet seven.

'A little early, Holmes, don't you think?'

'It will not surprise you, Watson, I have not yet retired to bed. I have reached an impasse in my thinking and would welcome a little distraction. Should you require an incentive, I can offer a cup of Arabic coffee. I brought up a small quantity from Baker Street.' I sighed and nodded my acquiescence.

As was his custom, Holmes prepared his coffee in a silver pot on a small stove. He had set up the chessboard and was preparing his gambit. I did not hold out much hope of success. My form had suffered of late, thanks mainly to the many hours I had devoted to my medical practice. What little time remained I squandered on itinerant frames of snooker at my club – my sole vice beyond a weakness for the fairer sex.

As an opponent, Holmes was utterly mercurial. Just when you believed you had fathomed his strategy, he threw you off with an entirely unforeseen attack. He once remarked that excellence at chess was 'one mark of a scheming mind,' and I am in no doubt that he was possessed of one, at least equal if not superior to the most formidable of his criminal adversaries.

Holmes had so far taken five minutes to make his move. 'I say, Holmes,' I muttered, to break the monotony, 'did you see that piece by Curzon in *The Times*?' Holmes shook his head and continued to stare, hawk-like, at my queen. I took up the paper and paraphrased the article for my friend's benefit. 'He has declared himself openly hostile to the notion of granting female suffrage. His principal arguments are twofold: one, that it will distract them from their highest duties of home making and maternity; two, that they lack the calmness of temperament and balance of mind to qualify them to exercise a judgment on political affairs.'

Finally, Holmes pressed his attack. 'Your queen is in jeopardy, Watson,' he smiled, sitting back and lifting his coffee cup to his lips. 'I suggest you move to her defence.' I glanced at the board and almost burst out laughing. 'Holmes,' I exclaimed, 'you have left yourself wide open.' I lifted my queen and swept her diagonally across the board, putting him into check.' My friend's face changed in an instant, from triumph to dejection. It appeared that in the brilliance of his attack, he had neglected the basics of his defence. 'Like our friend Lord Curzon,' I added, 'it is perhaps best not to underestimate the capabilities of a determined woman.' Holmes frowned and busied himself with his pipe.

Holmes kept his own company after our game and I half suspected him of sulking. Indeed his mood was only leavened by the arrival of our letters.

'Ah,' exclaimed Holmes, with a note of satisfaction. He selected a large, brown envelope from a haphazard pile of correspondence on his desk, removed a knife from the drawer, then sliced clean through the paper as if opening a bird's gizzards.

'Expecting something?' I muttered, glancing up from my book.

'Yes,' he confirmed, preoccupied, inspecting a page of newsprint and sliding out three large photographic prints, 'as a matter of fact I was. I would recognise Langdale Pike's handwriting from a hundred yards.' He held up the envelope for me to see. 'Look at the right slant, Watson, the narrow spacing – a shameless extravert if ever I saw one.'

Pike, that slippery socialite! He was a ghost of the fashionable clubs, his ear always to the ground; a strange figure who stood at the fringes of every important group in town. He somehow inveigled his way into every important party without being invited to a single one. Pike had a professed aversion to daylight hours that gave his skin the pallid complexion that made Holmes' own drained features seem positively bronzed by comparison. If there were any juice on anyone, Pike was the man to find it. My friend called upon his services whenever conventional channels were closed.

'Here,' he said, sliding the prints across the coffee table, 'what do you make of these?'

At first, I believed they were overexposed; yet the startling white revealed itself to be snow. Each photograph depicted a group of fashionably dressed people sledging high up in the mountains.'

'Tobogganing?' I queried.

'Precisely,' said Holmes. 'St. Moritz is my guess. The Alps. Now look more closely at the figure on the sledge.'

'A woman?'

'Quite so. But not just any woman.'

'Not... *the* woman?'

'No,' smiled Holmes, 'not her.' I studied the print more closely.

'God's teeth!' I cried. 'It's the woman on the platform.'

'Naturally,' smiled Holmes with no little satisfaction. 'Her name is Gertrude Cresswell, a woman of remarkable abilities. Look inside the envelope and you will discover a little more for yourself.'

I unfolded the article that had been torn from a newspaper and absorbed its contents.

The Times, 26ᵗʰ February 1896

Cresswell sets new course record on the Cresta Run

The notorious slopes of St. Moritz have claimed several lives already this season, but that did not deter the darling of the slopes, Miss Gertrude Cresswell, from setting a new course record on Monday last.

Ignoring warnings of treacherous conditions, Cresswell, a former nun, of Charing Cross, London, brushed aside her detractors to conquer the twisting, mile-long course in a record time of forty-three point four seconds.

Employing the new 'head-first' method, whereby the pilot of the steel sledge lies face down, Miss Cresswell reached speeds approaching sixty miles per hour, her chin never more than three inches above the ice.

The course has two notorious bends: Battledore and Shuttlecock, which have proved the undoing of some of Europe's best tobogganists. The former has shown itself to be a particular menace, having despatched both Henri Marcelle, the reigning French champion and Philip Glynebourne, the well-known British polo player who stated his intention to break the course record this year. Both Marcelle and Glynebourne left the course at Battlemore, flying more than twenty feet through the air into the soft snow below the run. While both were unharmed, there is some embarrassment that Miss Cresswell has so far recorded the season's fastest time.

Miss Cresswell had caused controversy earlier this week by appearing in a pair of jodhpurs, instead of the regulation skirt, which one club member described as 'very fast.'

However, no one could say a word against her form on Monday, when she executed a flawless navigation of the course and demonstrated an absolute mastery of the ice. She spoke exclusively to The Times a moment, after completing her record-breaking run.

'I do wish people would not refer to the conditions as "treacherous", she told The Times. 'It somehow implies that they were on our side in the first place.'

'I put my success down to clean air, fruit infusions and an absolute refusal of the concept of fear. When I am on the ice I am like an eagle swooping down from a great height. I have no more reason to be afraid than a bird descending from the clouds. I find myself thinking of all sorts of things when I am racing, but generally I sing to keep myself company.'

Miss Cresswell is expected to be a front runner in the Grand National sledge race this coming weekend, and her growing army of admirers will be following her progress with interest.'

I returned the article to the envelope. 'Well, well!' I concluded. 'But how did you manage to discover her identity?'

'It is wise,' Holmes counselled, 'to be aware of one's competitors. At King's Cross I recognised her in an instant. She has established a consulting practice of her own in London.'

'She is a medical doctor, too?'

'No,' Holmes chuckled.

'Then, what?'

'My dear, Watson. Is it not plain enough? She is a detective!' My eyes widened.

'Will wonders never cease! But what business has she here? Surely a straightforward matter such as this requires no more than the mind of Sherlock Holmes to find its resolution.' Holmes untangled himself from his chair, like a spider leaving the centre of its nest. He strode to the window.

'There are many players in this game, Watson. All with their own interests; each with something to gain from others' misfortunes. If there are two detectives at work, then it follows that there are at least two clients, perhaps more.'

I inspected the image again, the alpine sun glancing from those Amazonian cheekbones, finding myself beguiled by Cresswell's singularly determined expression. 'I confess, Holmes,' I muttered, almost unconsciously, 'I count myself among her admirers.'

'She is still a novice in this business,' my friend posited. 'Yet I have learned never to underestimate a woman of character. Proven ability in one field can easily transfer into another. And besides, competition, I find, sharpens the senses.' An old light rekindled in those deathless eyes.

'Watson,' he declared, 'once again, the game is afoot!'

He reminded me of nothing less than a vampire welcoming the new moon. Holmes produced the religious icon from his pocket.

'Data, Watson. That is the only thing that will give us the edge. Let us discover the identity of this sainted figure. Know that, and I believe we will be a step closer to a tranquil return journey to London.'

FIVE

The Priest

Holmes strode ahead, as if chronically late for a vital meeting, tapping his cane like a man prospecting for oil. His head was bowed, his narrow shoulders hunched together as if conspiring against him.

'I say, Holmes,' I gasped, 'steady as she goes. Are you in training for the Paris Olympics?'

'Not the Olympics, Watson,' he answered without breaking his stride, 'much as I admire the spirit of the games. I am all for conjoining the ancient and the modern.'

'Well, all the same,' I spluttered, 'ease up there, would you?'

'Watson,' he admonished, glancing back, 'can you not hear the ticking of the clock? We were thrown here on this lump of basalt by a chance of chemistry; let us not squander the miracle of our existence. In the great span of the universe we exist no longer than a single bubble in pot of boiling water. There is so much to do and so little time; our hours are already vanishing. There are a billion souls in this world; in the last hour a thousand more were born and a thousand have died. Now do you perceive my urgency?'

I shook my head and followed as best I could. A moment later, Holmes came to an abrupt halt and only a side-step prevented me from crashing bodily into him.

'A little warning would be helpful, Holmes!' We were standing outside a small house, situated next to the imposing Catholic Church of St. Mary and St. Modwen. It was a fine, but rather plain, red-brick building, not thirty years old, with the two stone saints conferring beneath a large, circular stained-glass window. My friend wrapped his knuckles against the door.

'If you want to know about the saints,' Holmes explained, 'ask a Catholic.'

A man of middle years, with a dented forehead and a broken nose, greeted us. He had hard, blue eyes; the kind that seemed to peer directly into one's soul.

'Father David?' asked Holmes. The priest glanced at me.

'I know who you are,' he stated in gruff, Glaswegian burr, holding the door only partially open.

'Then would you have a moment to assist in a small theological matter?'

'Do I have a choice?'

'We will not detain you long, Father. Besides, we may be able to share a tale or two of the fancy. I rather fear your career was ended by an unanticipated overhand right from a smaller fighter.' The man's brow furrowed for a moment. He glanced around the street, then gestured for us to follow him.

'Not everyone welcomes your visit,' the priest declared.

'We do not expect,' replied Holmes, 'a civic reception in every provincial town. Celebrity is an unwanted by-product of success. Naturally my friend Dr. Watson here shares some of the responsibility with his fanciful accounts.' He showed us into a modest sitting room, simply decorated with a crucifix, a painting of the sacred heart and, tellingly, a pair of boxing gloves.

'Do you mind if I don't offer you tea? I am preparing my sermon.'

'We simply require your expertise.'

'Perhaps. But I have many things on my mind. The building fund, for instance, finds itself well short of its target. A donation would jog my memory, I'm sure.' Holmes glanced at me. I rummaged in my pocket and reluctantly parted with a crown.

'Too kind, gentlemen,' he said, slipping the coin into his own pocket. 'I will remember you in my prayers. By the by, Mr. Holmes,' he added nodding in the direction of the boxing gloves. 'It was a straight right from a novice in Edinburgh. Just a wee lad. Thought I'd knock him into next week. Next thing I knew I was kissing the canvas. He packed a punch like a jackhammer.'

Holmes produced the pendant from his pocket and cleared his throat.

'Now to the matter,' he pressed. 'Do you recognise this figure?' The pugilist frowned, then held the pendant up to the light.

'Not one of the regulars,' he remarked, then went to his bookshelf and withdrew a thick volume. Flicking impatiently through the yellowing pages, he arrived at a colour plate showing two figures dressed in black and crimson smocks and stockings, one a reversed image of the other. They seemed alike in almost every way, though one wielded a sword. It matched the figure in the pendant precisely. 'Aye, there he is,' said

Father David, with a note of dour triumph. 'St. Abdon, patron saint of coopers.' In an instant, my friend's eyes clouded over.

'Grave,' he muttered, 'very grave.' Father David seemed perplexed as to how such an obtuse a piece of information could cause such consternation.

'We are in your debt, Father,' Holmes said, standing and shaking the man's hand.

'You are in debt to no one except the Lord,' he replied, still looking confused. 'I only hope that your investigations bring a happy conclusion.'

'Conclusions are rarely happy,' reported Holmes, 'but there is the consolation of justice. Come, Watson, we have work to do.' The priest gazed thoughtfully at Holmes.

'And what of your own soul, Mr. Holmes?' he asked.

'My mind,' he replied, turning back to him, 'has absolved my soul of all its duties.'

Once out in the street, we found ourselves at the mercy of a chill wind.

'The brewery, Watson,' he called, 'and if you see a four-wheeler, then for pity's sake, commandeer it: a man's life is at stake.' Pulling up the collar of his ulster, Holmes marched into the wind. I broke into a trot, pressing my hat to my head.

'A word of explanation, Holmes?'

'Arkham!' he called back. A weather-vane spun far above us, the darkening clouds turning day into night.

'I beg your pardon?'

'Eli Arkham,' he repeated, 'the head cooper. He is in great danger.'

Holmes burst into the brewery office, like a police inspector leading a raid.

'Arkham,' he stated. 'Has he reported for work today?'

The clerk implacably placed his pen upon the desk and smoothed a page of the ledger.

'And you are?'

'It's all right, Wiggins,' said Tolwood, appearing from a side office. 'These men are known to me – and no, Mr. Holmes, he hasn't.'

'When was the last time he missed a day's work?'

'In my experience, never.'

76

At Holmes' bidding, Tolwood sent a boy to the head cooper's home. We suffered an anxious wait before he returned.

'No sign, sir,' the boy reported. 'No one home, but he was seen at The Cooper's Arms yesterday evening.'

'By whom?'

'One of the other coopers, sir – Mr. Briggs.'

'Now is a critical moment,' Holmes posited, raising his hand. 'Unless someone has a coruscation to the contrary, then I fear Mr. Arkham has suffered one of two fates: Either he has elected to betray his lifetime employer and join this rogue band of coopers acting on behalf of an as yet unidentified power, or he has suffered at their hands. I do not mind admitting that I have already discounted my first theory on the grounds that it is entirely specious. My second, I fear holds more weight.'

'Good God, Holmes,' I muttered, 'those brutes would not think twice to slit his throat if they believed they would profit from the venture.'

Holmes held up one of his long, slender fingers.

'There is a chance,' he declared, 'but it is a slim one.' He glanced over to the manager.

'Tolwood,' he commanded, 'what is the nearest egress to your barrel yard?'

'The second door,' he indicated.

'Then, we must proceed post haste.' He swept through the door into the yard, his greatcoat flapping about him, much as a cormorant takes to the air. Tolwood and I exchanged a look, then bundled after him.

Once again, we were met by the sight of a thousand barrels stacked ten high in the yard. It seemed impossible that they could remain in such a parlous state, and not tumble to the ground.

'Let me in, Holmes,' I whispered. 'I can't help you if I cannot understand you.'

'Forgive me, Watson,' he said surveying the mountain, 'I believe that for one of their own, the coopers would reserve a particular fate. He would not have willingly parted with his talisman. It is my assertion that he was set upon by those fiends. But rather than murder him in their usual barbarous way, I believe they have contrived a fate fitting to their shared calling. Watson, my friend,' he said, clapping a hand on my shoulder, 'unless my powers have failed me, Arkham is inside one of these barrels!' I stood aghast.

'But which, Holmes?' He clenched his fist and stared hard at the multitude of casks, biting the corner of his mouth in concentration.

'Maybe,' he began, 'just maybe...' He dashed forward, scanning barrel after barrel. He finally lit upon one at the very end of a row, on the third tier.

'Here, Watson,' he called, 'this is the one.' He rapped hard on the side, with his cane, producing a hollow note; the same action on the adjacent cask produced something more akin to a thud. 'If confirmation were required, there it is.'

Tolwood summoned two lackeys, who were standing by, and together they extricated the cask from its position, lowering it onto its end.

'A crowbar,' demanded Holmes, 'quickly.' The implement was swiftly provided and my friend wasted no time levering off the end.

I took a step back, appalled, for we were greeted by Eli Arkham, his face contorted in a grotesque expression of panic and anguish.

'Arkham,' I exclaimed.

'As I feared,' cried Holmes. I rushed forward and helped Holmes pull the cooper from his confinement. He was stiff with rigor mortis. 'It is too late, Watson,' my friend sighed, 'even for your powers to revive him.' I removed my hat in respect, and the others did the same.

'Well, Tolwood,' remarked Holmes, 'let us not delay. Be a good fellow and summon the inspector. He will wish to view the body at the earliest opportunity.' The manager set off and Holmes waited until he was out of sight. He peered at the two workers, who swiftly resumed their labours.

'Cause of death, Watson?'

'Asphyxiation,' I declared, without the need to examine him more closely. 'The poor brute was alive when they bundled him in. Alas, he did not have the benefit of the air holes he fashioned for Butterworth.' Holmes nodded and narrowed his eyes as he examined the body. 'But Holmes,' I added, 'how in heaven's name did you know this was the barrel?'

'That, at least, was a simple matter,' he answered, without taking his eyes from Arkham. 'Each barrel in this yard was sealed in the same way, except for one. Naturally, every cooper employed by Houghton was trained by the master cooper, Arkham himself. Observe how the nails appear at one-inch intervals and are driven perfectly true. Yet on this barrel, they are driven in at a slight angle and at intervals of two inches. It was the work of an inferior cooper, most likely from another brewery entirely. Do you see? The slightest point protrudes at the edge of the lid, which catches the sunlight. It is as plain as day.'

'Remarkable,' I muttered.

'What is more remarkable is the fact that they missed the note clutched in his hand.'

Holmes knelt, and, with a little force, managed to extricate it from Arkham's grip. He scanned it once, turned it over, then handed it to me.

Enmerkar, Left for you at Etemenanki Victoria '44 at 44. Gilgamesh.

'An educated, legal hand, Watson. Expensive, black, iron-gall, nut ink. This is not the sort of note generally carried by a man who hammers wood for a living.'

'Gilgamesh' I muttered. 'Not a common sort of name in these parts.'

'No doubt, and what of these numbers, eh?' My friend's eyes danced with delight. 'The perfect brain food, Watson!'

A quarter of an hour later and we were finally reunited with the elusive Inspector Hubble. He was a wiry man of forty, with a long, rather drawn face-topped with jet-black, heavily oiled hair and distrustful eyes. He scanned the scene with the routine efficiency of a man who had established himself in his profession, drawing in the detail and alighting on one or two points of interest. He extended a blanched palm, then dipped it into his pocket, producing a small, white paper bag.

'Liquorice?' he enquired, proffering the open bag. 'I used to swear by Pontefract cakes, but I confess I am being increasingly wooed by the Liquorice Comfort. Will you join me?' We politely declined his offer. 'So, it's Arkham, is it?'

We led him to the corpse, lifting the blanket that disguised his contorted form.

'A wonderful rugby player in his time,' Hubble mused. 'I used to play with him at the football club when we were still at Peel Croft. He was a tidy little winger. He could put on a burst of speed like you've never seen; a slippery little fellow too. Coventry once accused us of plastering him in grease before a match to make him harder to tackle. We neither confirmed nor denied the rumour. Hubble gazed at him, as if privately reminiscing on these sporting glories.

'You will understand,' I put in, 'that we attempted to revive him. We found him hammered into that cask.'

'In the cask, you say,' the Inspector said. 'It is a mighty impressive feat to hammer oneself into a cask, even if you are a master cooper.' I let Hubble finish.

'Naturally,' I said. 'However, we believe he did not enter the cask of his own free will.' He considered this insight, chewing thoughtfully on his liquorice, then looked up at us, a more cheerful look on his face.

'Did you hear the club is moving to the Marston's ground? It is an appalling home for an institution as illustrious as ours, even if it is temporary.' I assured him that we had not heard this development. 'Still, we have proved we can succeed anywhere,' he declared with alacrity. 'We've won the Midland Counties Challenge Cup not once, but twice. And mark my words, we'll do it again.'

'Inspector,' broke in Holmes, finally tiring of this obfuscation. 'I would be interested in your view of the evidence.'

'There can be no doubt,' he said, glancing at the body, 'that this is more of Butterworth's work.'

'How can you be so certain?'

'It stands to reason,' he pronounced, selecting another confection from his pocket. 'He fled the scene the minute the poisoning was discovered. Old Arkham was probably privy to some information as to his whereabouts.' He levelled his gaze at Holmes. 'He may not have been the only one.' My friend did not so much as blink. 'It put Butterworth in jeopardy.'

'With the greatest of respect,' Holmes responded, 'that is entirely groundless speculation.'

'Besides,' I added, somewhat foolishly, 'that theory would depend on Butterworth returning to Burton. Do you think that's likely?'

'I can only tell you this,' Hubble replied darkly, 'to the best of my knowledge, Butterworth isn't a rugby man. He can hardly be trusted.' Holmes fought to suppress a laugh.

'You find something amusing, Mr. Holmes?'

'We may do many things differently in London, Inspector. But one thing surely we agree on is that evidence must be the foundation for our work.'

'Not necessarily.'

'Well,' countered Holmes, 'upon what do you base your assertion?'
Hubble stared at us as if we were imbeciles.

'Butterworth had help,' he said simply. 'He was one of the most popular men here. It would not surprise me if half the workforce is on his side. They will do anything for him. I will interview them one by one if I have to. One of them will break.'

'It is my belief,' said Holmes, 'that a gang of coopers from another brewery performed this work, acting on behalf of a rival concern or an enemy of Houghton's.'

'And your evidence?' asked Hubble, raising his eyebrows.

'They almost did the same to us,' returned Holmes, 'and what's more, I found this.' Holmes reached into his pocket and brought out a small, torn label, bearing the image of a silver unicorn.

'I retrieved this close to the barrel.' My friend pressed it into Hubble's hand.

'Something you found in a Christmas cracker?' suggested Hubble.

'Of course, in itself it proves nothing,' Holmes continued. 'However it happens to be the crest of Gibbons of London, the richest brewer south of the Trent. It may have been planted deliberately. Equally, it could conceivably have been stuck to the boot of the cooper, who entombed Mr. Arkham. However, it does have the benefit of being evidence. We are at the Crown Hotel should you need us.'

Holmes strode off towards the gate and I had little choice but to follow him. I raised my hat and hurried after my friend.

'I say, Mr. Holmes!' We turned to see the inspector holding up two pieces of white paper, no larger than betting slips. 'I have two complimentary tickets here to see Burton play tomorrow. Show up at the ground at noon and we can talk some more.'

'You are the rugby man, Watson,' put in Holmes as we walked away. 'Should we join him or pursue our own lines of enquiry.'

'Let us play the advantage,' I suggested.

'Then, beer and rugby it is.'

* * *

We stood on the touchline as thirty men hurled themselves at each other. Their bodies collided with the force of two omnibuses smashing head-on, and at each such occurrence a great cheer erupted around the

81

ground. From the entanglement of limbs emerged a small, stocky, red-haired fellow, sporting a pair of gigantic side whiskers. He glanced both ways, then down at the leather ball that he had somehow acquired in the chaos. No one appeared to have noticed that he had escaped with the item and he proceeded to squirrel it away before anyone reported the theft. The match had entered its final phase and I had found myself entirely absorbed by the play, which stirred memories of my own sporting endeavours at Edinburgh.

'It is quite plain to me, gentlemen,' remarked Inspector Hubble, without taking his eyes from the field, 'that our investigation cannot very well proceed without discovering the whereabouts of Harold Butterworth.' He inserted two wiry fingers into his pocket and removed a thin coil of black liquorice. He unravelled an inch, severed it with a thumbnail and gobbled it down. His teeth, I noted, were coated with a thin, brown film of sugar. He chewed quickly and swallowed. 'I am experimenting with this new form of flexible confectionary. Would you care to try some?' He uncoiled a further length and proffered this in my direction. I politely declined and instead found myself a battered cigarette from an inside pocket. In turn, Holmes located his pipe and began his time-honoured ritual of emptying and refilling.

'We all have our vices,' remarked Holmes. 'However, it is singular that, in a town celebrated for the crystalline quality of its beer, you follow a regimen of strict temperance.'

'Ah, so you have made enquiries,' replied the inspector.

'They are unnecessary,' my friend returned. 'You are a man of forty-one, yet still look to be in your mid-thirties. If I am not being too bold, I would assert that your father was rather too fond of the drink and you swore off it as a boy. You made a promise to your mother at sixteen that you would never touch it.'

Hubble turned to Holmes with a mixture of indignation and incredulity.

'And where did you turn up all this? Prying into my business.'

'Again, quite unnecessary,' explained Holmes. 'Every one of my deductions can be drawn from simple observation. Your white ribbon tiepin is the symbol of the Women's Temperance Association, is it not? Hardly a gift one could expect from a man. You wear no wedding ring, suggesting you are unmarried, and yet your shoes are polished, and you keep a freshly pressed handkerchief in your pocket, leading me to conclude you remain close to your mother. By the same token, your watch is of the older style. One may expect that a man of your middle years would still be possessed of a father. You inherited it when he died prematurely as a result of cirrhosis of the liver. Such a condition is likely to befall a heavy drinker in his fifties, giving me an approximate age for you at the time of his death, of sixteen.' Hubble frowned.

'Seventeen,' he muttered. 'I was seventeen when I made my oath.'

'Inspector, Inspector!'

Hubble turned to find the same urchin who had taken the telegram at the brewery tugging at his coattails.

'Whatever is it, boy?' he asked.

'A bad business at The Leopard,' he gasped. 'Three men. I think one of them is dead, sir. Mr. Tripp, the landlord, sent me to find you.'

'Dead?' frowned Hubble. 'Who's dead? You're making no sense.'

'One of the men is Constable Augustus.'

'What?' His face flushed.

'We must proceed directly, Mr. Holmes.' I exchanged a glance with my friend. 'Dr. Watson,' the Inspector added grimly, 'we may have need to call upon your services. You have your bag, I hope.'

We pressed through the crowd, pushing our way to the main road. Such were the numbers at the rugby match, the streets were almost deserted.

'You there!' cried Hubble to the driver of a passing brougham. 'Police business.' The carriage skittered to a stop. 'The Leopard, and hook it!' We leapt aboard and crammed in alongside the startled occupant. The horse shook its mane as it broke into a gallop, its shoes sparking as they struck the cobbles.

'Miss Bilton,' the inspector said, removing his bowler as he recognised the passenger, 'please forgive the intrusion. There's been an incident at The Leopard. Three men in a bad way.'

'Merciful heavens,' she muttered. 'Is that really a good use of your time? Mopping up the drunkards from the floors of public houses?'

'Augustus is one of the men.'

'Augustus? 'Then, let us not tarry. You there!' she bellowed at the driver. 'Shift your horse. Three men's lives depend on it.'

'The Leopard,' enquired Holmes. 'Is it one of Houghton's?'

'It's owned by the London brewer, Evercreech,' Hubble explained, coiling and uncoiling a length of liquorice. 'You won't find a true

Burtonian in there. It's mainly a haunt for the brewery's own workers to guzzle their wages.' He glanced at Miss Bilton.

'We have yet to discuss your protest,' the inspector muttered. 'You brought the town to a standstill.'

'That was precisely my intention,' she said curtly. 'I understand we made headlines in London. I only hope that the great statesmen choked on their devilled kidneys as they read their papers. We will only win the vote if we step beyond the bounds of society and convention.'

'Do you really feel it is wise,' provoked Hubble, 'emboldening every chambermaid and seamstress in the country, many of them do not even want the vote? Why burden them with the responsibility? Even for those that do, there are great matters of state, of war – how can they possibly know the best course of action as they stand, bewildered, at the ballot box?'

'You are a relic, inspector,' declared Miss Bilton. 'I used to warn my pupils that not every dinosaur was wiped from the face of the earth. Many walk the streets in broad daylight, and you, sir, are one of them!'

We careered through the streets, stopping twice for locomotives, which crawled across our path.

'A month ago,' began the inspector, peering at the fine municipal buildings, sweeping past, 'and I would have told you that the people of Burton lived a charmed life. There was cooperation and harmony; industry and happiness worked hand in hand. But over the last fortnight... it seems a kind of fever has gripped our town. We are blighted by violence, suspicion and unrest. There must be something in the water.'

'Or the beer,' Holmes added, pointedly. 'Miss Bilton,' he said, 'you are a woman of the world. How do you account for it?'

'Easily enough,' she exclaimed. 'It is the avarice of men. Bitterness and jealousy. Hubris and pig-headedness. Show me conflict and disharmony, and I will show you a man.'

'And so in a world,' speculated the inspector, 'where women made our laws and led our great institutions, this would not occur?'

She narrowed her eyes at him and raised herself in her seat. 'Are you trying to provoke me, inspector? Because if you are, you are succeeding.' Finally, we pulled up outside the inn. It was a fine, red-brick building on the corner, the pub's name in gold above the second storey and the name of the brewer emblazoned above the third-floor window.' The inspector wasted no time, kicking open the door and springing to the ground.

'If you don't mind, sir,' called the driver, 'this is my carriage and my living,'

We tumbled out after him. I turned briefly to Miss Bilton.

'Forgive the inconvenience,' I apologised, 'you may continue your journey.'

'Nonsense,' she dismissed, seizing her carpet bag, 'I'm coming with you,'

'I strongly advise against that.' Ignoring this, she accepted my hand and clambered out.

The door was ajar, a single leg and boot protruding onto the pavement. It was jerking in a series of erratic spasms, in much the same way as a frog's leg might when connected to an electrical charge. Holmes seized the brass handle and threw back the door. It was a desperate sight. Mr. Tripp, the stout publican was on his knees, attending to one of three men sprawled on the tiled floor, holding the man's arms to prevent him flailing. A third victim lay utterly inert, already overcome by whatever toxin he had imbibed.

'Good God, George,' cried the inspector, surveying the scene, 'is this what comes of serving London ale?'

'For pity's sake,' the man cried, 'don't just stand there, help me!'

'Augustus!' shrieked Miss Bilton, recognising the lanky constable, crumpled and helpless on the floor 'What is happening to him?' Each of the men were lying with their backs arched and limbs bent in the most grotesque fashion. Yet upon each of their face, was stamped a ghoulish smile, as if they were locked in some delirium or perversion.

'Holmes,' I called at once, 'strychnine!' I darted to the fireplace and seized a lump of charcoal. Crumbling it between my fingers I ran to the man nearest to Tripp and fed him as much as I dared without choking him. 'The lamps,' I cried, 'extinguish the lamps.' Tripp did as he was bidden. I dashed back to the man in the doorway and administered the same treatment. Rifling through my medical bag I lit upon a hypodermic then hurriedly measured out a solution of amyl nitrate, dosing both men with life still in their limbs. 'We must control the convulsions,' I explained, 'or suffocation is sure to follow.'

'Were there no others?' demanded Hubble.

'None,' the publican stuttered, his face pale with shock, his eyes transfixed by the body lying rigid on the cold tiles.

'Of course,' I realised. 'The others were all at the match; these poor souls must be the only three men in Burton who do not care for rugby football.'

'To their great disadvantage,' added the inspector.

Holmes eyed a half-drunk pint of ale on the bar. Two other glasses lay smashed upon the floor, the shards scattered across a wide radius. He pointed to the ale. 'Did they each drink from the same cask?'

'I had just changed the barrel,' Tripp managed, mopping his brow with the back of his forearm. 'I poured the first pint for myself, then three more. It was only because I entered into a fierce argument with one of these men that I neglected my own pint.'

'A fortunate oversight,' the inspector noted. 'One might say, suspicious.'

'How dare you!' Tripp shot back. 'And regardless, what sense would that make? Why would I destroy the reputation of my own establishment?' He glared at Hubble, his face flushed, breathing heavily through his nostrils.

'Gentlemen,' cautioned Holmes. 'There will be time enough for recrimination later. Let us get these men to a hospital.'

A pair of litters were summoned and accompanied by Miss Bilton, their fare and my written instructions, the men were spirited away to the Burton Infirmary. Holmes then began one of his meticulous inspections, pacing the floor in that slow, methodical way, which infuriates the impatient and unnerves the guilty. Hubble watched him with an intense interest. Tripp, possibly distracted by the day's events, absent-mindedly began to pull himself a pint. It was only my friend's intervention that prevented another disaster.

'Perhaps,' my friend cautioned, 'you would be wiser to take a glass of gin?'

'Surely,' Hubble said, at length, 'we should begin by taking a sample from the barrel?'

'Whatever for?' enquired Holmes without taking his gaze from the ground. 'Although it appears to have slipped Mr. Tripp's memory, we know their ale was poisoned.'

'But even so…' protested Hubble.

'There will be time enough for that,' Holmes muttered. 'Do you have a match?' My friend prepared a pipe then continued his search.

'Well, was it the barrel or only their glasses?' Tripp was busying himself pouring several measures of gin and either did not hear or was purposefully ignoring Hubble.

'Would you care for a drink, Mr. Holmes?' the publican asked. Holmes turned as if this were the most astonishing thing he had heard all day.

'How thoughtful,' beamed Holmes, accepting the glass at once.

'But Holmes...!' I cried. It was too late. My friend had drained the glass in a single gulp. Hubble and I stared at him, as if expecting him to convulse before our very eyes.

'You do not think Mr. Tripp would be foolish enough to murder me.'

'What about you, Doctor?'

After fifteen minutes of careful prowling, Holmes stooped and retrieved a small item from the floor. 'Well!' he declared. He held up a tiny, silver key.

'Had you mislaid this?' he asked.

Tripp examined the item.

'Why,' he said, 'it is the key to the polyphon.' He pointed towards a large cabinet on the wall.

'The music box?' I queried. We gathered around the cabinet and peered at the large, silver perforated disk that played saloon music and which was ubiquitous in these parts. Printed across it, in gothic text, were the words: 'Yn Chenn Dolphin.'

'It sounds German,' I suggested.

'Manx,' declared Holmes. Tripp's expression remained as blank as an unstruck sovereign.

'A traditional song from the Isle of Man,' Holmes elaborated. 'As chance would have it, I spent a week on the island in '89 and familiarised myself with some of the local customs and dialect. Do you recall, Watson, that ghastly business at the lighthouse at Chicken Rock?' I shuddered at the mention.

'All the keepers vanished,' I imparted, 'and a single, webbed handprint was stamped in blood across the front door.' Tripp's eyes widened at this vignette.

'Tell me, Mr. Tripp,' enquired Holmes, 'what prompted you to make such an esoteric choice?'

'I didn't choose the music,' muttered Tripp, recovering his wits. 'I can't stand the thing myself. It drives me half loopy. Besides, last time I looked, the songs were "The Honeybee" and "The Merry Copper."'

'Most instructive,' my friend said to himself. 'Now just one more thing.'

'Yes?'

'When did you first notice that each of your tables was missing a table leg?' The glass almost slipped from Tripp's hand.

SIX

The Suffragettes

I had already devoured the newspapers before breakfast was served. Now, as we engaged with our morning platters, the pages lay in a giant heap at his feet where he let them fall.

'Well, Watson,' my friend began, 'it seems bad eggs are as plentiful here as they are in the capital.

'Mine are splendid,' I returned, mopping up the yolk with a slice of quarter loaf.

'The other kind of bad egg,' he sighed. He glanced at the page open on the table, then began to read aloud: 'The police are searching for a William Morgan, last seen at the Burton horse fair, where he obtained a horse, paying with a worthless cheque. He was wearing a salt and pepper suit and had a crooked nose which veered somewhat to the left. He also has a half inch cut over his right eye, slanting up and to the right. I like that, Watson, very precise. Then there is Fred Bevington, forty, who obtained a situation by a false character reference, and is accompanied by his wife and seven-year-old daughter. He is distinguished by a deformed left thumb and an abscess at the centre of his back. I rather feel for the fellow. As the air and the ale suits you so well, Watson, you could do worse than to set up your own consulting detective agency here in Burton. With your emerging powers, I'd wager you would be turning a tidy profit by the year's end.'

'And neglect my patients?' I asked. 'They wouldn't have it.'

'Your practice is your crutch, Watson,' Holmes challenged.

'It is my livelihood,' I protested.

'Come, come, Watson,' he chided, 'it is obvious where your real passion lies. It is with the inkpot rather than the stethoscope.'

We were engaged in devouring our second pair of Scarborough bloaters when the door burst open. It was the landlady's son, a sandy-haired, enterprising fellow, who had amassed a small fortune in tips fetching newspapers, cigarettes and oranges.

'Pardon me, Mr. Holmes and Dr. Watson,' he panted, 'but there is a commotion at Houghton's. Would you care to look out of your window?' Holmes frowned, leaned back in his chair and parted the curtain with a finger.

'Well,' he murmured, 'there is a point well made.' I stood and went to see for myself. Running no less than fifty feet down the length of the tallest chimney was a strip of white cloth. Emblazoned on this, in black letters, was the legend: 'VOTES FOR WOMEN.'

'Upon my word, Holmes!' I cried.

'An audacious stunt,' remarked Holmes.

'In the same spirit,' I suggested, 'as Miss Bilton's antics on the railway. Do you believe she is behind this?'

'If she isn't, it must have her support. But I cannot imagine that Houghton would have willingly provided her with the advertising space.'

'Quite apart from anything, Holmes, I am intrigued as to how they managed it.'

'Agreed,' said my friend. 'A colossal, logistical feat. This may prove a distraction, Watson, but I believe this matter warrants further investigation.'

We joined a sizable crowd at the base of the chimney, peering up at the banner, its base still some thirty feet above us. Tolwood was directing operations.

'A ladder is on its way,' he relayed, gazing up still somewhat incredulously at the enormous letters, 'and make no mistake, Houghton is furious. He wants it down within the hour and has demanded a list of their accomplices.'

'He believes they received inside help?' I asked.

'Naturally. How else would these women have managed it?'

'We would be wise,' remarked Holmes, 'not to underestimate the ingenuity of a determined woman.'

'That may be,' Tolwood said, 'but we find ourselves a laughing stock. If you have ideas, Mr. Holmes, now is the moment. How did they climb the chimney unobserved?'

'Have you interrogated the night watchman?'

'Of course. He swears he was awake all night. A likely story. From his hut he could see the chimney well enough, but in his words "it appeared from nowhere."'

'A singular observation,' exclaimed Holmes. From the inside of his ulster he produced a small leather pouch which I knew to contain his opera glasses. He trained these on the top of the chimney, then followed the banner down to its end.'

'Ah,' he cried. 'Simplicity itself.'

'How so?' the manager demanded.

'There is a length of cord at the top of the banner and a much finer one running from its base.' I furrowed my brow and squinted up at the great structure.

Mr. Tolwood, no one climbed your chimney last night.'

'Explain yourself!'

'A strong tug on the extending wire would have been enough force to unfurl the banner. Gravity would have done the rest. It is my firm belief that the banner has been in place for some time, many weeks before, tightly furled inside the rim of the chimney. If you wish to find your accomplices, then I suggest you consult your records and discover who last serviced the chimney. They are the ones who took the package to the top.'

'Extraordinary,' remarked Tolwood, squinting his eyes. 'Ninety men in a hundred would have missed such a detail.' Holmes touched his hat and smiled.

'Elementary,' he announced. 'Still,' he said, his eyes fixed upon the banner, 'one cannot fail to feel sympathy with the cause of the suffrage. Without the women, the cogs of this great empire would soon grind to a halt. Their voices are growing louder, and inevitably they must be heard.'

Lethargic, I made my excuse and returned to our rooms. Holmes meanwhile adjourned to the Post Office to collect our mail. I was still combing my moustache when my friend swept in brandishing a piece of paper.

'We must return to London immediately. It's Mrs. Hudson.'

'My dear Holmes,' I cried, abandoning my ablutions, 'whatever is the matter?'

'She has...' He seemed for once at a loss for words, as if the trauma were so great that it had deprived him of speech, '...ideas!' He stood against the illuminated curtain like the villain of a murder mystery in a regional production.

'Here,' he announced, visibly weakened, 'read it for yourself. It is nothing short of a catastrophe.' I took the letter, confused at my friend's summary of the disaster.

Dear Mr. Holmes,

You will know I am a woman of regular habits and familiar ways. Doubtless, you will have noticed over these long years that I am less susceptible than others to the winds of change. I have long convinced myself that experiencing your adventures vicariously provides me with sufficient excitement.

In these many years of our acquaintance, I have had no need to purchase a single volume of sensational fiction, secure in the knowledge that that very afternoon a count with a limp and dark secret will appear at our door.

However, I cannot help but feel that the tide of history is turning. With it, I find myself caught in its powerful current. I am, I admit, in strong sympathy with the women's suffrage. It has given me cause to reflect on my own position, both in society and within my own household.

I have spoken little of my early years, when I championed the causes of imprisoned, destitute and fallen women. I feel these radical roots stirring. As your landlady, it is my duty to provide you with board and lodgings. Yet, the countless hours in the kitchen preparing meals have subdued my spirit. It is, therefore, my duty to inform you that I wish to move on from Baker Street.

The affection and respect I hold for both you and Dr. Watson of course remains, but you will understand that on this matter, my mind will not be turned.

I remain, nonetheless, sincerely yours,

Mrs. Hudson

'Watson,' Holmes declared, 'there are few certainties in this world, but one of them is that Mrs. Hudson can reliably be found at home at 221b Baker Street. If she departs, it will be akin to the ravens leaving the tower. England will fall.'

'Then,' I reasoned, 'let us solve this affair with all haste and convince her that she has taken leave of her senses.' Holmes pressed a finger to his lips, then raised it into the air, as if electrified by a thought.

'Quickly, Watson, a pencil. Take down this telegram:

'Do not leave Baker Street. STOP. Grave danger. STOP. More anon.''

'Grave danger?' I repeated, raising an eyebrow.

'Desperate times,' he explained, 'call for desperate measures.'

'So much,' I remarked, 'for championing the suffrage.'

'If you are acquainted, Watson, with any other woman in London who can prepare Brown Windsor soup quite like Mrs. Hudson, then give me her name.'

'I am not,' I confessed.

'Then, we have no choice but to send the telegram.'

SEVEN

Ingleton Hall

Houghton's invitation to dinner came around soon enough. The daylight was fading as Holmes and I sped in a four-wheeler towards Ingleton Hall.

'Three legs,' Holmes declared, apropos of nothing.

'I'm sorry?'

'What is the significance of the three legs?'

'Plainly,' I concluded, 'our antagonist has a signature; the three legs are his calling card.'

'Then,' smiled Holmes, 'your tale already has its title: 'The Adventure of the Three-Legged Man'.'

'Perhaps,' I nodded, attempting to appear indifferent to his excellent suggestion.

'You do not care for it?' Holmes probed.

'You look after your end of the business,' I stated, 'I shall attend to mine.'

From the carriage window, I watched a cloud slip across the bright moon like a fan passing across a woman's face. Hurriedly, we had managed to acquire dinner wear from a shop a little way along from our hotel.

'What precisely are we looking for, Holmes?' I enquired. My friend glanced up, as if surprised to see me in the carriage.

'We are searching for that elusive substance which illuminates in the same way lit magnesium lifts the gloom of a laboratory. It is data, my friend! We do not yet know what form it will take. It could be a black beast that stalks the grounds. It could be the incriminating stub of a cigarette. We shall know it when we see it.' I nodded at this.

'Are you here in your capacity as consulting detective?'

'For the purposes of this evening, Watson, I think not. We are enjoying a holiday in the Peak District and are house guests at the personal invitation of Michael Houghton.'

'I see,' I nodded, peering out into the darkening lanes.

'However, while we may speak of frivolous things, naturally our senses will be as alert as ever.'

The road bent round and we were suddenly afforded a magnificent view of the hall. It was a breathtakingly grand house, constructed in pale stone in the Italian style. It sat atop a hill on the far side of a silver lake and the building seemed to extend on either side to an almost infinite degree. Even in the diminishing light, it was obvious that the sweeping grounds were meticulously and expensively maintained. Clumps of conifers and birches vied for our attention, while here and there trees and shrubs of more exotic providence rose mysteriously from behind the brow of the hill.

'Two hundred years ago, Watson,' remarked Holmes, following my gaze, 'we would be arriving at the family seat of an earl or a feudal lord. No so today. Every brick of that house was paid for in blood, sweat and beer. The world is turning, my friend. The inheritors of England are no longer the descendants of ancient French knights. They are men of vision and courage with an endless appetite for labour.'

Two bright torches flanked the front entrance and I discerned a figure, standing waiting for us in half shadow, as we approached. The windows were illuminated throughout the ground floor.

'They could host a party for five hundred people,' I gasped, 'and still have room to play a football match.'

'If one's success is measured by the size of one's accommodation,' opined Holmes acerbically, 'then I declare myself an abject failure. However, there are a thousand more rooms in my mind than in the house you see before you.'

'No doubt,' I murmured.

The carriage door swung open and we were greeted by a jowly, heavy-framed fellow of middle years, who introduced himself as Houghton's butler. Shrubs of hair sprang from each side of his head, although with less vigour on the summit. Besides this, he affected a curious squint, which, combined with exceedingly luxuriant eyebrows, succeeded in almost entirely obscuring his eyes. To compensate for this impediment, his head was tilted at a permanent forty-five-degree angle, which clearly afforded him little vision.

'This way, gentlemen,' he said, stepping in the opposite direction to the front door.

'Are you quite certain?' I asked.

'Perhaps not,' he agreed and switched tack. 'If you would be so good as to follow me, Mr. Houghton has a small surprise for you.'

If Caligula had been born in 1812 instead of 12AD, you could imagine he might have built a residence such as this. We entered a world of conspicuous grandeur. Thick carpets of intricate design adorned the floor, Chippendale chairs and mahogany bureaux lined the walls. Ornate crystal chandeliers were suspended from the ceilings and familiar-looking paintings hung upon the walls; no doubt the originals of those I had seen in books. A second manservant was waiting with a pair of champagne flutes on a silver tray.

'Well, Watson,' said Holmes, with some amusement, 'it appears these beer barons drink wine behind closed doors.'

We were shown into the drawing room, a sweeping space, crammed with every conceivable comfort and luxury. At the far end were three figures, seated, who rose as we entered. The first we recognised immediately as Michael Houghton. The second was a formidable fellow in late middle age with trim silver hair and whiskers. His was a look of ferocious determination and quiet, inquiring, pale-blue eyes. The third was a portly fellow and the last to rise to his feet. He had a high forehead, swept-back hair and mutton-chop whiskers that only served to draw attention to the excess flesh upon his chin.

'The star attractions,' the fellow declared. 'Houghton, you spoil us with the quality of your guests.' We exchanged pleasantries and settled down to join them.

'First, some introductions,' Houghton began.

'I have heard stories about Sherlock Holmes,' the large man broke in, 'but perhaps a small demonstration of your powers would assure us of your identity.'

'Then, I am sorry to disappoint,' my friend stated, 'but I do not perform on command. You mistake me for a conjurer or palimpsest. If that is your fancy, then I observed a travelling fair on the outskirts of the town. For sixpence, they will be only too happy to oblige your whimsical requests.' The man scoffed and threw back a glass of champagne.

'I can only conclude, Houghton,' he retorted, 'that we are in the company of imposters.'

'On the contrary,' parried Holmes, 'it is perfectly obvious that we are in the company of brewers. You, sir, for example, are Geoffrey Gilbert, the chairman of Gilbert's of Brick Lane. You arrived this afternoon by the four-twenty train. You sat on the right-hand side of the carriage, facing forwards in the seat nearest the window. You drank a glass of

Bordeaux, ate a lemon curd tart and read *The Daily Telegraph*.' The man's lips formed into an astonished 'O.'

'Touché, Geoffrey,' laughed Houghton. 'Now do you believe this is Sherlock Holmes?'

'Wonderful!' Gilbert exclaimed, throwing himself back in his chair and shaking his head. 'Simply wonderful. Every word of it is true.'

'Now, where is Burrows?' asked Houghton, glancing at his pocket watch. 'His valet arrived an hour ago. Dinner will be ruined.' He shook a little bell and the butler, who had met us at the door, reappeared.

'Ah, Giblin,' said Houghton. 'Will you ask Mr. Burrow's valet to come here, please? His master is insufferably late.' Giblin bowed low then vanished through a side door.

'I apologise for my tardy friend,' said the third man.

'You will do no such thing!' retorted Gilbert.

'He believes manners belong only to women and the gentry. But would you indulge us with an explanation? How for example did you know which newspaper Gilbert read on the train?'

'It is laughably simple,' smiled Holmes, collecting his pipe from his pocket and beginning the slow process of assembly. 'Imprinted on his thumb is the clear impression of the 'h' of 'Telegraph'.' Gilbert glanced at his thumb as if it belonged to a stranger.

'So it is,' he murmured.

'For the ink to be wet enough to make such an impression,' explained Holmes, 'it would have needed to be an early edition, which indicates that it was the first train. The scantiest knowledge of the train timetable tells us that it was the seven o'clock, rather than the ten-past ten.'

'What of his choice of seat?'

'Again,' continued Holmes. 'It is the simplest process of deduction. You will recall that we enjoyed unseasonably good weather today, with strong sunshine. If it shone from the east during the morning train journey, it is perfectly logical that there would be a little light sunburn on the left side of the face of northern-bound passengers. For the rest of my deduction, you will note there is a trace of tannin on Mr. Gilbert's lower lip. I happen to know from my own experience that the only red wine served on the service is the Bordeaux."

'What is to say,' questioned Gilbert, 'that I did not have it at lunch?'

'Because at lunch, you sampled a glass of Houghton's pale ale. You are here on business and part of that business is to assess the quality of the competition. Wine would play no part in the working day for a beer brewer.' The brewers exchanged a glance.

'Right again, Mr. Holmes. And the final piece of the jigsaw?'

Holmes leant forward and removed an item attached to Gilbert's ear.

'Since eight o'clock this morning, a piece of lemon curd tart has been attached to you your ear. No doubt your friends here were on the cusp of informing you.' Gilbert turned a mild shade of crimson and looked accusingly at the other two.

'Far too amusing to let you know, old man,' Houghton explained.

The far door opened and Giblin re-emerged with a slender young gentleman standing beside him. He wore a neat moustache and his hair was meticulously parted, employing a considerable quantity of oil.

'Mr. Smesler, isn't it?' asked Houghton.

'That's correct, sir,' he answered. 'Joseph Smesler, valet to Mr. Burrows'

'An American, eh?'

'Correct again, sir. My home city is Philadelphia.'

'The cloth capital of the United States,' Gilbert put in. 'A hard-working city. I had the pleasure of attending the World's Fair there in '76. Quite a show.'

'Now,' said Houghton, 'more to the point, do you have news of Mr. Burrows? There is a saddle of lamb for dinner and the cook cannot hold it back indefinitely.'

'He is proceeding with all speed,' Smesler assured him. 'He has had business in Manchester, which I believe concluded at three o'clock. Withstanding mishap, he should be here any moment.' Holmes tapped his pipe against the ashtray.

'Remind me,' he said, 'of Philadelphia's most famous son.'

'Why,' responded Smesler, 'he belongs not just to Philadelphia, but to the whole world. Surely you are referring to Mr. Benjamin Franklin. But why do you ask?'

'Only,' added Holmes, 'that he was responsible for one of the great *bon mots*. "Beer is living proof that God loves us and wants us to be happy."'

'I want that for Houghton's advertising,' our host put in.

'Too late,' chided Gilbert, 'we are already using it!' With a wave of his hand, Houghton dismissed Smesler and, after a moment of confusion wherein Giblin failed to locate the door, we were once more left alone.

'Now, let us come to the point,' said Houghton. 'Our business is under siege. We at Houghton's have already suffered a hammer blow with the poisoning of a regiment in India. We have tested our remaining stock and have ascertained that it is entirely without contamination. But either of you gentlemen and your businesses could be next. Thus far, I have managed to contain the scandal. Using my influence, I have persuaded the local inspector, a competent, but uninspired man named Hubble, to allow Mr. Holmes time to make his own assessment. But I cannot keep this back forever. I have invited you here in a spirit of openness and cooperation. Tell me, who do you believe is behind this?' The two men shifted in their seats and drew thoughtfully on their cigars.

'The French,' proposed Gilbert, apparently without humour.

'Explain?'

'For every pint of English beer drained by the world's drinkers,' he said, 'there is a glass of wine that is left untouched. It stands to reason.'

'A capital theory,' mused Houghton. 'But where is your evidence?'

'We have punished their wine with taxes; naturally, they will have a thirst for retaliation. It is perfectly logical.' My friend listened to all this with an expression of great amusement.

'You appear to find this funny, Mr. Holmes?'

'Forgive me,' my friend answered, 'but this is akin to pointing fingers in the schoolyard. This is a scientific problem and we must find a scientific solution.'

Once more, Giblin returned to us.

'Mr. Burrows,' he announced with some fanfare, 'has arrived.'

'Not a moment too soon,' said Houghton. 'We were about to resort to cannibalism. Shall we move through?'

Collecting our drinks, we were ushered into a sumptuous dining room, laid out with more silver and crystal than one might ordinarily find in a dragon's lair. 'I apologise,' continued Houghton, 'for the lack of ceremony. I thought an informal supper would suit us better.' Holmes raised his eyebrows.

Burrows was a Bristolian of immense age and surliness. Wisps of white hair rose from his otherwise bare head like smoke from a barren moon. His face was deeply lined, his mouth permanently downturned. He staggered in, stiff legged from his journey, and eyed the company with the contempt of a man facing his executioner.

'My dear fellow,' said Houghton, 'delighted you could join us.' Burrows grunted a greeting, then dropped painfully into his seat, grimacing as he did so. There was a round of perfunctory introductions, although from his dour expression, Burrows made it clear that Holmes and I were less than welcome.

'We had the pleasure of meeting your charming valet,' I put in. He frowned at this remark.

'Barstow?' he asked.

'Smesler,' corrected Houghton. Burrows glanced up.

'Never heard of him.' Gilbert emitted an amused snort.

'Come, come,' he said, 'one must not become embroiled in the detail. We are big-picture men, naturally, but I would draw the line at forgetting the name of my own valet.'

'I have not forgotten the name of my valet,' growled Burrows. 'I am simply informing you that my valet is called Barstow.'

'An American fellow?' Houghton enquired.

'Cornish.' We stared at Burrows in something close to bewilderment.

'You have never heard of an American called Smesler?'

'No.' With a look of alarm, Houghton rang the bell and Giblin materialised through a hidden door. 'Would you kindly fetch Mr. Smesler?' he asked.

The butler coughed gently into his fist. 'I'm afraid he seems to have disappeared.'

'Good God, man!' cried Houghton. 'Go and find him.'

'Would someone,' drawled Burrows, 'like to explain what is going on? It appears I have entered a madhouse.'

An excellent mock oyster soup was served, which we supped in silence.

'Gentlemen,' intoned Houghton, red-faced, returning to the room, 'we have been hoodwinked. We have had an infiltrator.' Gilbert returned his spoon to its place.

'Good Lord. Has he taken anything?'

'My man Giblin is establishing that, now. I most sincerely hope not.'

'Then, what the devil did he want?'

'Devil if I know,' muttered Houghton, returning to his seat. 'But I feel a blasted fool. When Smesler arrived earlier this afternoon I had no reason to suspect he was not Mr. Burrows' valet. It was unusual, of course, that he was American, but he seemed a straightforward enough fellow. What do you make of it, Mr. Holmes?' My friend pressed a napkin to his lips.

'It was a first-class fraud,' he said. 'A perfect accent and he did not hesitate when I asked about Benjamin Franklin.'

'Then you suspected?'

'In my line of work one must always be a little circumspect.'

'Are you suggesting he was not an American?'

'It remains a possibility. Only, his shoes were English, which puzzled me for a moment, but an American is entitled to spend his money over here.'

'Confound it,' said Houghton. 'What did he want?'

'The same thing I seek: data. Would you allow me to conduct a brief inspection of the ground floor?'

'I should be obliged, Mr. Holmes. Should I call Hubble? Who know what's been taken. It's an outrage.'

'Let us defer that until I have made my preliminary observations.'

We left the barons to their cigars. In silence, Holmes stepped from room to room absorbing everything through those attentive eyes, much as a hawk peers down on the earth from the heavens, alert to every shiver of the grass below. We returned to the men shortly before they retired. Holmes promised to present his report in the morning after he had reflected on his findings.

A distant owl hooted its warning.

'Look alive, Watson!'

'Holmes,' I cried, reaching for my pocket watch, 'whatever is the matter?' A full moon peered into the room between the curtains.

'We have work to do,' he said.

'It's four in the morning!' I hissed.

'So it is,' he agreed. Still wearing his evening suit, he smelled intensely of tobacco. I knew my friend well enough to know that this meant he had sat up half the night, turning over some problem in his mind. I hurried into my clothes, stumbled into my shoes, then followed Holmes out into the corridor.

To my eyes, it was pitch black. Yet, Holmes had powers that exceeded other men. Instructing me to place a hand on his shoulder, he led me at great speed down the labyrinthine corridors, descending staircase, and passing through rooms. Occasionally I saw the flash of a painting – the face of an angel or admiral or the glint of a candlestick, but otherwise it was akin to journey to the centre of the earth. Finally, we slowed and came to a stop before what I assumed to be a door.

'A locked door, Watson,' whispered Holmes, 'is no obstacle to a resourceful man.' I heard a click and the whine of the hinges as the door crept open. Once inside, Holmes switched on the electric light.

'We may talk freely,' said Holmes. 'This door is two inches thick.' Awake for only a few minutes, I felt somewhat discombobulated, and badly in need of some coffee.

'Where are we, Holmes?' I asked, testily. 'And is it quite necessary to prowl around like this?'

'It is,' he confirmed. 'Secrets do not generally reveal themselves, Watson. They need to be coaxed like salmon from a river. I took the liberty of studying the layout of the house before we arrived. I noticed this room next to the library and correctly identified it as Houghton's study.'

I peered at Holmes, my thoughts now becoming clearer. 'Surely you do not suspect Houghton himself? He would not tamper with his own beer. It would be a work of madness.'

'There is more to this than beer, Watson,' my friend muttered, his eyes searching the paraphernalia that lay strewn across the room. On the wall was a watercolour of a stone figure, naked from the waist up, with a long, squared-off beard and wild, staring eyes. Upon the desk was a large sheet of parchment etched with what appeared to be hieroglyphics.

'So Houghton is an Egyptologist!' I cried.

'These ciphers are not Egyptian, Watson,' stated Holmes. 'If I am not very much mistaken, they are Sumerian.'

'Sumerian?'

'The first of us all, Watson! They were the first great civilised people of the earth, building their cities seven thousand years ago, when London was nothing but mud. They created huge ziggurats, great angular temples that rose from the dust of Mesopotamia.'

'Quite the Renaissance man,' I noted. 'Still, correct me if I'm wrong, Holmes, but there is no crime in taking an interest in history.'

'None at all, Watson,' my friend agreed. 'But my suspicion is that his interest is not merely academic. He stared at the papers, as if in a trance, and I knew at once he was committing it all to memory. It was then I heard footsteps on the other side of the door. Holmes gestured towards the cupboard. With some difficulty and a certain degree of haste, both of us clambered inside.

The door opened, however it was not Houghton but Gilbert who stepped inside. Had I not been holding it in the first place, no doubt I would have taken a sharp intake of breath. The baron paused for a moment, perhaps detecting the scent of Holmes' tobacco. However he himself reeked of cigars and port and it seemed unlikely in this state he would know the difference. The brewers clearly had not retired as early as we had.

Through the narrowest of gaps I watched the man size up the room as we ourselves had done, not minutes earlier, swaying slightly from his evening's indulgences. Despite his inebriation, I detected a singularity of purpose, as if he knew what he was looking for. He swept back his iron-grey hair then began opening drawers, pulling books from the shelves and feeling behind pictures, no doubt searching for some safe or concealed hatch. He worked for five minutes or so, before betraying his obvious exasperation, hurling a book to the floor. Shaking his head, he made a haphazard attempt to cover his tracks, then turned and left the room. For a minute or two we remained where we were, perfectly silent in case the man had a change of heart and resolved to continue his search. Only when it was clear that he would not return did we emerge from our hiding place.

'Good God, Holmes,' I muttered, 'there will be hell to pay in the morning. Houghton will know for certain there has been an intruder.'

'True enough, Watson,' he agreed, 'which is why we are going to restore this place to its original condition.' My friend, it transpired, had memorised not only the document on the desk, but incredibly the location of each object in the room. He worked quickly and methodically until he declared the work done. It was extraordinary – as if a clock had been wound back ten minutes.

'Now, Mr. Gilbert has done us some favour,' Holmes declared. 'He has conducted the search we would not have dared to. However I note that he left one stone unturned. Holmes approached the statue of the man with the beard, examined it more closely before placing his hands on its head and neck. Slowly, he turned the head, which to my astonishment unscrewed and detached. Inside the hollow neck was a thinly rolled piece of parchment. This too was covered in a series of strange hieroglyphs, too numerous surely even for Holmes to commit to memory. I handed Holmes a notebook and pencil, which he received with a nod. At speed, he jotted down the sequence, before returning the roll back inside the neck and replacing the head.

'We have what we need,' declared Holmes, 'now let us remove ourselves from the equation.'

From the diary of Miss Gertrude Cresswell, 10ᵗʰ October 1899

My accent did not fail me! The summer spent with my mother's cousin in Philadelphia served me perfectly. I will admit to a small thrill as I parried with Mr. Holmes as the beer barons looked on, none the wiser. The world's greatest detective was so preoccupied with my shoes that he failed to discern I was a woman. Perhaps I have overestimated him; perhaps he was well-aware of my subterfuge. We shall see in time. In any case, I was long gone before any of them could do a thing about it. Naturally, the great house was not without its secrets, although it did not yield them easily.

And so to return to the mundane. Once more I had cause to return my kippers to my landlady. I was only sorry they could not be returned to the sea itself. Such was the stench, I had to fling open the windows and exchange one set of fetid air for another. The moment I pulled up the sash, my room was infused with that infamous Burton snatch: one part egg, one part wet soil. It only took a morning to realise that by choosing lodgings on the southern side of town I had placed myself in the path of the prevailing wind, which sent the air away from the management and towards the worker bees. The workers, I divined, lived in the terraced dwellings to the pungent east; the managers and skilled artisans live in the grander dwellings to the west.

For breakfast, I raided my own supply of crackerbread and chewed joylessly while considering my next line of enquiry. It was then that I noticed the envelope lying just inside the door. Evidently it had been slid beneath it. My initials were printed in elaborate calligraphy on the front of the envelope – a heavy, yellow stationery of excellent quality. I located my pearl-handled paper knife and broke through the glue. Inside was printed a single short phrase in what appeared to be Russian:

Давайте выпьем за здоровье!

Beneath this was printed the numeral '8', and a perfunctory drawing of a man, upon a hill, bearing a cup. Within the hill were the initials 'W.C.' It was signed off by a further set of initials 'A.S.' I stared at this for a moment, immediately engaged by its cryptology, then returned the note to its envelope, collected my umbrella and quietly made my way downstairs.

'A peculiar bird she is,' I heard the landlady gossip to a stout, red-faced woman with a headful of tight, springy, black curls, crushed beneath a white bonnet. 'And particular too. She's turned her nose up at cook's kippers again. I had them myself this morning. On the turn, perhaps, but perfectly edible.' As I rounded the corner she stopped mid-sentence; the pair of them stared at me, a little embarrassed, no doubt. 'Ah, Miss Cresswell,' my landlady remarked, 'will you be requiring dinner?'

'No thank you,' I replied curtly. 'I have received an invitation.'

'I see,' she returned smartly. 'I hope they will find something you like.'

I narrowed my eyes a little, preparing to give them a piece of my mind, then stopped myself.

'I wonder,' I said, 'whether perhaps you can assist me?'

'We can try.'

'Do the initials 'W.C.' mean anything to you?'

'It's along the corridor.'

'No, I rather fancy it is the name of a hill, or at least somewhere close to a hill.' The two ladies stared at each other.

'Is this,' my landlady enquired, 'some sort of parlour game?'

'Not at all,' I assured her. 'Someone I believe has assumed I have rather more local knowledge than I do.'

'Winshill?' Mrs. Toller suggested at length.

'That doesn't allow for the 'C,'' said the other.

'Oh, wait a moment,' the woman in the bonnet exclaimed, raising a stubby finger. 'I wonder whether it could be Waterloo Clump?'

'That sounds promising,' I said. 'Where can I find that?' She pushed open the front door and pointed towards the west.

'Just look up.'

EIGHT

The River

'I have been reflecting, Watson,' said Holmes, returning his teacup to its saucer. 'Your holy ghost may indeed warrant some further investigation.'

'Why the change of heart? Not twelve hours ago, you were dead set against the idea.'

'Because I believe it may have a bearing on our present case.' Our landlady was an adventurous cook and it was half-past nine before we had disposed of several poached embryo chickens and a quantity of anchovy paste. We then considered our constitutions sound enough to head down to the river.

The customary murk was in the air; clouds it seemed, struggled to keep themselves aloft above the town, preferring to linger at street level. A pervasive cold damp suffused the skin and succeeded in penetrating even the most tightly buttoned tunic. We passed beneath the magnificent wrought-iron gates of the new ferry bridge, a gift to the town, we noted, from the wealthiest of the great beer barons. The numerals '1889' announced themselves above our heads in gold calligraphy. An elegant lantern hung directly beneath the date of construction and on either side rose an ornamental tower, each topped with a fancifully carved lion, supporting a flag.

'Why, Holmes,' I remarked, 'it is something of a miniature Tower Bridge, built with the patronage of the local patriarch.'

No sooner had we ventured twenty yards along the structure, when a gentleman with sandy-grey, coloured whiskers and a shabby suit appeared in the mist directly ahead of us. His hands were plunged into his pockets, a hangdog expression on his face.

'Thomas Whitney, if I am not mistaken,' began Holmes. The fellow looked up in surprise.

'And who are you, sir?'

'My name is Sherlock Holmes,' my friend announced. At this, the man assumed a querulous expression, placed his feet a distance apart and folded his arms in a rather obstructive fashion. It seemed either that my friend's fame had not extended to the North Midlands, or that his exploits singularly failed to impress him.

'You are a Londoner, then,' the fellow stated, brusquely.

'I would agree with your assertion only so far,' smiled Holmes. 'My ancestors were country squires and I fancy there is a soupçon of French in my make-up, but why this enquiry into my lineage?' The man seemed a little taken aback by my friend's bold manner.

'Only because you may be aware that this is a toll bridge,' he informed us. My friend smiled more broadly at this.

'Then, you are Charon,' he laughed, 'the ferryman of Hades. Tell me my friend, what is the charge, an obolus? Or are my friend Watson and I fated to walk the shores for a hundred years?'

'There is a half-penny charge to cross,' the man declared, now a little less sure of himself.

'Is that so?' cried Holmes.

'Watson, will you be so good as to summon an officer of the law?' The man now looked wholly flummoxed. 'This man is correct in every respect, except that this bridge was declared toll free in 1898. It is my assertion that this is the former toll keeper, now deprived of his income. He waits now for unsuspecting strangers, wheedling a halfpenny out of them by fear and deception.'

'But how could you know?' the man asked.

'Because,' replied Holmes, 'you were given a formal warning for such conduct only last week. A helpful description of the fraudster was provided for visitors such as ourselves. It pays to read the local papers.' We left the man, chastened and scowling in the mist.

We negotiated the hire of a small rowing boat from an underemployed fellow with a limp and a mouth organ at the bank side, who seemed most surprised to have any custom at all on such a grim morning. Assuring him of our ability to handle such a craft, I took the oars while Holmes reclined at the other end, busying himself by knocking the spent ash from his pipe.

'I find flowing water highly conducive to the mental process,' he informed me. 'It is no surprise that the greatest advancements in human knowledge have taken place in the bath. I refer you to our friend, Archimedes. Now, be a good fellow and take us downriver. Let us aim for that clump of overhanging willow trees where I fancy we lost our friendly ghost last night.'

I paddled quietly while Holmes expanded on one subject or another. I recall that the problem of longitude, English bowling techniques, a mathematical formula to determine the discolouration of textile dye and the diameter of cigar ash were among those topics broached as we cut through the blue-brown waters of the Trent, dispersing the ducks and swans that ordinarily held right of way on this stretch of the river. The oars dipped and lapped, the only other sounds being the occasional flutter of wings as a sandpiper or wagtail migrated from one tree to the next. My friend was studying the banks intently when suddenly he let out a small cry.

'Over there, Watson,' he announced. 'Do you see? There is a small arrow formed from a twisted branch.' I turned my head to examine the phenomenon. 'A somewhat fanciful notion,' I suggested, pulling hard on the oars. 'Do you not feel that is simply a branch broken by some careless walker?'

'To my eye it appears to be deliberately manipulated,' he said lightly, 'but I have no desire to impose my fanciful notions. Let us continue with our journey.'

We had not progressed another hundred yards when we saw the curious sight of a stick figure drawn playfully in chalk on a tree trunk, pointing downstream.

'Well, well,' remarked Holmes, 'does the style seem reminiscent of something we have witnessed in one of our earlier adventures?' I examined the figure and confirmed to Holmes that it did indeed feel uncannily familiar. We pressed onward, Holmes quite animated by now, sitting bolt upright in the boat, scanning the riverside for signs of the unusual, as alert as a curlew searching for its supper.

To our right, we passed a row of run-down boathouses, each in a state of advanced dilapidation. 'That takes the biscuit,' announced Holmes as we drifted past. 'Would you mind confirming something for me, Watson, in case my eyes once again have deceived me? Please examine, if you will, the words scrawled upon the door of that yellow boathouse. Tell me exactly what you see.

'It is the word "RACHE", Holmes,' I said falteringly. 'But surely, I added, that was the legend we found daubed upon the wall in that astonishing business I recorded as 'A Study in Scarlet.''

'Precisely,' agreed my friend with an impish smile. 'And what of the stick figure? Cast your mind back.'

'The Adventure of the Dancing Men!' I exclaimed. 'The style is the same exactly.'

'These markers were left by a student of my methods and someone who has more than a passing familiarity with the accounts of my investigations. What's more, Watson, I believe it is a woman.'

We rounded a corner and saw her in plain view. Gertrude Cresswell sat languidly upon a folding canvas chair in the long grass, a bone-china teacup in her hand and a quizzical expression on her pale, symmetrical features. She wore a white dress with a high collar, in something of the French bohemian style. Beside her, a yellow umbrella lay against the chair. On a small camping table lay an instrument I recognised as a Hawaiian ukulele and perhaps most remarkably, a copy of my book, 'The Sign of Four.' It took only a moment for me to recognise her as the same formidable woman I had seen on the platform at King's Cross.

'Gentlemen,' she called, in a clipped, amused tone, 'I was expecting you ten minutes ago.'

'Forgive us,' returned Holmes. 'My friend insisted on second helpings at breakfast, causing us a small delay.' I glanced between the woman and Holmes, feeling somewhat doubtful.

'You had arranged to meet?' I asked, gliding the boat up to the shore.

'Not at all,' laughed Holmes, stepping deftly onto the riverbank. 'This remarkable lady is familiar with our routine. She is a student of my methods and merely anticipated our movements. She laid one or two considerate, although ultimately redundant clues, providing the final indication of her whereabouts.'

'Would you care for some tea?' she enquired.

'Certainly,' I replied, tying up the boat to a tree. 'I don't believe we've had the pleasure.'

'Gertrude Cresswell,' she returned sharply. 'Consulting Detective, 212a Charing Cross Road. I confess it is no small thrill finally coming face to face with Sherlock Holmes, not to mention his faithful chronicler, Dr. Watson.'

'If I am not mistaken,' I asserted, 'it was you who was credited with making the breakthrough in that curious business of "The Copper Owl."'

'It was bronze, Dr. Watson,' she returned, 'the bronze owl.'

'Of course,' I returned.

'If I recall from the papers,' noted Holmes, 'the owl was the only item left behind in that notorious Mayfair burglary. You correctly surmised that the burglar had a pathological fear of owls. An incisive piece of reasoning, although perfectly evident for anyone with a logical mind who was availed of the relevant data.'

'Do I detect a note of professional jealously?' she asked playfully.

'Miss Cresswell,' retorted Holmes in a somewhat prickly tone, 'I assure you, there is more than enough murder, blackmail, fraud and larceny to go around.' She poured two cups of hot tea, a welcome pep given the morning's chill.

'A remarkable piece of detective work...' I began.

'For a woman?' she enquired.

'Well,' I spluttered.

'Believe it or not,' she explained, 'some of us are equipped with powers of reasoning.' She gave me a sharp look. 'Or is reasoning in women something of which you do not approve, Doctor? Perhaps using one's mind to solve difficult problems is not considered 'women's work?'

'Not at all,' I protested, weakly.

'I apologise,' she continued, 'but it appears I have left my crochet in London.'

'And how is business?' enquired Holmes, testing the damp ground with the end of his cane.

'You will be aware my agency is not long established. I recently returned from Switzerland, where I was making something of a reputation in the field of tobogganing.'

'Tobogganing?' I repeated.

'Precisely,' she said. 'It was a pastime I took up shortly after leaving the convent.' My incredulity was stretched to breaking point. 'As it transpired, my frame is perfectly suited to the physical demands of the sport. Apparently I have limbs of timber, but alas the same could not be said for my joints. Only when I sustained a knee injury did I retire reluctantly from the slopes.' I sipped at the tea and considered this remarkable revelation.

'Gracious,' I said, returning my cup to its saucer, 'this is an unusual blend.'

'Is it to your liking, doctor? It should be. It employs the leaves of the *Camellia Sinensis*, The Chinese swear by it. It has life-giving properties; drink enough of it and you will live forever. You might know it by another name: Green Tea.'

She suddenly swiped her field binoculars from the table and brought them to her eyes. 'Good gosh,' she exclaimed, 'that's a lesser whitethroat. He's a tricky little customer. When he takes flight against a white sky it is as if he vanishes into thin air.'

'I hope I am not speaking out of turn,' I said, taking another experimental sip of the brew, 'but is it not an extraordinary coincidence that two London consulting agencies are operating within the same square mile in the same provincial town?'

'Not if you consider,' my friend broke in, 'that we are working on the same case.'

'Sakes alive, Holmes!' I exclaimed. 'Is it true?'

'Of course it is,' Miss Cresswell confirmed, returning her binoculars to the table. 'I have been employed by Evercreech Brewery to investigate the same matter.'

'What possible business is it of theirs?'

'If there is a poisoner at large,' assisted Holmes, 'is it not conceivable that he will target another brewery?'

'I suppose it is,' I conceded. 'But why the subterfuge? The cryptic messages?'

'Hardly cryptic!' she insisted. 'I saw you gentlemen stumbling around last night up on Waterloo Clump.'

The penny dropped. 'Then you were the apparition on the river!'

'It was obvious that you would see me and investigate in the morning. I merely laid a few friendly markers in homage to your work. However, there is one important consideration. We cannot be seen to be conspiring by our respective employers. That is why I thought it better to arrange our meeting in an out-of-the way spot.'

'Miss Cresswell,' said Holmes stiffly. 'While I am flattered by your attentions, it is not my method to work in tandem. Mine is a solitary vocation.' As if to underline the point he took several paces to the river's edge and peered into the waters.

'You seem happy enough to work with Dr. Watson,' she countered.

'With all due respect to the good doctor,' he said, 'ours is not a partnership of equals.'

'Really, Mr. Holmes,' she scolded, 'that remark is beneath you.' I felt, I admit, somewhat stung by Holmes' words.

'Dr. Watson has the wit of Voltaire and the loyalty of a dash-hound,' Holmes proceeded, stooping to study a plant. 'But he is not a partner in my agency. His role is that of catalyst, sounding board and companion. But the responsibility for the success or failure of my investigations rests with me.'

'Then, a straight exchange of information,' she concluded, 'seems the fairest settlement, even if that will be to your advantage.'

'My advantage?' scoffed Holmes.

'Naturally, I am aware that you suspect the brothers, the cooper and the assistant brewer.' My friend raised his eyebrows, evidently impressed despite himself. 'However, I confess I do not yet know the role of Butterworth in all this. If you were to assist, I am willing to trade theory for a place or name.' A pair of swans drifted past, imperiously ignoring our little tea party.

'I am not in the business of purchasing information,' declared Holmes. 'Nor do I solve cases by a system of barter. I can honestly attest that not even suspects interest me. Only data. Naturally I am curious about the disagreements between the brothers, and Anaxagoras is certainly a rare bird, but all our options remain open.' Miss Cresswell frowned and peered at my friend in something between fascination and disappointment.

'They always say it is inadvisable to meet your heroes.'

'It appears we have reached something of an impasse,' noted Holmes.

'A great pity,' she said. 'I had rather hoped we could combine our complementary talents.' She took up her ukulele and strummed a melancholy chord.

'If there is nothing further,' my friend concluded, 'then I wish you good fortune with your investigations, your bird watching and musical adventures.'

'Before you leave,' she began, 'I wonder if you would glance at this.' She held up what appeared to be a small, iron cog. 'Tolwood found this outside the gates of the brewery on the day Butterworth disappeared.' My friend's eyes fell on the object.

'Have you presented it to the police?' he enquired.

'Not yet. Tolwood assured me it is not part of any mechanism connected with the brewery.' I have made numerous enquiries with various other places of business, but it appears entirely unconnected with any machine used in the town.'

'A singular problem,' stated Holmes. 'May I?' He took out his handkerchief, picked up the item and held it before him.

'I would suggest that it was removed from the mechanism of a municipal clock. Have you observed whether any clock is telling the wrong time?'

'No, I confess, I haven't.'

'Then, you have a new line of enquiry.'

'You see,' she said brightly, 'perhaps we can work together after all.'

'I think not,' said Holmes, and returned his topper to his head. 'Good day, Miss Cresswell.'

'One more thing,' she added, rising from her chair. 'Would you sign a book for me, Doctor?'

'Delighted!' I said, and fetched a pen from my pocket. She gave me a curious look as I returned the book.

'Beware the Americans,' she said. 'They will make you a rich man one day, Doctor and money may prove your undoing.' I nodded warily at this curious remark, then tipped my hat. She was as charming and composed as any woman I had encountered, but I could not help feeling we were dealing with a dangerous intellect. Holmes and I returned to the boat and slowly pulled away from the shore. As we departed she broke into song in a contralto voice. It was, I recognised, the music hall song, 'The Man Who Broke the Bank at Monte Carlo.'

'A charming woman,' I remarked, as soon as were out of earshot.

'You are easily flattered, Watson,' Holmes declared.

'And you are easily affronted, Holmes,' I returned. A raft of ducks divided around our boat, before reuniting on the other side.

I could see my friend needed some cheering. 'An extraordinary deduction about the clock mechanism,' I remarked.

'Whatever are you talking about?' demanded Holmes.

'The cog from the clock,' I said.

'That was no cog. It was a sprocket from a motorcar.'

'But what about the clock?'

'What of it?' enquired Holmes. 'So far as I am concerned every clock in Burton is keeping perfect time.'

'Then, you lied to Miss Cresswell?'

'So it appears.'

'Holmes!' I admonished. I pulled heavily on the oars, quietly seething at my friend's behaviour. 'She may be a rival,' I muttered, shaking my head, 'but better to say nothing than to mislead. I'm afraid to say I think it's been a poor show.'

'I would pick you up on one point only.'

'Oh yes?'

'I do not consider her a rival.'

'Pride comes before a fall,' I added.

Holmes lit his pipe with excessive ceremony then perched at the far end of the boat with his eyes fluttering shut, as if in meditation. I could not say for certain, but I rather felt that he was feigning this state following our contretemps to avoid a fracas. As I heaved on the oars, I considered the increasingly perplexing series of events that had led us to this point: the brewer in the barrel; the incident with Mycroft; the woman on the line; the eccentric astronomer not to speak of the coruscating Miss Cresswell. Yet we were no closer to identifying the man who had poisoned the beer. It seemed such a mundane business for one, let alone two brilliant minds. Why should we not accept her offer to pool our resources? It seemed absurd.

Lost in this reverie, I had failed to notice the steamboat that was puffing steadily through the water behind us. I glanced over my shoulder. It was a small launch, perhaps the kind that ferried pleasure seekers during the summer season, yet there was no one on deck. I tugged on the left oar to bring us close enough to the bank to allow it to pass safely, but was astonished to note that it too had altered course.

'Sakes alive, Holmes,' I exclaimed, 'they are coming right for us!'

'Watson,' cried Holmes sitting bolt upright, shaking off all signs of lethargy, 'row straight for the left bank and keep as low as you can.'

The sound of the steam pistons was almost in my ear. There was still no one on the prow and I could see nothing but thick plumes of smoke billowing into the sky.

'We will be splintered to driftwood!'

'Nonsense,' parried Holmes, 'we are twice as agile.'

I slew across the water as Holmes instructed, but by now I was convinced we would be crushed at any moment. We ploughed through a dense stretch of water reeds and ducked beneath the imbrications of outlying branches, which more than once almost toppled us into the water. We bumped against the bank and I almost lost an oar in a patch of brambles, yet, agonisingly, there was nowhere to land; the banks

115

were too steep. I veered again to avoid one particularly gargantuan alder tree that leaned out into the Trent.

'Hurl yourself down, Watson!' called Holmes. He did not need to ask again. No sooner had my head crashed against the wooden floor when a gunshot blasted a hole clean through the side of boat. 'There goes our deposit,' he added with a wild laugh. 'Now stay down!' Though at first, at such close quarters, I could only see Holmes' Tennant-Stribbling patent leather shoes, glancing up I saw that he had risen to his feet, was clutching his cane and had assumed his Bartitsu position, one foot forward, the other setback for balance, with his arms set in the same arrangement. A moment later, he had hurled his cane through the air, with an expertly delivered throw and had succeeded in hitting his mark. There was a growl of pain, followed by a splash as one might expect when a sack of flour falls from a barge.

'Row for your life, Watson!'

The boat slackened off its speed to pick up the brute and I lost no time in seizing the advantage. Despite an agonising throb from the old ache in my shoulder, I pulled back hard, fairly launching us through the waves.

'Bravo, Watson,' called Holmes, 'not far now. Up ahead there on the left, we can land without obstruction.' Water gushed in through the hole in the side and our feet were now fully submerged in the murky water.

'I have a mind to send them the bill for my shoes,' Holmes remarked, lifting each foot in turn, water pouring through the holes in his brogues. We were now listing heavily to starboard. Every oar-stroke sent another flood of water on board.

'I don't believe we will make it,' I panted, red-faced. The pursuing boat had built up a full head of steam and was upon us once more.

'Desperate times, desperate measures,' Holmes muttered. He reached into his ulster for his Webley Bull Dog and took aim. 'Don't move an inch, my dear fellow,' he said, squeezing one eye shut. I heard a mighty crack, followed by a high-pitched whistle as steam escaped at high pressure. 'That should keep them busy,' he said.

Just as we were about to pitch over, we drew alongside the bank and Holmes leapt like a panther onto the grass, landing in an athletic crouch, one hand flat on the ground to steady himself. Another shot, more powerful this time, blasted clean through the stern and the boat disintegrated around me. Just as I was about to plummet into the waters, I was seized by the scruff. With the strength and dexterity of an ancient Olympian, Holmes succeeded in lifting me clean from the beleaguered vessel before sweeping me in a single clean turn onto dry land. I had barely a moment to register I was standing once again on terra firma when my friend darted into the undergrowth, issuing an unequivocal instruction for me to follow him.

'It is somewhat amusing for me to observe, Watson,' gasped Holmes as we emerged through the trees, 'that once again I have led you into mortal danger. What began as a simple investigation into an ale of questionable quality has become a thoroughly unpleasant imbroglio. If you wish to return to London by the next train and leave this matter in my hands, I would perfectly understand.'

'Not for a moment, Holmes,' I said, my handkerchief pressed to the jagged cut on my forehead. 'Whoever it was who has just taken pot shots at us, they have thoroughly got my dander up.'

'Splendid, Watson!' my friend remarked. "Under the bludgeonings of chance, my head is bloody but unbowed." It is your qualities as an adventurer, and your spirit, as indignant as it is indomitable, that make you a first-rate conspirator.'

'Even if,' I broke in, 'ours is "not a partnership of equals?"'

'Pah!' scoffed Holmes. 'Do not be fooled by my repartee with the singular Miss Cresswell. She is possessed of a first-class mind, of that I am in no doubt, but I am not yet certain of her loyalties in this matter. Now let us fill a glass with an ale of less redoubtable providence and consider our next move. The game is afoot and we are being played, Watson!'

From the diary of Gertrude Cresswell, 11th October 1899

Sherlock Holmes! Face to face, he is every bit the sinewy, hawk-like figure of Watson's stories. If anything, he is leaner and more ascetic. He is as pale as Banquo's ghost and has less flesh on him than a shilling pork chop. But he is more alert too. His mind darts and flashes before you like a hummingbird. Watson has captured his waspish, supercilious air precisely. But far from feeling that he was merely scoring points against me, there was an outrageous twinkle in his eye. I had the unnerving feeling that he had read my mind in an instant. There was also the strong sense that the substance of the case was in fact immaterial. What matters is the chase. It is all about the game! Oh, what perfect fun. I believe I have aroused the competitive edge in him.

But to the matter of these brewers. I do not believe for one moment Holmes' false assertion that the sprocket from the Marquess' motorcar came from a clock. He knows the providence of the item as well as I do. Nonetheless, it is important that Holmes brings his own knowledge of the case on a parity with my own. Only then can he help me make a decisive breakthrough. But on no account must he suspect that I am assisting him. He may be a man amongst men, but he shares their great Achilles' heel: that inescapable pride. It is their undoing!

And what of Dr. Watson? I was expecting another man entirely. The caricature he sketches of himself underplays his qualities. One thing is clear: He is not the dullard in the room. He has a thoughtful, sensitive, almost moral presence. But he is a man in a way Holmes can never be. I saw his eyes linger on mine for half a moment, a certain animal instinct that public-school manners cannot suppress. It is the red-blooded beast within him that he has tamed into submission. But I saw it, just for a moment, and confess myself momentarily attracted. But he is open to the simplest flattery. I produced my copy of 'The Sign of Four' for him to sign, which caused him half to melt.

Spent the afternoon thinking over the matter and occupying myself with birding. I had sufficient tea to sustain me until supper and my patience was rewarded with the sighting of a green woodpecker and a yellowhammer. I felt something of an exotic bird myself sitting there in the long grass. A small barge crawled past while I was playing 'The

Man Who Broke the Bank at Monte Carlo'. The captain almost fell overboard when he saw me.

Two letters of interest. One from the manager of the Burlington Hotel, Sheringham, complaining of an empty room that locks itself and smells of cinnamon each morning. He wonders when I will be available to pay him a visit (and that he does not believe he can afford Mr. Holmes' fees!) Another from Evercreech Brewery advancing my expenses. Will spend half on my arrears at my boarding house and half on a new fuchsia hat I saw in a window yesterday, which leaves me in exactly the same state of destitution in which I awoke this morning. The glory of life lies in birds, melodies – and new hats.

NINE

The Coopers

A litter of amber leaves swept across our feet as Holmes and I emerged into the thin morning sunlight. The town was teaming with life: Schoolchildren hopscotched their way to their lessons; newspaper sellers waved the front pages of the freshly inked Burton Mail; rake-thin workers in flat caps stumped along the pavement to their breweries. For all the ale we had seen imbibed since our arrival, I noted, few of the men had the pot bellies one might associate with such a habit. Meanwhile, bustling matrons propelled enormous prams ahead of them, like small, powerful, steam engines shunting carriages into sidings.

'What do you say to a short constitutional, Watson?' suggested Holmes. 'I would like to conduct another inspection of the track where we found Mrs. Bilton. There is something that troubles me.'
'By all means,' I agreed, 'but let us be wary.'
We proceeded along the High Street
'These, Watson,' declared Holmes, with a sweep of his hand, 'are the great fortresses where the beer barons preside over their empires. Mark my words, there is as much wealth, power and influence along this street as there is in all of Whitehall. And what is more, I would wager there is twice the efficiency!'
'I do not doubt it.' Presently, we heard singing.
'Ah,' exclaimed Holmes, his face suddenly brightening, 'Mozart! He was sent to lift our spirits and put life in our veins.'
'The Marriage of Figaro,' I remarked.
'Quite so,' said Holmes. 'Mozart's music is the nearest humanity has come to creating something to rival the great works of creation.'
'Can you name another such example?'
'The pipe,' responded Holmes in an instant. 'As a conveyance of pleasure and contentment, it is almost without equal.'
We paused and peered along the street, attempting to identify the owner of the voice, wondering perhaps whether it was a cheerful brewer reviewing a healthy sales ledger.
'Over there, Watson,' pointed out Holmes.
Sure enough, we saw a lone figure, standing outside the door of one of the great brick buildings. A cloth lay on the floor in front of him,

meanly covered in ha'pennies, pennies and farthings. Singing with great poise and gusto, he was a middle-aged fellow wearing a shawl collar dinner jacket, purple bow tie and cummerbund. Incongruously, he also sported a soft, green velvet hat. We drew closer and stood ten yards back, listening intently. There was something uncanny about the man. While his attire was ostensibly smart, it was also grubby and ill-fitting. He had gone to seed somewhat; his shirt was pulled tight across a sizeable paunch and there was an unhealthy red hue about his cheeks.

Holmes stood quite spellbound before the man and remained so until he had concluded his aria. My friend gestured towards the fellow's upturned hat and I reluctantly obliged with some coins.

'I think we can do better than that, Watson,' my friend suggested, watching the pair of pennies applaud like castanets as they landed. 'You had one pound, eight shillings and four pence in your pocket.' Curious at my friend's exactitude, I rummaged for my change, counting it quickly on my palm.

'Perfectly correct,' I agreed, somewhat annoyed that Holmes had gone through my pockets.

'But, why do you look so infuriated, Watson? Because you believe I searched your pockets?'

'Quite so!'

'An appalling suggestion!' he said. 'I was merely aware of the sum with which you left London and have stood beside you while you made each purchase. It is a not a question of deduction, merely arithmetic.'

'Not true, Holmes,' I announced with delight. 'I bought a packet of humbugs while I went to look for Brushwood on the train.'

'Indeed,' my friend agreed. 'I smelt them on your breath when you returned to our carriage and later took a moment to make a note of their price. I factored them into my calculation. I also noted that you did not offer me one.'

'You once told me,' I protested, 'that confectionary was a tool of socialist control!'

'That is beside the point.'

'By the way,' I asked. 'Where are my humbugs?'

'Here,' said Holmes, throwing me a white paper bag.

'So you did go through my pockets,' I declared.

'I picked your pocket, not searched it. There is a difference.'

'Gentlemen,' the singer broke in, 'if you don't mind, I have a living to make.'

Forgive us,' apologised Holmes. 'But before you resume, would you be so good as to satisfy my curiosity and explain how a man schooled at the Royal College of Music comes to sing in the street?'

'But, how did you know?' he asked incredulously.

'You were taught by Jenny Lind, were you not? The Swedish Nightingale.'

'Yes, but that is hardly common knowledge? I did not amount to much.'

'The deportment of her pupils is entirely recognisable. It was a feature of her training was it not? The head, shoulders and abdomen should be relaxed and knees and hips aligned.'

'Remarkable,' he said. 'She insisted on precisely those instructions. Well, since you ask, my first public performance was a disaster, the second was a catastrophe and there was no third. One might call it stage fright. Others called it the end of my career.'

'Yet you sing with such ease out here in the street.' The man shrugged.

'A curious predicament,' noted Holmes. 'Have you sought professional help? I am no psychotherapist, but I am convinced in the powers of hypnotherapy.'

'I fear,' he said, 'it is little late for that. I am now more convinced by the powers of the bottle.'

'My friend,' Holmes consoled, 'we are all passengers on the ship of life. Our talents are the oars. Only they will take us to our destination. Do not let them slip into the water.' There was a look of appalling despair in the man's eyes. 'Let me pay for lunch at the best hotel,' continued Holmes more brightly, 'but first I would appreciate your assistance in a small matter. Tell me, were you singing on the morning of Monday last?'

'Who is to say,' he said mournfully. 'One day folds into the next. But I begin each day at seven to catch the morning crowds.'

'Then, perhaps you remember a motorcar that stopped outside Houghton's that day?'

'A motorcar, you say?' he repeated.

'Quite.'

'Well, yes, of course,' he stated as my friend was stating an obvious fact. 'You are referring of course to the Marquess.'

'I am?' asked Holmes.

'How could I forget the man who dropped a five-pound note into my hat? He paid a short trip to the brewery then drove away, but not before comparing me favourably to Arvid Odmann.'

'High praise indeed,' said Holmes. 'Do you happen to know his residence?'

'The family seat, I believe, is Beaudesert House in Cannock Chase.'

'Was he alone?'

'No, he was accompanied by a heavily bearded man, dressed in what I can only describe as Roman robes. They made quite a pair.'

'Hardly inconspicuous!'

'Anaxagoras!' I exclaimed.

Holmes and I clicked our way along the High Street, making frequent stops at the railway crossings that made rapid travel across the town almost impossible. The locomotives shunted back and forth incessantly, bringing in the hops, and ferrying the barrels on their journey to London and thence to every corner of the world. They hissed and grinded with an indefatigable power, obeying their masters. Priority was given to beer over people at every turn and the townsfolk seemed to exhibit almost superhuman patience at this arrangement, perhaps conscious that their livelihoods depended on the success of their industry.

'What exactly are we looking for, Holmes?' I asked.

'Anything and everything,' he returned, distracted, searching the hedgerows and gutters for anything out of the ordinary. Yet another white crossing gate closed behind us.

'Don't turn or even slow your pace, Watson,' my friend informed me, 'for it appears we are being followed.'

'Good Lord, Holmes,' I exclaimed, feeling instinctively for my service revolver. 'Are you quite sure?'

'I have deliberately crossed over the road twice as if we were about to turn off,' informed Holmes. 'Each time they followed us across. There are five of them, three walking in front and two a short distance behind. Even with my powers and your service revolver, I feel a confrontation would be unwise.'

'Then, what shall we do?'

'We continue at the current pace until the next gate begins to close.'

'And then what?'

'Then we run!' At this, Holmes put on a terrific burst of speed and I had little choice but to follow. Both the near and far gate were closing slowly, but inexorably in front of us. 'Faster, Watson!' Holmes urged, his coat-tail snapping behind him. We reached the near one just as it closed and Holmes deftly vaulted it, leaping high into the air, one hand planted on the top. I followed suit, after a fashion, tumbling over the gate and landing hard on the other side. I had barely a moment to collect my wits when I saw the vast iron hulk of a locomotive bearing down on me. I scrambled to my feet and hurled myself over the next gate, just as it thundered past. My hat, a handsome bowler not a month old, I noticed, was a casualty.

'Too close for comfort,' I noted, feeling a small pang of loss for my hat. Through the blur of trucks we saw the five men, grimacing like a pack of hounds. They were a motley crew with gnarled features, faded suits and missing teeth. The man at the centre, more bristled than the others, appeared to be the leader. He glared at me with a malevolent purpose. I could not be sure, but it seemed he was missing a considerable portion of his left ear.

Holmes seized my arm. 'I would caution against further delay, Watson. Perhaps we will find you a new hat this afternoon.' He hauled me aside and we dashed down a side street to safety. Narrowly avoiding a collision with a shoe shiner and his stall, we rounded a corner and stopped for breath.

'We appear to have made more enemies than friends,' I panted. 'Any idea who they are?'

'I believe,' asserted Holmes, 'that they are coopers. Did you see the adzes swinging from their belts?'

'I confess I did not,' I admitted.

'Well,' returned Holmes, 'you seem to have another opportunity.' I looked up and to my chagrin saw that the brutes were upon us again. Three stood at one end of the lane; two others approached slowly from the other.'

'Can we help you, gentlemen?' enquired Holmes. Slowly, I reached for my revolver.

'You can leave that right where it is,' hissed the man with the torn ear. 'Now, unless you want to be fish food at the bottom of the Trent, I suggest you come with us.'

'I say,' remarked Holmes, 'what in devil's name is that on your shoe?' Instinctively, the man glanced down and with this, my friend upended the shoe shiner's stand and sent it directly into his path, causing him to reel backwards.

'This way!' shouted Holmes.

We bundled onwards, back towards the High Street, sending pedestrians spilling into the road. I pulled my revolver and glanced behind me. Despite their shambolic appearance, the coopers seemed remarkably fleet of foot and were gaining on us. A stone flew past my ear and, from around the corner, three more of the devils appeared, each bearing a sharpened implement of some sort and a look of malign intent. 'I can't risk a shot, Holmes,' I cried, taking a step back to the wall. 'Too many people.'

'Our position I agree,' muttered Holmes, assuming his Bartitsu posture, 'is not without its disadvantages.'

'Gentlemen,' a familiar voice called, 'climb aboard!'

From a cloud of noxious black smoke emerged the absurd figure of Anaxagoras Houghton sitting at the wheel of an 1899 Daimler motorcar. He had appeared as if from nowhere, and had swerved in towards us. His beard was as luxuriant as ever and his flowing robes owed more to Roman than Victorian tastes. He was an unlikely saviour. The engine panted with the keenness of a cheetah.

We did not wait for a second invitation and, stepping onto the footplate, we threw ourselves in and careered back down the High Street, with Holmes up front and myself sprawled in the back, fumbling in my jacket for my revolver. The gang, it seemed, was not deterred by our apparent escape and continued to lumber after us with the deadly zeal of a lynch mob, perhaps knowing that our progress would be impeded once again by the railway crossing. I fired a warning shot into the air, but they knew I wouldn't risk a public massacre. I heard a bell sounding and at once knew the gate was closing ahead.

'We will never make it across,' I bellowed.

'Oh, I don't know about that!' exclaimed Anaxagoras, and accelerated towards certain oblivion. Holmes was hunched forward, his steely gaze on the white gate, his face fixed with hawk-like intensity, while the monstrous hulk of a locomotive moved in from the left.

'No!' I protested, but already it was too late. The first gate splintered in front of us, sending our headlights spinning away, before we tore with equal ease through the second gate. The train skimmed the rear bumper and I felt its heat against my skin.

'Collateral damage only,' proclaimed our driver with a wild laugh, but half paralysed with fear, I did not respond.

'An impressive display,' smiled Holmes, 'although I believe you have succeeded in removing one of my friend Watson's nine lives. I imagine some brandy will be required to restore his wits. Can you direct us to a place where such a thing can be obtained in relative safety?'

'I know the very place,' he confirmed, and belted onwards, heading uphill and out of town.

The road, I realised, was the same one we had taken to meet him that first time, rising steadily upwards. To our left, the great peaks and dales grew in the distance. A church tower rose up like the head of a needle darning the patchwork of fields.

'There's no place like it, Doctor!' shouted Anaxagoras over the din of the engine, 'except perhaps Mesopotamia.'

'No doubt!' I shouted back.

'How are you, Mr. Holmes?' our driver demanded. 'Unruffled, I hope.' Holmes smiled and nodded.

'I feel like I am travelling through time,' our driver continued in a distracted sort of way. 'One age has ended and another has begun. But to which do we belong?'

We thundered on, swerving around a four-wheeler being hauled by a pair of weary mares, our pursuers now left far behind. Never having ridden in a motorcar before, I felt a pleasant and unexpected feeling of exhilaration, the wind blowing in my hair. It was a feeling quite different from train travel, but not dissimilar to sailing.

'Not long, now,' Anaxagoras shouted. At that moment, there was an alarming bang from somewhere in the inner workings of the machine, and we began to slow. A pungent smell announced itself, which we assumed was the engine seizing up. 'Just our luck,' he said, slapping the wheel with the flat of his hand.

'It seems entirely probable,' my friend put in, 'that the mechanical failure is directly related to our misadventures in Burton.'

'So what now?' I asked. 'Continue on foot I suppose and harangue your car dealer when you see him next?'

'My car dealer?' he repeated. 'My dear man, you don't suppose for one moment this is my motorcar?'

'Is isn't?'

'No, I don't have two ha'pennies to rub together. This is one of Toppy's toys.'

'Toppy?'

'Henry Paget, the 5th Marquess of Anglesey.'

'Be that as it may,' I said, 'the motorcar is inoperable.'

'I agree,' conceded Anaxagoras. 'While I have great pleasure operating the machine, I have little knowledge of its workings.'

'And you have no horses?' I pressed.

'I do not believe in the slavery of noble beasts.'

'Then how do you propose we continue our journey?' He held a finger in the air. 'One moment gentlemen.' He returned momentarily, clutching three machines, each about the size of a bicycle wheel.'

'May I present,' he said, 'the best thing to come out of France since the 1881 Bordeaux. Gentlemen, I introduce you to the Gérard folding bicycle.' He busied himself with the mechanism for a moment, then, in a single deft movement, succeeded in doubling its length.

'A marvel!' I cried.

Half an hour later we found ourselves ensconced in the drawing room of a magnificent country house.

'No doubt,' I said, glancing up at the extraordinary decoration, 'this all belongs to the Marquess.'

'No doubt,' answered our host.

'What do you know,' enquired Holmes, holding his glass up to the light, 'of the Sumerians?'

Anaxagoras shifted his head slightly to one side. 'That is a curious line of questioning, Mr. Holmes.'

'It is an interest, we have discovered, of your brother's.' Anaxagoras nodded thoughtfully, then took another sip of his wine.

'It does not stop there,' our host elucidated. 'It was the great passion of our father's life and as a result, consumed our lives too. In fact, he died in Iraq, itself named after Uruk, the great Sumerian city, while on a quest to discover the origins of the race.'

'An astonishing people,' he mused, 'and one we came to loathe as they consumed my father's attentions, leaving no room for his own children.'

'But, why, then, does Michael maintain such an interest?'

'It is not, I assure you,' he said, 'one born out of any intrinsic love. Did you know, Dr. Watson, they were a race of beer lovers?'

'I did not,' I confirmed.

'You are familiar, no doubt, with the great text, the 'Epic of Gilgamesh'?' Holmes nodded in the affirmative.

'Let me see if I can remember this,' Anaxagoras began, closing his eyes. "When Enkidu first tasted Gilgamesh's beer his spirits were transformed. Drink the beer, as is the custom of the land... He drank the beer-seven jugs! and became expansive and sang with joy!"'

'I had no idea,' I said, 'that beer had such pedigree.'

'It is as old as the land itself. They say, Doctor, that the first recipe ever written down was one for beer. To my palette, at least, it is a coarse beverage to slake the thirst of the peasant. Wine, I need not remind you, is the drink of the gods.'

'As you say.'

'One moment,' he added. 'I have something which may be of interest to you.' Anaxagoras left the room, returning a minute later holding a small, wooden box. He laid it upon the table and pushed it towards me.

'Please do the honours, Doctor.' I frowned and glanced at Holmes who gave a slight nod of approval. Releasing the small gold catch, I flipped up the lid.

'Egad!' I cried, clapping eyes on the object.

'You express considerable surprise, Watson,' remarked Holmes, 'given that it is merely a drinking cup. There are two glasses on the table. It was natural that our host would bring a third.'

It was a cup of astonishing craftsmanship, with a copper hue, decorated with asymmetric patterns. The singular feature was a curious, thin spout curving sharply upwards.

'A Sumerian beer mug,' stated Anaxagoras. 'It is four-and-a-half-thousand-years old and made of solid gold.'

I heard a clattering from along the corridor, not unlike the sound of roof tiles falling to the ground. I threw my newspaper aside, then followed the noise until I found myself standing outside the library, the door left slightly ajar. Pushing it open, I came upon a surprisingly well-lit room with bookcases lining every wall; the amber ceilings seemed to double the sunlight. Given the otherwise gloomy demeanour of the house, this was an unexpected discovery. My friend stood with his back to me, balancing upon a small mahogany stool, cheerfully plucking volumes from the shelves and allowing them to fall into the cradle of his arm and thence to the floor.

'Ah, Watson,' he said, without turning around, 'immaculate timing. Perhaps you would be so good as to help me transport these volumes to my room?'

'Great heavens Holmes,' I remarked, 'you must have over fifty books here. Are you so short of reading material?'

'Research!' my friend declared, continuing to pilfer the shelves. 'As you are acutely aware, there are some lamentable gaps in my knowledge. These do not concern me until such a time when this ignorance sets me at a disadvantage.' Hopping off his perch, he proceeded to load my arms with books until I could only just peek above the topper-most volume. My moustache absorbed an inch of dust and when I sneezed, it was all I could do to avoid dropping the entire consignment. Similarly loaded, Holmes led me towards his room, the two of us like men escaping a fire at the British Library.

'What is this gap in your knowledge?' I enquired, once we were alone. I attempted to read the spine of the book nearest my nose. 'Are you finally to acquaint yourself with the heavenly bodies? If memory serves, you were unaware that the Earth travels around the Sun.'

'I hold by my assertion that it matters little to me what goes on even a mile above the spire of St Paul's Cathedral.'

'What then is this area of urgent study?'

'Sumerian history,' Holmes remarked. 'The answer to this riddle lies somewhere two thousand miles and four thousand years from here. I plan to indulge in a little time travel. I have upon my person a pound of rough shag tobacco and a pint of port. These will be my companions as I embark on this odyssey in space and time.'

My friend did not join us for lunch, nor supper that night, instead keeping to his room. He made one journey only to the library to retrieve another consignment of books and to obtain an additional box of matches, avoiding any communication with either my host or myself. It was noon the next day when I finally felt compelled to check upon his well-being. Knocking, I received no answer; similarly, calling his name yielded no response.

If you have ever opened the door on a burning room, you will have some idea of the atmosphere that greeted me that day. I was repelled by a wall of thick smoke and an intense heat. There was a darkness relieved only by a bright burning point of light at the centre.

'Holmes,' I called again, 'are you there?'

Hearing nothing and seeing less, I ventured into the room, tentatively, as one might explore the scene of a crime where the murderer is still at large. My friend's chair was turned towards the window and I had an irrational fear of what I might discover. Assuming Holmes had fallen asleep, my most immediate concern was that he had set light to his chair with a stray cigarette end. The smoke had an almost tangible presence and I pushed it aside like a velvet curtain. Only as I drew face to face with Holmes could I make out his features. He was smiling weakly, his eyes as rheumy as those of an aged man.

'Hello, Watson,' he said in something close to a whisper. His skin, ordinarily pale, had assumed a hideous grey pallor.

'Holmes!' I exclaimed, 'you are awake.'

'Naturally, I am awake,' he confirmed, tapping ash into his lap.

'And you are quite well? I am sorry to say it does not appear that way. Missing meals is not something I condone.'

'Asceticism,' he pronounced, 'is the path to the truth. By denying the body, one empowers the mind. But I would also remind you, Watson, that I am your friend and not your patient.'

'Quite, quite,' I muttered, 'but for God's sake, allow me to open a window and fetch you some tea.'

'As you wish.' I did my best to decant some of the poisonous fumes outside.

'Well,' I enquired, 'pulling up the shutter, 'did you find what you were looking for?'

'After a fashion.'

'But you didn't read all those books?'

'Of course I read them,' he retorted, sounding somewhat affronted. 'I read two of them twice.'

'And, what now?'

'I must go away for a while alone.'

'Can you tell me more?'

'Not at present.' This reticence was not entirely without precedent, and I did not press him further. 'No doubt,' he added, 'Anaxagoras and you will find subjects of mutual interest in my absence.'

Anaxagoras was singular company. He shared a number of Holmes' traits: the manic energy, the rampant egomania and flights of fantasy that hovered somewhere between madness and brilliance. He speculated about the composition of the stars and the entomology of the hippo. One morning he roused me from bed at five to glimpse an amber moon; another night I woke of my own accord and saw him playing croquet alone in the moonlight. But, like Holmes, he suffered from those sudden and debilitating bouts of melancholia. For long periods during these episodes, I barely saw him. He confined himself to his room or else sat at the end of the garden in his makeshift observatory, sitting motionless beside his telescope. His conversation in these dejected states was reduced to mumbles and incoherent grunts. During that interminable week, I spent long hours in my room with my thoughts.

It was not without some relief therefore when the doorbell sounded that Tuesday morning. I very nearly tripped over my feet, in my haste to answer the door.

'On my way,' I declared, seizing a half-empty bottle and a pair of whisky tumblers, as I passed the drinks cabinet. A dark shadow filled the doorway.

'Good day, Dr. Watson.'

'Miss Cresswell,' I stammered.

'You were expecting Mr. Holmes?'

'I confess I was,' I managed. She cut an imposing figure, leaning on her yellow umbrella, her piercing green eyes fixing me like a sorceress. 'Well, may I come in?'

'I'm not sure that would be appropriate,' I cowed. 'After all, we are working on the same case. There are sensitivities...'

'Oh, don't be such a ghoul,' she scoffed, taking a step forward. 'Our interests coincide exactly.'

She glanced at the tumblers in my hand. 'You were about to have a drink,' she noted. 'Anaxagoras is in one of his funks again, no doubt. Well, no one likes to drink alone.' Wearily I pulled open the door. She marched into the porch, deposited her umbrella in the stand, and handed me her coat. Glancing about the place, she pulled off her gloves a finger at a time and handed these to me too.

One sometimes hears stories of how enemy agents succeed in infiltrating our nation's institutions. Through a potent mix of charm, flattery, cunning and invariably strong liquor, they succeed in winning the confidence of those possessed of our most valuable secrets. Time and again, those who consider themselves the safest pair of hands, the most sober of mind, fall most disastrously into their clutches. Such a parallel was not so inappropriate to the situation in which I found myself in that day. Wary of revealing any of our progress in the case, I advised Miss Cresswell in the strongest terms that I could say nothing of the matter of the poisoned regiment.

She agreed readily to this arrangement, promising not to speak of it until Holmes himself returned. In the intervening time, she regaled me with stories of her exploits in Switzerland, her second career as an ornithologist, and third career as an interpreter of musical hall songs. From the voluminous carpet bag she carried with her, she produced the ukulele I had first glimpsed at the riverbank and delivered accomplished renditions of my favourite musical numbers.

I began to lose my inhibitions. After all, what objection could Holmes possibly have to such innocent badinage? Indeed, it was possible that I might learn something from her if she lowered her own guard. After a glass or two, I convinced myself that Holmes would even applaud such a move.

Astonishingly, her interests *did* seem to coincide with mine, from the science fiction of H.G. Wells, to the plays of George Bernard Shaw and the basest form of music hall. Throughout this diverting evening, we continued to fill our glasses until the point when I began to lose my grip on events, to speak nothing of my resolve. Naturally, flattery formed the central plank of her strategy. She commended not only my medical and literary endeavours, but also my burgeoning abilities as an amateur detective, pointing to my modest successes in 'The Adventure of the Norwood Builder.' Despite my protests to the contrary, I could not help but enjoy her attentions.

Such were my thoughts the next day as we sped toward the shadowy hills of the Peak District. Miss Cresswell sat back behind the wheel of the Marquess' motorcar as if she drove such a thing every day, and appeared to be enjoying herself exceedingly well. Anaxagoras could not be persuaded to join us, so the two of us found ourselves alone.

She sang at the top of her lungs, slapping the wheel in time and suffering it seemed, not the slightest ill effects from our evening's excesses. As for myself, I was nursing my cranium, attempting to prevent my brain from expanding beyond the threshold of my skull; that is to say, mitigating the after-effects of the single malt.

'I cannot help but feel,' I muttered, 'that Holmes would not approve of this recklessness. Do you not perhaps think we are being a little hasty?'

'Nonsense!' she laughed, swinging the motorcar around a corner. 'Besides, there is no time to lose. This is simply a splendid example of your initiative. It's not as if you haven't dabbled in a little private detective work of your own. What of 'The Hound of the Baskervilles' or 'The Adventure of the Lady Cyclist?'

'The Solitary Cyclist,' I corrected.

'Yes, of course.'

'Well, that was an appalling fiasco,' I added. 'I say, do you mind if we stop for a moment?'

Once I had recovered my wits, I clambered back aboard the infernal machine, dabbing my lips with my handkerchief.

'Tell me,' I said, taking my seat, 'where did you learn to handle a motorcar?'

'Switzerland,' she declared. 'They're mad about them over there. Surprising, given that the place is stuffed full of mountains and riddled with lakes. Not the most obvious spot for a run in the motor.'

As we ventured further into the countryside, I found my senses momentarily befuddled by the vivid colours and intoxicating scents of the turning season. As we rounded yet another corner, narrowly missing a dry-stone wall, we found ourselves in something of a rural idyll. Trees bowed to meet us, their autumn finery draped from their boughs; vacant-looking sheep paused mid-mouthful to register the clank and growl of our engine. We coasted down narrow streets through remote working towns, their dark Satanic mills casting shadows across the road. Faces of strangers flashed past, many with the haunted look of the enslaved, quite different to the benign, open faces of the country folk we saw resting at the edges of fields. I found myself in reflective mood. Were we really so happy in our great cities? Does the human soul only find its true peace when refreshed by fields and trees? And yet, and yet...'

'Dr. Watson,' I heard Miss Cresswell call, 'the map!'

'What?' I spluttered. She reached down and threw a mass of folded paper into my lap.

133

'Find me Matlock Bath,' she commanded, 'then tell me how to get there.'

With a little concentration and some assistance from a long-haired gentleman tramp we found asleep in the road, we put ourselves on the correct path. Soon the road began to incline and presently we were surrounded by cliff faces that rose incongruously around us.

'Much like Switzerland,' remarked Miss Cresswell, gazing at the alpine scene that had emerged about us. 'Just think of the winter tobogganing! Bring me hills and snow, Doctor, and you find yourself in the company of a happy woman.'

'The road!' I cried, reaching for the wheel as she let her attention wander. She emitted out a kind of wild laughter as she corrected her course. It reminded me of Holmes. She was cut from the same cloth: independent of mind and utterly disconnected from convention. We passed a sign and at once found ourselves motoring sedately through a street of fine, three-storey houses, shops and hotels. A large painted mural advertised the Fish Pond Hotel and stables. As the road grew busier, we found we had to take great care to navigate safely between the four-wheelers and horses, not to speak of the cyclists and pedestrians.

'We are like visitors from the future,' Miss Cresswell confided. 'Just look at how they stare. In twenty years you will not see a single horse in the street.'

'Impossible!' I laughed. The town had the same curious feel of a seaside resort; a sort of mini Scarborough without the sea. The bandstands, tea parlours, novelty shops and street entertainers were all in place, albeit with a little end-of-season atmosphere about them.

'Let us find some rooms, Doctor,' my companion suggested. 'We can then begin our investigations.'

We drew up outside the Fish Pond Hotel: a long, white-fronted building advertising luncheons, teas and Bass on draft. 'Good Lord,' I remarked, as I manhandled the luggage from the motorcar. 'Look over there. It's the gentleman tramp we met on the way.'

'So it is,' agreed Miss Cresswell, 'but if you don't mind, I'm gasping for a raspberry infusion.' She disappeared into the lobby. The tramp was loafing against the wall, his swarthy face upturned to the autumn sun.

'You made good time,' I informed him. He turned and cracked a grisly smile, exposing his green teeth.

'Got lucky with a lift on the back of a beer wagon,' he confided, then broke into a hiss of giggles. 'What they didn't know was that I was helping myself all the way. Drank 'alf a barrel!'

'Now, look here,' I said, fishing in my pocket for a crown, 'you're robbing the barber. You've got hair as long as Moses. It's not hygienic, man. Why not get yourself a trim and shave? You'll feel all the better for it.' His fingers closed covetously over the shilling.

'I thank you for your advice,' he deliberated, 'and I fear I shall ignore it in favour of a glass of beer.'

'As you wish,' I muttered, then followed Miss Cresswell inside.

'Yes,' I heard her announce to the manager, 'Dr. and Mrs. Watson.'

'I say!' I remarked.

'Yes, dear?' she asked, turning to me and blinking her soft, bovine eyes. The lashes opened and closed like Venus flytraps. I coughed, momentarily flummoxed by her advances.

'Just to say, that's all the luggage.'

'Very good, dear,' she returned. 'Now our luck is in. They've found us a room with a four-poster.' I felt blood rush to my cheeks.

'Splendid,' I managed.

We followed the porter in near silence up the musty stairwell. He was a bored-looking man in his late thirties, with a long face, and terrifically small ears, his hair parted neatly down the middle. With a ponderous gait, he showed us to what I can only describe as the honeymoon suite, sliding open desk drawers and pulling out wardrobe doors as if we had never encountered such furniture before. It was only when I caught Miss Cresswell's eye that I realised this elaborate performance was designed to elicit a tip.

'Ah,' I said, fishing into my dwindling supply of loose change and handing him a modest reward, 'most kind.' He was turning to leave when my companion raised a finger.

'One moment, please,' put in Miss Cresswell.

'Yes, madam?'

'You know how to handle a shotgun, don't you?'

'Whatever gave you that idea?'

'Just an answer will suffice,' she returned smartly.

135

'Well, yes,' he replied. 'I have a second job on the Chatsworth Estate flushing out game from the woods.'

'And how are the two spaniels?'

'I beg your pardon, madam?' he started.

'You do own two English Springer Spaniels, one with brown forelegs, the other predominantly white?'

'Well, yes, as a matter of fact, I do.'

'And the one with the injured back leg,' she continued. 'A little better?'

'Yes, thank you, Mrs. Watson,' he responded, looking utterly bewildered, 'he is. But how could you possibly know? My home is ten miles off and you are strangers in these parts.'

It was a scenario I had watched play out a thousand times: the observation, the deduction swiftly followed by the gaze of astonishment; yet the vital difference was that Sherlock Holmes was conspicuous by his absence.

'Deliciously simple,' she cried. 'As you bade farewell to your two beloved pets this morning, they left strands of hair on each trouser leg; the left one brown, the right one white. This is clearly a daily ritual, and the tiny indentations of their claw marks have damaged the fabric of the trousers. You will note that the impressions on the right leg are lower down, suggesting a weakness in the legs.'

'But what of the shotgun,' I asked.

'Spaniels are gundogs, dear!' she chastised. 'You really have spent too long in the city.' She turned to the porter.

'That will be all now, thank you.'

He closed the doors ceremoniously behind him with what I can only describe as a knowing look.

'Good gracious, Doctor,' said Miss Cresswell swinging her legs up onto the bed, 'we find ourselves alone at last.'

'So we do,' I nodded, determined not to let her get the better of me. I sat down at the bureau and selected a piece of foolscap from the drawer.

'Whatever are you doing?' she enquired, sitting up.

'I'm writing to Holmes,' I informed her brusquely, scratching the address of Stapenhill Hall at the top of the page.

'To what possible end?'

'To inform him of my whereabouts, naturally,' I explained, dipping my nib into the pot of ink. 'In my haste, I left no message.' My companion let out a shriek of laughter that seemed to combine delight and derision in equal measure.

'Doctor, you seem to forget this is Sherlock Holmes. I do not think for one moment he needs a note from anyone to determine our whereabouts. He read the same note I did and no doubt divined exactly the same information. It would not surprise me if he were sitting downstairs, at this moment taking tea and perusing *The Times*.'

'I very much doubt that,' I countered. 'We read the note together and I can assure you, he betrayed no clue that he understood its contents.' It was at this juncture that I heard some commotion below us. I ventured to the window and pulled back the curtain.

'It's that devil of a tramp,' I muttered. 'What's he up to now?' The tramp was engaged in a violent tussle with a much larger man who was wielding a knife and carried a hessian sack in his other hand. He was using the stick from the knapsack to parry the blows in something of a haphazard, but otherwise seemingly effective, manner. A crowd had gathered and was standing well back from the pair as they squared up to each other.

'Will you excuse me,' I said. 'I believe my medical knowledge will be imminently required.'

I arrived outside at a critical juncture. The larger man was making wild swipes at the tramp, slashing the front of his dark waistcoat, a shower of tin buttons raining to the ground. Yet, the vagrant seemed unperturbed. With a deft turn and twist of his arm, he succeeded in landing his stick across the wrist of the larger man, sending his knife clattering into the gutter. With a shout of rage, the beast threw himself onto the tramp, who again displayed remarkable agility, side-stepping the man's enormous bulk, sending him plummeting to the ground. Kicking away the man's knife, he then sat upon his back and beckoned for others to do the same. Now, assured of their safety, the public came to his aid, happily adding their weight to the tramp's own, while the aggressor issued a torrent of expletives. Finally, there was the unmistakable sign of a custodian helmet bobbing up and down behind the heads of the assembled crowd.

'Make way there,' we heard a deep voice call, 'coming through.'

Clearly anxious not to attract official attention, the tramp took this opportunity to excuse himself, tipping his ancient top hat at the crowd, revealing his long shanks of hair, before flashing his gruesome smile and hopping away down the road.

'You there,' I called. 'Are you hurt?'

'Not in slightest,' he answered, before adding this cryptic parting shot: 'Beware the darkness within.'

Miss Cresswell set off up the steep incline, tapping the road ahead with her folded, yellow umbrella. Suffering with my old Maiwand wound, I lagged a little way behind, taking every possible opportunity to retie a shoelace, take in the view or otherwise malinger so as to catch my breath.

'I say, Doctor,' my companion cried, pointing up at the sky, 'a buzzard. Is there a more majestic sight?'

'A public house?' I suggested. For a moment we watched the bird of prey, circling above the rocky crags, its handsome, auburn plumage just visible against the bright sky.

'They are one of nature's supreme creations,' she said, resuming her relentless stride. 'They have such beauty, such grace, and yet in an instant they transform into a killing machine.'

'A terrifying combination,' I agreed.

'There is something of the hawk about Sherlock Holmes, would you not agree?'

'In appearance or manner?' I queried.

'Both, I would suggest,' she returned. 'He seems to operate with the same ruthless efficiency, and yet not without a certain grace.'

'I would describe him as a thinking-machine rather than one designed to kill.'

'Quite,' she replied. 'What is it about him? Why have you thrown in your lot with him so completely?'

'It is perfectly simple,' I returned. 'He is my friend. Now, how much further to the top?'

A little further on, we agreed to stop for a short rest. Miss Cresswell reached into her coat and withdrew a small paper bag. From this she pulled four sticks of celery.

'Good for the teeth, good for the brain,' she explained crunching into one.

'Good for the rabbits,' I added, declining her offer, instead taking a nip from my flask.

138

'You know Sherlock Holmes better than anyone alive,' she began, chewing enthusiastically. 'Are his powers really so remarkable? Surely you employ a certain licence in your written accounts?' I lay down on the grass, my elbows planted in the soft ground.

'Miss Cresswell,' I instructed, 'I have committed a mere fraction of our adventures to the page. If I were to share the case notes of our most remarkable investigations, the public would reject them as an outrageous fiction. Believe me, his powers are twice what they appear.'

'It is bad form to tease a woman, Doctor,' she parried, selecting a second stick. 'You cannot make such a claim without evidence.'

'Well,' I muttered, gazing up at the clouds, 'where could I begin? The singular case of 'The Clairvoyant Bookbinder'; 'The Genie of Islington'; or perhaps the baffling affair of 'The Haunted Organ'?'

'Dr. Watson,' she laughed, 'you are toying with me?'

'I assure you, madam, I am not,' I replied, 'but you will see my difficultly. Such cases stretch the credulity of the most broadminded reader.'

'A fascinating insight,' she reflected, gazing at me in a slightly unnerving way. 'Are you sure I cannot tempt you with a stick?'

'Perfectly. Now a question for you,' I added, 'if I may.'

'By all means,' she grinned.

'Are we climbing for a specific purpose, or are you hoping to stumble upon something pertaining to our case?'

'Oh, I have something quite specific in mind,' she explained.

'That comes as a relief,' I remarked. 'Would you be so good as to let me in on the secret?' She delved into her pocket and retrieved the cryptic note found in the cooper's hand.

Enmerkar, Left for you at Etemenanki Victoria '44 at 44. Gilgamesh.

'Are you familiar with the Tower of Babel, Doctor?'

'Mais, bien sur,' I joked.

'Perhaps you are less familiar with Etemenanki, the fabled ziggurat that is said to have inspired the myth?'

'You have me there,' I confessed. 'But isn't that the word in the note? You didn't mention you understood its meaning.'

'You didn't ask,' she parried. 'A profitable ten minutes in the library provided me with the answer.'

We rounded the corner and were met with the impressive sight of the Victoria Prospect Tower. I cannot say that I had heard of it before this date, nor that it had any particular charms to recommend it. Spoiled as we were in the greatest city on Earth, in London one only has to raise one's head to observe some new architectural glory. In contrast, this was a remarkably plain, round tower, which, save for its bottle-top lid, was untroubled by decoration of any kind. Its single advantage was its location atop the cliff, with remarkable views of Matlock below and the wide vista of fields and trees that covered the hills.

'It reminds me,' remarked Miss Cresswell, 'of those melancholy Norman towers one sometimes sees in Norfolk, where the rest of the church has fallen away.' I peered down into the valley.

'I believe this was only ever a tower.'

'Quite, Doctor,' she attested. 'My information is that this was a charity project to keep men in gainful employment after the lead mines closed.'

'And you believe a solution to this baffling affair lies inside?'

'I do,' she confirmed, peering at the construction with unwarranted excitement.

'I follow your logic to arrive at Victoria Tower, but what of this business of the double '44'?'

'Look there,' she said, and advancing on the tower, pointed halfway up its length. I squinted and could just discern a date: 1844.

'Well, that accounts for one of them,' I agreed. 'But what of the other?'

'All in good time, Doctor,' she assured me. 'I find that a solution often presents itself, if only one keeps one's eyes open. Shall we ascend?'

The staircase was not for the faint-hearted: a steeply spiralling sweep of pale stone. I climbed first, with one hand flat against the cold stone, the other steadying me.

'They clearly had smaller feet in 1844,' I remarked, as I laboured towards the top. The lack of a central column was particularly disconcerting. However, while I fought to control the onset of vertigo, Miss Cresswell seemed entirely unperturbed, instead humming some jovial melody to herself. As we reached what I supposed to be the three-quarter-way point, she suddenly called out.

'Stop there, Doctor!' I froze.

'Forty-four,' she called in delighted.

'What of it?'

'You are standing on step number forty-four.' I glanced down at my feet.

'What do you see?' she asked.

'Nothing at all,' I confessed.

'Have you tried lifting your foot?' I took a step back and peered at the stone.

'Only some graffiti, and illiterate at that.'

'Let me see,' Miss Cresswell said, moving forwards.

'I'm not sure you should.'

'Really, Doctor, don't be so priggish. I am a woman of the world.' I sighed and made room for her.

'Remarkable!' she exclaimed.

'You think so?'

The letters hidden beneath my foot read: 'SHT'. She knelt to get a closer look, and in so doing misjudged her balance and slipped backwards. Without thinking, I seized her jacket with both hands and the two us tumbled together down two or three steps, a descent into the abyss only averted by her yellow umbrella wedging itself between the stairs and the wall. For a moment we lay there, face to face, breathing heavily.

'Splendid reflexes, Doctor,' she remarked coolly, getting to her feet and smoothing her jacket. 'Now, shall we return to work?'

'Certainly,' I said, but could not disguise my racing pulse and flushed cheeks.

'Can you see how the 'T' is so much thicker than the other two characters? It is also oddly formed, with a heavy crossbar and thick ligature at the bottom. The other two letters are comparatively lightly formed.'

'Forgive me,' I said, still struggling to regain my composure, 'I cannot very well see the benefit of analysing the script of some ignorant vandal. Shall we continue?' We ascended the remaining stairs until we finally broke out into the sunlight.

'The summit!' I declared, heaving myself up the final step. 'Perhaps the fresh air will allow us to think more clearly.' The view was stupendous, the ancient landscape unfolding into the distance. 'I cannot help but feel,' I added, 'that the solution to this mystery lies far from here.' However, Miss Cresswell did not appear to be listening. Her eyes were glazed over in that stupor of concentration I had seen overtake my friend, Sherlock Holmes, on so many occasions.

Returned to earth, we sat with our legs overhanging the edge of the granite cliff, peering down at the Derwent valley below. Miss Cresswell produced some more celery. Concealing a grimace, I reluctantly accepted a stick. While engaging with it in a desultory fashion, I watched a sheep meander like an idle thought from one end of a field to the other.

'Would you ever abandon London?' I enquired.

'For good? Never. The hills and mountains are all very well, but frankly I would be bored to death.'

'Holmes once remarked that there is as much mischief in the country as there is in the city. Or words to that effect.'

'Is that so?' she smirked. 'Well, personally, I doubt it.'

'You really are very much alike,' I put in. 'Except for the umbrella, and perhaps the ukulele.'

'Kingfisher!' she suddenly cried. Whipping out her binoculars, she followed a blur of blue and green sweep across the sky. 'In my book,' she said, 'that's a good omen.' While I busied myself with the indigestible vegetable, I saw her scratching white letters with a jagged stone onto a large slab of granite.

'Oh, really,' I scolded. 'That's not graffiti is it?'

'You really are a prig,' she laughed. 'I'm thinking about the letters on the step.'

'Oh, yes?'

'Suppose,' she mused, tapping her stone against the rock, 'that one of them isn't a letter?'

'Go on,' I said.

'Suppose the 'T' signifies something else entirely.'

'Such as?

'A hammer.'

'You don't say.' She began drawing something else; larger and more intricate in its design – an upturned 'T,' with an interlacing pattern in the interior.

'It has been nagging at me; as if I had seen it somewhere before.' Finally, she laid down her stone.

'Mjolnir,' she sneezed.

'Bless you,' I muttered.

'No,' she laughed. 'That is its name, Mjolnir. It is the hammer of a god: Thor's hammer.'

I peered at the strange design.

'Extraordinary,' I concluded. 'Perhaps you have something there. But that still doesn't explain the 'SH'.' She stared at me in the most unnerving way.

'Whatever's the matter?' I asked in alarm. 'Why are you looking at me like that?' She glanced again at the letters and then back at me.

'No,' I said slowly, 'that's impossible!' She formed a tight-lipped smile and nodded. 'Sherlock Holmes!' I cried.

'But what does it all amount to? It is as if we have solved one puzzle to be immediately presented with another.

'Then let us apply a little more science,' she proposed. 'The hammer was scratched with a flint possessed of an exceedingly fine edge. The letters 'SH' were autographed using a different stone with a rounded end. What does this tell us?'

'That they are the work of two different people?'

'Precisely, Doctor,' she exclaimed, tapping the stone again emphatically. 'It is my belief that until a few hours ago, all that was to be found on that step was the depiction of a hammer. The stone with the rounded edge was two steps below it. In fact, that is what caused me to slip. The tower is a popular attraction; another visitor would have disturbed it if it had been left longer. This suggests only one thing.'

'Go on,' I pressed.

'Your friend, Mr. Holmes, has beaten us to it. With these letters he is telling us he is on the same trail. He may very well have just left us a friendly greeting.' I examined the letters more closely, now recognising the shape of the characters. I had spent more than a decade in the company of that inimitable script and yet I failed to recognise it.

'So, where is he now?'

'I can only assume he has made the same deduction as me.'

'Which is?'

'He has gone to Thor's Cave.'

A low mist hung like a dispirited cloud over the undulating hills. It gave the landscape an eerie, uncanny feeling, as if it were the setting for a Grimm's fairy tale. It was through this vista that Gertrude Cresswell and I motored along the long, lonely road. Dry stone walls snaked upward and I thought of the countless hours that had been spent in their construction. The monotony of the country life filled me a mild sense of horror. What must fill the rural mind while enduring the endless days, unremitting weather and interminable seasons?'

143

'Still, I began, 'you have not revealed how you made the link between the small image of the hammer to Thor's Cave?'

***

'"Ward Lock & Co's. Guide Book to Buxton, Leek and Surrounding Areas with pull out map',' she announced, a pair of amber-tinted snow goggles secured around her head. 'I happened to be reading it last night and found a little section on Thor's Cave. What, I thought, was a Norse god doing wandering around the outskirts of Stoke-on-Trent?'

'A perfectly reasonable question,' I agreed.

Miss Cresswell swerved around a sheep that had wandered into the road. 'The even-toed ungulate,' she declared. 'A menace of the public highway.'

'What do you believe we will find?' I asked, giving the beast a disapproving stare.

'Perhaps that should be who, rather than what,' she replied.

'That didn't occur to me. Do you really suppose that someone is using it as a hiding place? It is a tourist attraction, after all. I can think of better places to disappear.'

We drove deeper into the Peaks, the hills rising and falling around us. The trees were beginning to show their autumnal colours, decaying into copper and gold.

'What else did you learn about the cave from your guide book?' I asked. 'Any ghosts?'

'We know that people lived there as much as ten thousand years ago and it was still considered somewhat bijou until the Saxons. They've found axe heads and the Saber-toothed tiger teeth there.'

We abandoned our car at the foot of a steep hill, thickly carpeted in moss and grass. Miss Cresswell yanked a lever, presumably to apply a brake of some description, and in so doing, produced a sound normally associated with the wringing of a cat's neck.

'I think this is as far as we go on four wheels, Doctor,' declared Miss Cresswell. 'I sincerely hope you have sound footwear.' She glanced at my feet. 'I dare say my shoes are better suited,' I confessed, 'to the cobbles of Baker Street than the slopes of the Peak District, but they will have to do.'

'You can tell a man's character,' she opined somewhat disconcertingly, 'by his choice of shoes.'

Miss Cresswell struck out ahead, climbing steadily, planting the end of her umbrella in the grass at intervals, swinging her bag forward to gain some additional momentum. I slipped and struggled behind her, while the sheep observed my efforts with the scorn an expert mountaineer might reserve for the stumbling of an amateur. With the exception of our woolly-backed observers, we appeared to be quite alone on the hill. I turned and surveyed the valley. Again, not a soul could be seen among the reds, browns and greens of the vegetation below.

'Well, well,' she said, pointing with the end of her umbrella to something on the ground, 'take a look at this doctor.'

I joined her and examined the discovery.

'Footprints,' I stated somewhat nonplussed. 'Hardly unusual if I may say so.'

'You may,' she agreed. 'But less common is to find the footprints of a three-legged man.'

We ventured further up the path, finally entering the gaping mouth of the cave. I felt a cold chill as we were enveloped in shadow and my eyes struggled to adjust to the gloom. Inside, the floor sloped steeply upwards and to the left, slippery and printed with great swathes of lichen. The roof, meanwhile, arched high above us, like the vault of some roughly hewn cathedral. The walls were warped and gnarled, worn away by millennia of erosion. It was possessed of a silent menace, the drip of water only serving to amplify the silence. It was no great leap of the imagination to picture our ancient forefathers cowering in the darkness while beasts roamed the plains below, only the flicker of their fire warding them away. Miss Cresswell stepped forward, testing each foothold first, scrutinising the grooves and markings on the walls, poking the end of her brolly into the crevasses.

'Aha,' she exclaimed, 'I believe I may have just found the earliest owner of this delightful homestead.'

'Oh, yes?' She pointed to a series of concentric circles standing proud in the rock wall.

'A goniatite,' she declared. 'I would put this fellow at two hundred million years old.'

'Overdue his pension then,' I put in. 'Now, what is it we are looking for?'

'You may very well ask,' said Sherlock Holmes. I leapt a clear foot into the air as I heard the familiar voice at my shoulder. 'I apologise for breaking in on your excursion.' I spun to face my old friend, only to be greeted by the shambolic figure of the tramp who had dogged us these last two days.

'Well,' said Miss Cresswell, a slight smile forming at the corners of her mouth, 'you have finally decided to show your hand.'

'It was you!' I cried.

'Naturally it was me, Watson. How many vagabonds do you know who are skilled in the art of Bartitsu?' I shook my head, marvelling at the audacity of the man.

'I admit it was an enjoyable ruse,' Holmes confessed, peering down at a mark on the cave floor, 'but I felt that my assistance was required.'

'By the way,' stated Miss Cresswell, 'we received the note you left on the stairs.'

'Yes, I thought you would,' he said, somewhat distracted and pulling his glass from his pocket. 'They really ought to put a handrail in that tower – those steps are awfully steep.'

'I believe,' she went on, tapping the stone floor with the end of her umbrella, 'that we would have found the cave perfectly well without your assistance.'

'No doubt,' he said, crouching down, 'but as it was, you had the benefit of Watson's inestimable help.' I detected a trace of irony in his voice. 'One likes to think one can trust a friend with a confidence.' At this, I remembered the interrogation that had led me to divulge Holmes' deductions to Miss Cresswell.'

We stumbled up a hill, catching our boots on the rocks that protruded through the long grass. I heard a gun crack and a rock not ten paces in front of me exploded in a cloud of dust. My heart thumped in my ears. Pursued again? Already the recipient of one bullet, I was none too keen to host another. I consoled myself with the knowledge that if you hear a gunshot then it has already missed you. Nonetheless, I flung myself forward, clutching my hat to my head, while Miss Cresswell and Holmes took similar evasive action. Glancing back, I saw that we had at least succeeded in putting some distance between us and our pursuers, and that the accuracy of the marksmanship was the result of luck rather than proximity. We scaled a hillock as a second and third gunshot punctured the air and, for a moment, believed ourselves to be unseen. This was small comfort. A great plain stretched out before us, offering scant cover from the fiends. Surely we would be picked off like rabbits if we ventured forward; and yet there seemed little option. 'Down there,' Holmes commanded, pointing with his stick. 'A bolthole.'

Purely by chance it seemed, Holmes had alighted upon a natural opening in the rock. The entrance was small and dark, studded with loose stones. A little light spilled into the opening and showed a slope, rather than a sudden drop. One by one we scrambled in: Holmes first, followed by Miss Cresswell and finally myself just as I glimpsed a flat cap and the barrel of a shotgun emerge at the brow of the hill. My friend struck a match to reveal a narrow corridor of smooth, wet stone that widened as it deepened.

'Cover the entrance,' Holmes hissed. I reached up and pulled great armfuls of grass and bracken over the opening, then pushed up some larger stones to further conceal our hideaway. Observing my work, and apparently satisfied, Holmes placed a finger to his lips, flicked his wrist and the light went out. We cowered, staring into the dark, breathing in the dank, loamy air. Dimly we perceived footsteps, muffled shouts and, more disconcertingly, two rifle shots, then nothing.

We remained in our cramped positions for some ten minutes. I then detected Holmes at my shoulder, having crept silently up to me. It struck me that with his lanky frame, the confinement was of greater discomfort to him.

'I will hazard a look, Watson,' he whispered. 'Be ready with your service revolver should I have miscalculated.' With the stealth of a vole, he slithered back up the tunnel and removed no more than three small stones to provide himself with an eyehole. He peered for a few seconds, adjusting his position twice, replaced the stones, and then returned to us. Another flame stole the darkness from my friend's gaunt, stoic features.

'We find ourselves,' he began, glancing between us, 'in a grave situation – if not indeed, a grave.' He paused for us to register his witticism. 'I believe this to be the entrance to a burial chamber, quite possibly Saxon.'

'Spare us the archaeology lesson, Mr. Holmes,' sighed Miss Cresswell. 'Have our pursuers moved on?'

'On the contrary,' returned Holmes, 'they have positioned sentries around our position and are raking the ground with sticks. My reputation notwithstanding, they know that even Sherlock Holmes cannot vanish into the ether.'

We listened intently. There was a steady drip of rain soaking through the chalk, the gusting breeze over the entrance, like breath across the mouthpiece of a flute, but then something else too: a faint rattling sound. I pulled my ulster tightly around my shoulders, beginning to feel the cave's chill seeping into my bones.

'Merciful heavens, Holmes,' I whispered, 'I believe you've led us directly into a viper's nest.'

My friend allowed himself a thin laugh. 'As a medical doctor,' he returned, 'you are in the first tier. As a naturalist, I am sorry to say, you are at the back of the class. I believe the sound you can hear is the chattering of Miss Cresswell's teeth.'

'You're not wrong, Mr. Holmes,' she confessed, hugging her arms. 'I feel like a side of cold beef in the larder. How much longer do you believe we shall have to remain here?'

'At least until nightfall,' he replied, inspecting his pocket watch at close quarters. 'Some four hours away by my reckoning.'

'Couldn't we make a dash for it?' I put in. I had still not entirely banished the thought of snakes from my mind.

'Madness, Watson,' he scolded. 'With your old injury we would be easy prey. Not even a sporting chance. No, we must hold our nerve.'

Despite our eyes growing accustomed to the gloom, we were little more than dark shadows to each other. Suddenly Holmes raised a hand and we froze. We heard the rough-hewn voice of a local man, almost directly above us.

'There were three of them all right,' he grunted. 'A tall, lanky one, thin as a whistle and spry as a weasel. Small wonder he managed to get away. Then there was a shorter, stouter fellow with a limp too. Then a women, a strange old bird by what I saw of her. One of those suffragettes, I'd say. Too much to say for themselves in my view. A woman with ideas of her own is a dangerous creature. They need to stay put in the kitchen where they belong. Or the bedroom…' He chuckled, a wheezing cackle, which turned presently into a crunching cough, his chest echoing to his hacking pipes as he laboured for breath. I heard the first signs of emphysema. Once he had recovered sufficiently, he pressed his companion further: 'What do you think they're doing here, then?'

'Meddlers,' he muttered.

'Could just be tourists?'

'Impossible,' the second man said sharply. 'Why would they run? Besides, they've seen something. I overheard them talking about the three footprints.' The other fellow emitted a dry chuckle.

'And I wonder what they made of those. The devil himself didn't walk on three legs. They don't know what they're dealing with.' In the faint, grey light at the mouth of the cave, we saw the end of a shotgun nosing through, only a few feet away.'

'This ground is riddled with warrens,' the first man warned. 'Watch your step or your ankle will snap like a wishbone.'

'Confound it!' cried the other. 'Where the devil are they? He'll keep us out all night if they don't show.'

'They've gone to ground,' the first scowled. 'We'll smoke them out like rabbits if we have to.' Their voices grew indistinct again. I sensed a deep unease from Holmes.

'What is it?' I asked.

'Smoke,' he returned obliquely, with a forlorn note in his voice. 'I fear I shall not be permitted a pipe for some hours. This could be a trying evening, Watson.'

'Then, let us occupy our minds with the problem,' I began brightly. 'The three-legged man. Surely we have enough brainpower between us to unravel this simple conundrum. There are three possibilities,' I suggested.

'Go on, Watson,' encouraged Holmes. 'your reasoning always amuses, even if it does not elucidate.'

'Let him speak, Holmes,' scolded Miss Cresswell. My friend raised his brows at this reproach.

'Number one,' I continued, ignoring my friend's barbed remark. 'It is a three-legged man. This is a notion I have already discounted on the grounds of biological improbability.'

'I defer to your medical knowledge,' Holmes parried. 'Yet I speak only for myself when I say never rule out a theory until it collides with compelling proof to the contrary.' Once again, Cresswell gave him a disparaging look.

'Number two,' I persisted. 'There is a one-legged man assisted by a man possessed of both his legs.' Holmes pressed his fingertips together and nodded, as if granting permission for me to continue. I cleared my throat. 'Number three. It is a two-legged man being assisted by a one-legged man.'

'On the face of it,' Holmes pronounced, 'all of your theories are perfectly plausible. As is the possibility that it is three one-legged men supporting each other.'

'I have a fifth solution,' posited Cresswell.

'Then, let us hear it,' permitted Holmes.

'It is a two-legged man with a walking stick, on the end of which, is an artificial foot.'

'A capital notion, Miss Cresswell.'

Holmes clapped his hands with delight. He glanced at us both, with that outrageous twinkle in his eyes.

'I do not hesitate to pronounce this a three-foot problem.' I rolled my eyes at Holmes' rather laboured witticism, yet Miss Cresswell seemed thoroughly taken with it.

'You are more personable in the flesh, Mr. Holmes,' she observed, 'than Dr. Watson's accounts might suggest.' My friend poo-pooed this with a dismissive wave of his hand.

'Now, these deliberations may help pass the time,' he offered, 'but they bring us no nearer to the solution. Nor do they suggest a way out of this mousetrap.' Holmes struck another match. 'Three left,' he noted. 'Watson, are you possessed of any fire?' I patted my pockets in a rather helpless fashion. 'I suspected not,' my friend concluded. 'I note you have not smoked in the last two days, influenced, no doubt, by Miss Creswell's philosophy that celery and beetroot are all that is required to sustain the human body.' Miss Cresswell harrumphed at this.

'I will not disparage your habits if you refrain from remarking upon mine.' As if reminded of her supply of raw vegetables, Miss Cresswell took a stick of celery from her bag and bit firmly onto the stem. She returned our bemused stares.

'What?' she demanded. 'It helps me think.'

'I shall explore the tunnel,' declared Holmes. 'I believe I am the leanest member of the party and therefore would have an advantage in this endeavour.' I frowned at this.

'But, surely, Holmes,' I reasoned, 'it would make better sense that I, the stoutest of us conducts the investigation, because I will need to fit through any opening we discover. Camels passing through the eye of a needle, and all that?' My friend winced and dropped his match. 'Watson,' he sighed, 'your rambling, though amiable and well-meaning, has cost us a match.' I could not help but feel however, that I had scored a point against my old associate. Holmes turned and, planting a hand on the roof of the tunnel, made his way slowly and methodically down the passageway, probing the cave like an outsized mole. Presently, his footsteps fell away.

'Well, Doctor,' Miss Cresswell said at last, 'we find ourselves alone once more.'

'So we do.'

'I confess,' Miss Cresswell said, probing the rock with the tip of her umbrella, 'it is something of a thrill to be embroiled in one of your adventures. If I close my eyes, I can almost see the words upon the page. No doubt Mr. Holmes has already foreseen the outcome of the day? Surely his theatrical foray down the tunnel is for appearances and my benefit only.' I smoothed my moustache, feeling the evening damp encroaching.

'I rather think not,' I concluded. 'There are times when even Holmes finds himself at a loss.' Distantly, we heard the report of a military rifle. 'A Martini-Henry,' I observed, dolefully. 'Our chaps used them all the time out in Maiwand. A serviceable weapon, but it was a fiend to use. The cartridge was forever jamming and you couldn't shift the breeze block.'

'Is that so?' Miss Cresswell asked, a wry look of amusement in her eyes. 'Once a soldier, always a soldier.'

'Never really a soldier,' I muttered. 'Not really a doctor either; not at heart at any rate.'

'Then, what?'

'That I'm still trying to fathom.'

'Then, a writer, surely?'

'Perhaps.'

'But a friend foremost,' she suggested, 'I would wager.' I suddenly felt all this a trifle too familiar.

They're just trying to scare us,' I assured her, taking a brusquer tone. 'They're a quarter of a mile off at least.'

'A very precise estimate,' she remarked. I shrugged.

'In Afghanistan one tended to get the measure of these things.'

'It must have been difficult out there.'

'Well, at times it felt like a great game. But it certainly became more trying when I became the owner of a bullet from someone else's gun.'

We heard footsteps along the passage.

'Holmes,' I breathed, somewhat relieved, 'is that you?'

'No,' my friend remarked from the gloom, 'it is the inspector on the Bayswater omnibus to London Bridge.'

'I see. Any light at the end of the tunnel, Inspector?'

'The tunnel takes a sharp left turn,' Holmes informed us, 'then narrows to nothing. A field mouse would have no better chance of escape than us. In the grey light his expression was uncharacteristically grim. 'I would be delighted,' he continued, 'to hear alternative proposals.' For once, I felt a clear sense of purpose and resolve. I cleared my throat.

'I propose that I give myself up and negotiate our safe passage.'

Holmes smiled and shook his head. 'As honourable as ever, my dear Watson. It warms the very chambers of my heart to know that there are still gentlemen such as you in the world. But these are rapscallions of the first order,' he said. 'They would think nothing of putting a bullet through your brain.' Miss Cresswell listened to all of this with some amusement.

'This is not the first time I have found myself in such a tricky spot. I have a suggestion.'

'Then, let us hear it,' invited Holmes.

Miss Cresswell barked. Not a command, word or exclamation familiar to users of the English language, but a feral, guttural, animal noise. It was a violent rasping sound, somewhere between a dog and a deer. She scanned our faces for signs of a reaction.

'I confess,' my friend smiled, 'that was unexpected.'

'Then, allow me to explain. I once spent a summer dedicating myself almost exclusively to the study and practice of animal impersonation. I have since found it invaluable when conducting clandestine work in the field. My proposal is to venture out at nightfall in the guise of a fox.'

'One moment!' I interjected.

'Yes?'

'What about those of us who did not spend their summers perfecting the art of animal impersonation?' Miss Cresswell failed to suppress a giggle.

'I am not expecting you to attempt this, Dr. Watson. I shall go out alone. I will fetch help and return with some officers of the law.'

'Never!' I declared. Without thinking, I shot to my feet and instantly cracked my head on the roof of the tunnel.

'Your chivalry is your undoing, Doctor,' she noted, as I crumpled to the ground, nursing my bruised cranium.

'Nonetheless,' I muttered, 'it is preposterous that you should be the one to risk your life.'

'Preposterous? I appear to the most qualified, why is that preposterous?'

'Because...'

'Yes?'

'Because you're a...'

'Yes?'

'About to lose an argument,' observed Holmes. 'Miss Cresswell's plan is not without its merits.'

'Well, it's remarkably dangerous, that is all,' I managed. 'For example, you may be able to sound like a fox, but even to the amateur naturalist, you do not look like one.'

'I am very glad to hear it, Doctor,' she said. 'However you are also unaware that the winter before last I immersed myself in three short but intensely learned monographs on the arts of stalking, scouting and stealth. Mr. Holmes will be all too aware of this tryptic of papers.'

'Quite so, Miss Cresswell,' he said approvingly. 'For I was their author!'

'My point exactly!' I protested. 'Why not allow Mr. Holmes to make the attempt. His track record in matters of improbable survival is second to none.' My friend joined his fingers, perhaps weighing up the compliment against the fact that I had volunteered him for this fool's errand.

'Allow me to stage a small demonstration,' said Miss Cresswell. 'Mr. Holmes, would you be so good as to strike one of your two remaining matches? Please then move five paces away.' We did as she instructed while she made some preparations, rearranging her dress and opening the umbrella a little and placing it by her head. 'Close your eyes. Now count to three and open them again.' Once more we indulged her, only to find that she had vanished entirely. I glanced at Holmes, who pushed past me and proceeded to the entrance. I quickly joined him.

'What can you see?' I asked.

'Nothing yet.' Presently, we heard the bark of a fox. Our eyes followed the sound and were met with a quite remarkable sight. For there, on the horizon, was the unmistakable form of a fox, its snout in the air, silhouetted against the thin, silver light of the fading day. In shadow, we saw the flash of its back as it darted into the bracken.

'Superb,' I murmured, 'simply superb!' Just then, a single shot ricocheted across the tundra, followed by the whinnying howl of pain.

'Great heavens, Holmes,' I cried.

'Hush, Watson,' my friend snapped, covering my mouth with his gloved hand.

'But Miss Cresswell...' I began.

'Surely, if she had been shot she would not have had the wherewithal to continue her impersonation.' I accepted this logic begrudgingly, then continued to peer into the darkness for any signs of our companion.

'I don't like it one bit, Holmes,' I said, finally retreating into the cave. 'Suppose she was shot?'

'Suppose,' my friend countered thoughtfully, 'she was working for the other side all along? Suppose she will lead them directly back here?'

'Then there is no time to lose?'

'Calm yourself, Watson,' my friend cautioned. 'We must trust in our new friend and accept whatever hand fate deals. Now, if you would be so good as to block up the entrance, and at the risk of asphyxiation, I am going to venture a smoke.'

Awake since the early hours, I felt the cold from the bare earth work its way into my joints. I glanced across at Holmes who appeared to be scribbling in the half light.

'You didn't sleep, Holmes?

'No. A sudden inspiration took me.'

'Oh, yes?' I asked, rubbing my shoulder, stiff and sore as ever.

'I conceived an idea for a monograph on eighteenth century tiepins. Extraordinary how often they appear as critical evidence in my work.'

Once more, I was astonished how Holmes was able to separate the workings of his mind from the discomfort of his body.

'You are not fatigued?'

'Brainwork, Watson, that is what invigorates me. Not the inanity of sleep. Besides, a fanciful dream about becoming a fox and being chased across the moors would be an unwelcome distraction to my thought process.'

'Upon my word, Holmes!' I started. 'But I did not breathe a word about my dream? Did I talk in my sleep?'

'An animal utterance and the characteristic twitching and cowering you exhibited as you lay there was enough to furnish me with the narrative.'

I shook my head, then began to breathe life back into my frozen fingers.

'I hope I'm not intruding, gentlemen.' Inspector Hubble's long, pale face appeared at the entrance to the tunnel. 'I received word that you would benefit from some assistance.'

'Too kind, Inspector,' said Holmes, returning his pencil and paper to his pocket, 'and not a moment too soon.' He edged past me and out into the dawn light. I followed my friend out, blinking as the sun's glare seemed to burn into my brain.

'It was an anonymous telegram,' Hubble continued, 'but when I saw your name and the singular location, I felt it was too outlandish not to be true.'

'Well, we're very glad you came, Inspector,' I said, stamping the ground and looking about me. A group of constables was standing in a convivial circle a few feet away, smoking and discussing the morning's business. One of them, I noted, was the constable who attended Miss Bilton on the railway line when we first arrived in Burton and whom we had found stricken in the public house. I was gratified to see that he had apparently made a recovery.

'Any sign of them?' I asked. 'We spotted four, colourful-looking characters when we arrived,' explained Hubble, 'all carrying rifles. But when they saw my men, they cleared off soon enough. They had too much of a march on us to give chase.' The inspector peered off into the middle distance and dipped absent-mindedly into his pocket. He retrieved what appeared to be a handful of magic beans. 'Liquorice comforts,' he explained, holding out his palm. Liquorice contained within a delicious shell of colourised sugar. I'm afraid I can't get enough of them.'

'I can't imagine your dentist approves,' I murmured.

'I thought you would like to know that we are closing in on Butterworth. We believe he is here in Burton. A landlady has provided some useful intelligence. Another tip-off led us to a house in Stapenhill. I think perhaps it's time that you closed down your more fanciful lines of enquiry and accepted that this business of the contaminated beer is simply a case of a disgruntled employee.'

TEN

The Angler

The morning brought with it a light breeze and the inescapable, rich scent of hops. We had returned to Burton to consider options and lick our wounds after the debacle at Thor's Cave. I could not conceive what advantage we had gained except for making new enemies and discovering a fraction more about the three-legged man. Still, there was a small consolation: Miss Cresswell had, mercifully, taken the motorcar, allowing Holmes and myself to have a more civilised journey by rail.

'What say you, Watson,' my friend put in, finishing his morning toast, wiping breadcrumbs from his lips and laying down his newspaper, 'to another helping of fresh air?' I peered at him quizzically.

'For my own part, I would be pleased never to see a blade of grass again.'

'Come now, Watson. It is you who more often pushes me through the front door. Let us escape from our funk and greet the day. I have perused the map and propose Newton Solney as our destination. It is little more than two miles off, affords splendid views of the surrounding area and, what's more, has at least two excellent public houses where we can restore our energies in readiness for the return journey.'

'Very well,' I capitulated. 'Lead on.'

My friend was in an expansive mood and possessed of remarkable energy. Days such as these were less common than they were at the beginning of our acquaintance.

As we marched, Holmes' coattails struggling to keep up, he expounded variously on the untapped potential of tidal power and the possibilities offered by the five-string violin, while offering his reflections on A.E.J. Collins' astonishing prowess with the cricket bat, having notched up 628 not out earlier in the summer. While maintaining this verbal *tour de force*, he busied himself studying the flora and fauna: the delicate purple and yellow flowers that sprang from gaps in the dry-stone walls. 'There is a theory, Watson,' he advised, 'not widely held by established Christian thinkers, that we were never cast out of the Garden of Eden. Look about you: See how the hills slip away into the mist in a hundred shades of green; imbibe the citrus notes from sweet-smelling grass, the languorous cows treading the fields; silver ribbons of water and the drowsy sun offering us its warmth and light. If this is what it feels to be banished, then it is a curious sort of punishment.'

Holmes and I stood with our hands flat upon the bar, awaiting the attentions of the landlord, a jowly fellow with a flannel of damp, grey hair spread across his brow.

'It is a fact, Watson,' my friend opined, 'that men do not wish to spend too much time in their own minds. The reason beer has remained ubiquitous across millennia is that it provides the genial distance between a man and his troubles, and between himself and reality. It permits a benign contemplation of the world in contrast to the effects of whisky or gin, which encourage introspection and melancholia. I myself have little taste for beer, not merely because it does not represent a poison of sufficient strength, but because I have no desire to disconnect from my mind. Indeed the opposite is true; I choose vices which lead me to the innermost chambers of my mind.'

In circumspect fashion, the landlord peered at my friend, then back at me.

'I take it from that,' he said, with a weary look, 'that it's just the one beer then?'

After disposing of two agreeable partridge pies washed down with a pint of claret, Holmes and I felt suitably fortified for our return to Burton. We had not long left the establishment when we encountered a middle-aged couple heading in the same direction. The woman wore a large bustle, and had a remarkable poise and formidable manner. The gentleman was a tall, unusually upright fellow with greying hair, a monocle and a hacking jacket. He glanced over at us and I returned a nod of acknowledgement. While I was certain we had not encountered him before, there was something in the strong jaw and intelligent brow that seemed not entirely unfamiliar. I remarked as much to Holmes, who explained he had made the same observation.

'What is more remarkable, Watson,' he added, as we let them walk a little way ahead of us, 'is that he is Mr. Samuel Houghton, brother of our friends, Michael and Anaxagoras. I suggest we take this opportunity to make his acquaintance.'

'I say,' called Holmes, 'the *lonicera periclymenum* is positively rampant in these parts.'

The woman turned her head sharply, then gave an approving smile.

'To say nothing of the *viola riviniana*,' she returned. 'The fields are simply teeming with it.' The fellow I noticed had furrowed his brow in exactly the same expression of bewilderment as my own. 'That's 'honeysuckle' and 'dog violet' to the layman, darling. How charming to have a botanist with us, wouldn't you agree?'

'Not just a botanist,' he growled, 'a consulting detective too, if this is who I believe it to be.'

'Quite so,' my friend granted. 'Sherlock Holmes at your service and this is my companion, the good Dr. Watson.' He reluctantly returned our handshakes.

'Now, is this a delightful coincidence,' asked Samuel with a note of cynicism in his voice, 'or do we find ourselves part of your enquiries? I have already provided a statement to Inspector Hubble. I have little interest in repeating myself.'

'I would not dream of asking you to,' Holmes replied. 'Naturally, I am curious about your view on the matter pertaining to the poisoning of the Queen's men in India, but, in actual fact, it is Watson who has a question for you.'

'I do?' I asked. Holmes flashed me a look.

'Watson is something of an angler, as I believe are you.'

'On what evidence?'

'There is a small nick above your left eye,' my friend explained, 'which I believe was caused by a lure striking the socket. I would put the wound at no less than a week old. I also noticed when I shook your hand that there was a pronounced stiffness in your right shoulder and elbow, a classic symptom of an overuse injury. Do you favour the thumb on top technique when fly casting? I rather fancy that you do.'

'Remarkable,' he murmured. 'Intrusive and entirely brazen, but remarkable none the less. Now what is your question, Doctor?'

'In the matter of bait, do the local trout favour mealworms or salmon eggs?

'Neither,' returned the fellow. 'The secret is marshmallow. They can't get enough of it.'

'Remarkable,' I returned.

'Perhaps, gentlemen,' his wife proposed, 'you would care to join us for tea and a slice of pistachio cake?'

'Why ever not,' Holmes smiled.

We passed a convivial hour with the couple, forcing in two large slices of the rich cake. Closely following the partridge pies, capacity became a serious issue. Yet for the sake of appearances, we enthusiastically devoured the baking.

'It is a sorry state of affairs,' declared Samuel, after we had dispensed with the pleasantries. He dabbed his lips and returned his fork to his plate. Michael grows the business ever larger, and naturally I receive a generous income from my shares, but I otherwise play no part. It gives me great sorrow to admit that Michael and I do not speak, and as for Anaxagoras…' He trailed off and his wife placed a hand on the back of his palm. I have done everything I can to help him, but he is set against any kind of reconciliation.'

'Allow me to speak plainly,' asked Holmes.

'I tolerate nothing less,' replied Samuel.

'Anaxagoras is convinced you are behind the poisoning of the regiment. He believes you wish to discredit your brother and assume control of the brewery.' Samuel leaned forward and lifted a small book from the table. I craned to read the title: *A Modern Treatise on Practical Coarse Fish Angling* by Henry Coxon.

'I have no more desire to run a brewery,' he declared, 'than to fly to the moon. Besides the happiness of my wife, fish are my chief preoccupations. Why would I jeopardise a reliable income that allows me to spend my days on the sun-dappled shores of the Trent?'

'Why indeed,' I broke in. 'Now, is it really true about the marshmallows?'

As we made to leave, Samuel shook Holmes' hand. 'If there are any answers,' he said solemnly. 'You will almost certainly find them at the family home. We must all live with our conscience.'

Like gentlemen of the road, my friend and I found a quiet bench by the muddy Trent and loafed back on our perch, luxuriating in the unexpected warmth of the afternoon sun. The return from Newton Solney had felt longer than the outward journey. We had trudged most of the day and relieving the weight from our feet was a delicious indulgence. As was his custom, Holmes busied himself in the preparation of a pipe, while I ransacked my pockets for a flask and matchbox. 'We are at the tipping point, Watson,' averred Holmes, plucking the matches from me, while watching the swans glide down the river. He lit his pipe, shielding it from the wind, then planted his hands, one upon the other on his cane.

'How do you mean?' He issued a great plume of silky, white smoke.

'The old order will be swept away,' he began. 'The age of the aristocracy is at an end. Without doubt, the new century will see in a new one: the age of meritocracy will reward only intellect and enterprise. New money will trump old.'

'You are in a philosophical humour today, Holmes,' I laughed. 'Come to your point.'

'Observe the children throwing bread to the ducks and the swans. Notice how the ducks snap at the bread as if their lives depend upon it. The swans hold back, as if too proud to stoop to charity. See how they glide serenely away, as if they do not require sustenance; as if they can survive on their grace alone. At some point, the swans will weaken and die.'

As we talked, I noticed a child of eight or nine ambling towards us in an ill-fitting, shabby suit, with trousers that stopped short above his bare ankles. A great section of his jacket was torn off and hung loose like a flap over his makeshift belt. Like his clothes, his face looked older than his years. Mud and tears were streaked across his cheeks and his eyes bore a hollow weariness. I was overcome with pity and immediately began searching my pockets again for something that might improve his lot.

'Here,' I said, beckoning him over, 'try one of these. They're called Allsorts from Bassett's. Entirely new this year.'

'What happened to your humbugs?' enquired Holmes.

'I ate them. But these are much better: sugar, coconut, liquorice. Absolutely delicious and look, each one is different.'

'He could, I believe, make better use of a shilling or two,' muttered Holmes. The urchin continued towards and us and then stopped a few feet away, standing directly before us. He addressed us in a faltering voice:

'I am your worst nightmare and your most earnest friend. I am he that appears in the night and is gone in the morning. I have controlled you from the beginning. I see everything that happens. You will believe yourself alone, yet find me beside you. I have you in my sights. Let these matters alone and you will live. Tamper with my affairs and you will most certainly die.' Concluding this astonishing speech, he hung his head and stared sorrowfully at the ground. I stared, flabbergasted, while Holmes peered at him gravely.

'Tell me who sent you,' I blurted, 'and we will pay double.'

'Spare your breath, Watson,' said Holmes. 'He will have sworn with his life not to tell. Give him a coin Watson, and send him on his way.'

I did as instructed and the boy scurried down the path, glad, no doubt, his ordeal was at an end.' We were alone once more.

'By great Gordon's ghost, Holmes!' I ejaculated. 'What is the meaning of this?'

'No empty threat, I'd wager,' my friend muttered, glancing about him. 'Ingeniously delivered, but I believe it is a riddle too.'

'Meaning what?'

'Watson,' my friend laughed, 'my mind is agile I grant you, yet I am not Plato. Results will come but they are rarely instantaneous. A problem plus data, plus time equals results. I often find that they need some jollying along.'

'What do you propose?'

'That we get some neck oil. The Barley Mow is within striking distance. I suggest we adjourn there to consider our next move.'

Once again, we found ourselves ensconced in the embrace of a public house. How many had we patronised since arriving in Burton? I had lost count.

'What can I get you, love?' I was rather taken aback by this familiar, somewhat feminine term of endearment, particularly as it came from a bristled publican.

'A pair of pale ales,' I returned. He peered at me with a benign curiosity as he pulled our pints.

'You're the gentlemen from London,' he said. 'There's been a bit of talk about you.'

'Oh, yes?' I enquired. 'All good, I hope.'

'Not all of it, no,' he said laconically, but did not elaborate. 'Now then,' he said, slopping our pints on the bar, 'let that tickle your innards.'

I returned with the drinks to our small wooden table by the window. Holmes had placed a pound of shag tobacco before him and was now harvesting a quantity for his next pipe.

'Any inspiration?' I enquired. 'I confess I found it unsettling in the extreme. Who was that boy?'

'Who he was is of no consequence. He could have been anyone who would do something for money and ask no questions.' Holmes drained an inch of his beer. 'Discounting my earlier thoughts, I confess, I am developing something of a taste for this,' he said admiringly. 'There's a certain sparkle to it, wouldn't you say, Watson.'

'You're not wrong,' I said, wiping my lips. 'Now may I speak frankly, Holmes?'

'Always!'

'I fear they are pitting us against each other.'

'They?'

'The sender of the message. "You will believe yourself alone, yet find me beside you." Surely, the implication is that it is me.' Holmes stared at me for the longest time.

'My dear Watson,' he smiled. 'Your loyalty is beyond question. Besides if you did not have me to alleviate the boredom of your medical practice, you would be done for.' I shook my head, then put my glass to my lips, this heavy weight off my mind. Holmes' trust, I saw, meant more to me than I realised.

'It is a baffling affair,' I put in. 'Still, this has told us that there is some criminal mind behind it. If they do not mean to break our friendship, then what is the meaning of "I am your worst nightmare and your most earnest friend?" Do they perhaps infer that we already know our enemy?'

'Excellent, Watson,' congratulated Holmes. 'You are, I believe, working along the right lines.'

From the diary of Gertie Cresswell, 13ᵗʰ October 1899

A fitful sleep! I was awoken at around three by a curiously soft but persistent knocking outside my bedroom window. I stumbled to the window with a candle, whereupon the knocking abruptly ceased. I returned to bed, only for it to start up again. I repeated this rigmarole on three more occasions, upon the last of which, I flung open the window, quite ready to tear a strip out of my bobby knocker. Then I saw them. It seemed impossible to conceive, but two black bears stared up at me, their savage eyes darkly reflecting the moon, each exposing its bloodied jaws and each dragging what appeared to be a coffin. Upon seeing me, they let out a cackle, inhuman but utterly unlike a bear.

163

Instinctively, I recoiled at the phenomenon, then pulled the window shut. Like a child I ran back to bed and hauled the covers over my head. I listened again, but there was nothing.

Reading over the passage I have just written, it feels like a discarded page from Mary Shelley's 'Frankenstein'. Now feeling rather foolish – plainly I was in the throes of a lucid dream, which conjured these strange apparitions. I found the candle burnt down and the evidence of my labours at the window. I was neither awake nor asleep when the moonlight and the lateness of the hour conspired to play tricks on me.

A pot of coffee has succeeded in restoring some semblance of order to my mind. It is clear I am being harassed by the same malign forces that pursued us on the moors. They appear in different forms, but a central intelligence no doubt controls them all. A tangled skein, indeed.

***

We found Miss Cresswell waiting for us in our rooms. She appeared markedly less sure of herself than on our previous encounters; more pallid of skin and perhaps even a little nervous. No doubt her reckless actions on the moors had shaken her to a degree, although my offer to provide a medical opinion was politely declined. She did however request that she work from our rooms, citing the poor quality of the mackerel served at her own boarding house. Naturally, it occurred to me that this was the cause of her malady, but I did not push the matter.

The rain rapped its knuckles against the glass as if demanding to be admitted. I set another log on the hearth and poured myself a second measure of single malt. Ale, endless ale! With beer occupying my every waking thought, I was pleased at last to be back under the civilising influence of whisky. I allowed the amber liquid to sting my lips and sighed a note of satisfaction. Setting out a hand of solitaire, I settled into the sort of slumberous reverie I had not permitted myself to enjoy since leaving Baker Street. It was a welcome respite after our disturbing adventures across the moors.

Holmes and Miss Cresswell were absorbed in their work: Holmes applying himself in that single-minded way of his, to his monograph on tiepins; the latter picking out a plaintive melody on her ukulele. Neither felt the need to disturb each other, although more than once I heard my friend murmur a word of appreciation, complimenting our new partner on a particularly fine phrase.

Presently, Miss Cresswell started to sing. Her voice was possessed of an exquisite, expressive quality; the song was a beguiling ballad that, while melancholy, had a singular effect on the mind. It suddenly occurred to me that I had fallen in love. I stared at the cards, attempting to refocus my attention, to little avail. These few minutes of sublime calm had now vanished; my thoughts were thrown into disarray. At once, I attempted to rationalise the situation. It was the intoxicating effect of the whisky, the plaintive song, the comfort of the fire. Any man would find himself prone to such thoughts. I admonished myself for my sentimentality, my weakness, but it was as if a switch had been flipped. On the face of it, it was obvious. Her quixotic energy, acerbic wit, brilliance of mind, and the hours we had spent together driving into the hills before we were reunited with Holmes. But thinking back, the attraction had been there from the start; that first glimpse of her at St. Pancras; the flash of her green eyes, the dark hair. It was an unwelcome complication.

Miss Cresswell's voice seemed to permeate my very being. It was as if she were speaking the words directly to me, in expectation of an answer.

'Watson,' called Holmes from his bureau, without lifting his pen from his page, 'you are vexed by some question. You have raised and lowered your glass four times without it reaching your lips. You are torn by some dilemma. We have considerable brainpower within these four walls. Perhaps we could be of some service?'

'It is nothing, Holmes,' I returned unconvincingly. 'I have merely contrived a position for myself, which seems unplayable.'

'I rather think,' my friend deduced, 'it is something else. Your cards are still in the position in which you laid them out.'

'Are you unwell, Doctor?' Miss Cresswell asked pointedly, returning her instrument to the table. 'Perhaps a chill from the moors? Or else some other spectre hangs about you?' I felt my cheeks prickle with heat.

'Merely some concerns about my medical practice,' I fabricated, rising to my feet, circulating my whisky. 'My patients will be beginning to note my absence. I have appointed a stand-in, but he is a man of limited abilities. I rather fear my best patients will find alternative arrangements.'

'Nonsense,' barked Holmes. 'Those with any sense would wait a year for a man like you to return.'

'Some, I fear, will not last a year,' I replied. 'Besides, there is a colonel with a weak heart and a healthy pension whom any doctor would welcome to his list. I would be sorry to lose him.' The light flickered across Miss Cresswell's face. She was staring directly at me, with a mixture of amusement and affection, reading my every thought and seeing through each of my decoys. In truth I did not care a moment for my practice; I would drop it in an instant if some other form of income presented itself. At present, I could think of nothing but Miss Cresswell. I could not conceive of a future in which she was not part.

Presently, there came two smart knocks on the door. Holmes glanced across at me.

'Expecting someone?' I shook my head. He called out: 'Is that you, Mrs. Todder?'

There came another pair of knocks.

'Inspector Hubble?' he demanded. Yet another two knocks sounded. Holmes gestured to Miss Cresswell and myself to stand at the far side of the room.

'Reveal yourself or my friend, Dr. Watson, will put a bullet through the door.' In fact, my service revolver was in the pocket of my ulster, hung in the bedroom closet. I flared my eyes at Holmes and displayed my empty palms, indicating that I did not have my gun upon my person. My friend seemed unperturbed at this.

'He has it trained on the door as I speak.'

At that moment, there was the crack of rifle fire and the door splintered cleanly down the middle. In the same instant, the window behind me shattered and I felt the light rain of a thousand splinters on my neck. Along the corridor I heard a woman scream. There followed a stampede on the stairs as other guests fled down to the street. The three of us were already on the ground, our hands flat on the floorboards in full expectation of a second shot. When it came, it arrived with terrible precision, shattering the bottle of single malt I had transported so carefully from London.

'Fiend!' I cried, seizing a vase from a low table and hurling it towards the door. The room, I noted with more curiosity than alarm, was filling with smoke. A glance to my left revealed a canister spewing a thick, white matter, a screen they had devised to cover their attack. Holmes, who was still stranded in middle of the room, rolled to one side and joined us in the corner. Plainly, he was without his own Webley revolver, or else, surely, he would have returned fire. I cursed our lack of readiness.

'Miss Cresswell,' I shouted. 'Into the bedroom!'

'A trifle forward, Doctor,' she returned.

Ignoring my call, instead she took up her yellow umbrella from the basket. 'Please, Gertie,' I implored, 'do as I say.'

'Hold your nerve and keep your heads low,' instructed Holmes. 'Now each of us must play our part.'

Not a second had elapsed since that first shot, when three men burst into the room, each brandishing a rifle. Three more shots exploded at close quarters. A lamp shattered throwing the room deeper into darkness.

Holmes may not have had his firearm, but he had a far deadlier weapon: his walking cane. Any half-interested follower of my chronicles of Holmes will need no reminding of his prowess at the obscure martial art known as Bartitsu.

With a leg planted behind him, and his stick raised above his head, he stood ready for the attack. In a moment, Holmes was upon his nearest assailant, cracking his stick against his neck, felling the man with a single blow. Without thinking, I charged at the second with the mad courage of a wounded bull, barrelling his legs from under him. I leapt on the man, grappling for his rifle, which he held in a death-like grip. We found ourselves eyeball to eyeball, an inch from each other's face, but without exchanging a word. I smelt beer on his breath. He was thick-set lout, with dull, grey, unfeeling eyes, a flattened nose and a horizontal gash across his forehead. It occurred to me, in that strange manner the brain has of suggestion at the least appropriate moment, that I was tussling with Frankenstein's monster itself.

In brute strength, my assailant had a clear advantage, but his wits were slow. Reaching up, I managed to tug a heavy clock from the mantelpiece and brought it crashing down on his head. He roared with pain and I pulled myself free, only to hear another shot crack against the wall just an inch or so past my left shoulder. What of Miss Cresswell? My eyes searched frantically in the smoke-filled room. She was equipping herself admirably, indulging in the same practice as Holmes, and with equal expertise. The central column of her umbrella it appeared was quite detachable from the gaudy yellow canopy and the end tapered to a single sharp point. At the very moment I looked up, I saw her plunge it into the thigh of the third man, sending him into a spasm of fury. He reeled away, the gun falling from his hand as he fought to staunch the wound.

A minute later, and remarkably enough, we found ourselves alone once again in the room. My senses returned, I ran to Miss Cresswell, who lay prostrate upon the floor.

'My dear Gertie,' I cried, stooping and holding her gently by the shoulders. 'Say something!'

'A new dress, perfectly ruined,' she returned curtly, picking herself up. 'It was my belief that I would be safer in your company. I can see that this was a miscalculation.'

I checked myself for injury, my heart racing.

'A miracle!' I cried, my face smeared with a thick grease of dust and blood.

'A spirited defence,' agreed Holmes, dusting broken plaster from his jacket, 'but no miracle.' He surveyed the room, the splintered door, the shattered widows and holes blown in the brickwork. 'I fear, nonetheless, that we may have lost a portion of our deposit.'

'Nowhere is safe,' Holmes declared as Miss Cresswell boarded her Hackney carriage bound for the station, 'but in London at least, there are the millions to hide amongst, and the proximity of Scotland Yard. I suggest you lie low for a while and do not return to your address until this matter is resolved.'

It had taken some persuasion to convince Miss Cresswell that a spell away from Burton was a sensible course. Following assurances that we would keep her informed of developments, she eventually capitulated.

I had given her the name of a friend in Islington, who I knew would ask no questions and keep her safe until such a time as the threat had passed.

'I will write,' I said, offering my hand to help her into the carriage.

'That is what you do best, Doctor,' she returned. 'I look forward to it.'

With a whip crack, the carriage pulled away and Holmes and I were left alone once again on the pavement.

ELEVEN

The Mirror Man

Holmes and I paced the market square, having replenished our supply of tobacco. My friend reached into his wallet and produced a small piece of folded paper. Scrawled across it was a message in a child's spidery hand.

'What do you have there?' I enquired, attempting to read it upside down. 'Is it perhaps a letter from a young follower of your work? Surely, by rights, such correspondence should come to me.'

'I do not believe it is a fan letter,' said Holmes. 'See for yourself.' This is how it ran:

Will you meet me at Elsie Parker +, noon tomorrow? Leave answer same place.

'Somewhat cryptic,' I remarked. 'Where did you come across such a thing?'

'It was dropped by the child who visited us by the river. In his haste to get away, he did not notice it slip from his pocket.'

'Excellent spelling and punctuation for one so young,' I noted.

'A lucid observation, Watson,' congratulated Holmes. 'What does that tell us?'

'A solid education?'

'I rather think not. The handwriting is laboured and irregular, as if executed with great concentration.' I smoothed my moustache and peered at the note, which seemed more baffling by the minute.

'An adult has disguised their handwriting by impersonating a child's?'

'Better!' cried Holmes, 'However, an equally unlikely theory. Undoubtedly, it is the work of a child even if not composed by one. The paper is a legal type, typically unavailable to a child. It therefore suggests it has been provided by an adult. Similarly the implement is a good-quality fountain pen, although used in an entirely amateurish way, as if the author were unused to the flow of ink. All this points to a controlling hand.'

'I see,' I mused. 'But this leaves us unenlightened about the meaning. Who or what is Elsie Parker? A café, a pub perhaps?'

'Entirely possible, but unlikely.'

'And what of the cross?'

'What indeed!'

'Let us take a stroll, Watson, and consider the matter further. I find that such activity can often facilitate brainwork.' I was astonished at this assertion.

'Yet,' I suggested, 'ordinarily you spend hours entirely inert when considering a problem.'

'The deepest problems require utter concentration,' my friend returned. 'I do not place this in that category. An answer will come momentarily. This is what I call a "jogger." Instinctively we can already see the answer. It is merely a case of tipping the information forward from one part of the brain to another more easily accessible to the conscious mind.'

We set off across the main stone bridge, admiring the fine house that stood a little lower, which appeared as if it were floating in the water.

'I must confess,' I put in, 'that I struggle to connect the different strands of our case.' Holmes permitted himself a thin laugh.

'As you well know, Watson, a case must unravel first before we find the correct thread. Think of it another way. It is much like tidying a house. It must become a good deal more untidy first, while the detritus is extracted, the old books are piled up, the unwanted pots are pulled from the cupboard and the pictures are stacked against the wall. All this must occur first before order can be established.' A pair of swifts swept past us, causing us to pause momentarily in our footsteps. Holmes watched as they bobbed and glided away over the rooftop before disappearing behind a church tower.

'Let us set out what we know. The consignment sent to India travelled on the Liverpool Canal. It originated in Houghton's brewery. Our theories can be divided into two categories: accidental and deliberate. Let us work on the latter first. Michael Houghton has a longstanding dispute with his brother, Samuel. Yet Samuel's income derives from the same business. It would be an act of self-harm to destroy the brewery's reputation. Then there is Anaxagoras, estranged from both brothers and somewhat disconnected from reality. He cannot be entirely ruled out, but you have as much experience of him as I. His energy is benign, but he has an intriguing connection with the mad Marquess.

Butterworth has protested his own innocence and the evidence seems to point elsewhere. That leaves us with the rival brewers, namely Everard of London. They have everything to gain from Houghton's demise; they would certainly be in position to instruct a crew of savage coopers to scare us off the scent. Did you note their accent? The vowels were more Bow than Birmingham.'

'Then, the solution lies back in London?'

'It is entirely possible.'

'Good Lord,' I mused. 'You mean we could have conducted this investigation from the comfort of our own beds?'

'I would not go that far. Now, do you see that church, Watson? It has given me an idea.'

'Let us suppose Elsie Parker is not a cafe or a pub, but a person.'

'That does seem the obvious solution,' I concluded, glancing up at the gathering clouds. 'Should we make some enquiries? It is a common enough name, but there cannot be so many Parkers in a town as small as this.'

'A fair enough assumption,' agreed Holmes. 'Yet the cross is suggestive. What could it mean?'

'Is there a town cross or memorial?'

'I do not believe so. But let us say it denotes a church.'

'That seems plausible. So Miss Parker is a parishioner then?'

'Or was a parishioner.'

'Was?'

'Look at the construction, again, Watson. 'Meet me *at* Elsie Parker. An odd grammatical construction. I own that Elsie Parker is dead. The meeting place is her gravestone.'

'Wonderful!' I said. 'But which church? There must be ten churches at least within two square miles.'

'Let us preserve our shoe leather and consult the register of births and deaths.'

A profitable half hour in the town hall provided the answer we needed. Helpfully, there was only one Elsie Parker buried in Burton-upon-Trent, late of the Parish of St. Peter's. It was armed with this information that we found ourselves returning across the bridge taking us from Staffordshire back into Derbyshire. The church itself was a high, handsome building of light stone and a tower made higher with short stone spires at each of its four corners. It was also of surprisingly recent vintage, having stood for only ten years, replacing the previous, smaller building.

As we wandered amongst the gravestones, Holmes noted that no memorial was dated more recently than 1866. 'It is as if,' I remarked, 'dying went out of fashion in this parish in the last forty years. There must either be a sizable population of elderly folk or the streets are filled with vampires.' I stared at the stones in puzzlement. 'Perhaps there was simply no more room,' I added.

'A large cemetery is situated less than half a mile away,' Holmes explained. 'It clearly proved a more desirable destination.' A minute or two later we came upon Miss Parker's stone.

'Poor soul,' I remarked. 'She died at only nineteen.' A spray of lavender-blue daisies was left at the graveside.

'How singular,' my friend remarked. 'The grave is more than fifty years old, and yet fresh flowers have been left in the last few days. Note that there is not a single flower on any other grave.'

'Curious,' I agreed. 'Still, it is possible an old friend or admirer remembers her; a childhood sweetheart perhaps, or even a lost daughter.'

'The writer's mind is always whirring,' smiled Holmes. 'How quickly you transform a name into a life.' We stood for a moment contemplating the tragic circumstances of her life and death.

'Now, to work,' Holmes instructed. He pushed the flowers aside to reveal a folded note:

The churchyard is no longer safe. Instead we will meet at the old maltings tower. 8pm tomorrow.

'Now,' he said with satisfaction, 'we know the time and the place. We can observe the rendezvous under cover of darkness. We shall make it our business to eavesdrop on the meeting. But first let us retire to see who recovers the note. It is ten minutes until noon and our visitor will soon be with us.'

Retreating behind a towering stone memorial, we waited in silence. Presently a man in a fawn jacket and flat cap arrived at the gate. Glancing around, he lowered the brim of his cap and turned up his lapels to conceal his features. Satisfied that he was both unrecognisable and unobserved, he furtively approached the graveside, retrieved the note and scanned its contents.

'Ah,' murmured, Holmes, somewhat mournfully, 'a grave disappointment.' The man departed swiftly enough, and we were alone once again.

'Well,' I pressed. 'Who was he?'

'Surely, Watson,' Holmes sighed, 'the signs were plain enough. You must have recognised him.' I shook my head. 'Then you will need to wait a day to satisfy your curiosity.'

The following morning I awoke late and staring up at the ceiling, both infuriated with Holmes, and wondering indeed whether my medical practice was still a going concern. It seemed that I had left it in the hands of my associate so long I would soon relinquish my claim. I often accompanied Holmes on his provincial adventures, yet they rarely took us away from the city for more than a day or two. We had been away for some considerable time now, and Baker Street was becoming something of a distant memory. How strange that the address continued to exert such a hold on me. Even when I lived happily with Mary I would think of Holmes' rooms at the centre of the great metropolis.

I tied the cord of my dressing gown then threw some cold water on my face before going to seek out my old friend, hoping against hope that there was still hot coffee in the pot.

'We have a day in hand, Watson,' Holmes said. 'The rain has begun, I see. I fear the onset of the black dog. I shall retire to bed. Would you be so good as to rouse me at seven?' I nodded my consent.

I spent a restless day walking the streets of Burton, returning the nods and glances of acquaintances we had acquired across our eventful week. My only encounter of note was the pugilist from St Mary and St Modwen's.

'Good afternoon, Father,' I remarked politely. The priest stopped and placed his hand on my shoulder. He peered directly at me.

'See to it,' he returned, 'that no one takes you captive through hollow and deceptive philosophy.' He continued on his way, leaving me not a little disturbed by the warning.

Returning at six, I found a note from Holmes instructing me not to disturb him. After a fruitless half-hour leafing through the Bible for the origin of the quotation, I dined alone on eggs and hock, the great book propped up against the salt cellar. At precisely a quarter to eight,

Holmes appeared at the door. Naturally, he was immaculately dressed, but his face was supernaturally pale and drawn.

'You have eaten, Holmes?' I pressed. He waved away my concern.

'In my present state, Watson,' he said, dabbing his brow with a double-folded handkerchief, 'brain food is sufficient sustenance. Now lead on.'

We found ourselves on a deserted road by the old brewery. The rain fell in an arrow shower and the street was in flood. It gushed over our shoes and trickled down our collars.

'Curse this weather, Holmes!' I exclaimed. 'Stand here much longer and we shall drown.'

'Patience my friend,' my companion assured me, his voice still a little doleful. "For the rain it raineth every day."'

In our glistening black ulsters, we resembled nothing so much as a pair of waterlogged beetles. We stood before the great door of the maltings tower, which loomed over us in the darkness. There was a faint glow of light illuminating each of the tall, narrow windows.

'Is this really such a good idea, Holmes?' I struggled to make myself heard over the deluge.

'I suspect we will find out soon enough.' He rapped twice on the door with the end of his cane. 'Now, look alive, Watson.' We darted along the alley and hid in the shadows.

A few second later and we saw the door fall open. Butterworth glanced out into the street, checked, then checked again, then satisfied it was nothing, closed the door and returned inside.

'Upon my word, Holmes, did you see that? It was Butterworth! What the devil is he doing here?'

'Waiting for someone, evidently. Just as he was at the grave. Now, hello, who's this?' From the shadows, we saw a hackney round the corner, the horse straining at its halter as it drew to a stop outside the gates. Jumping down, the driver opened the door and a slow, lumbering figure climbed down. He walked with a stick and approached the door. He too knocked twice.

'Through here,' hissed Holmes and pointed to a rotting door, half fallen from its hinges. A sharp yank and it fell open easily enough. My friend and I slipped inside and out of the rain. My first impression was the smell: that pungent, moist scent of hops; almost overpowering at first.

We waited until our eyes grew accustomed to the gloom. Above me, I could make out the great gantries and iron staircase; the pipes and ladders and flash of light on the copper tanks. Presently, a cold, thin voice called out.

'Where is it?'

'It will be here tonight.'

'I do hope I have not wasted my time.'

We crept up some stairs and found ourselves a vantage point on the first level of the gantry. While still concealed by shadows, we could make out Butterworth, conversing with the stooped figure, clutching his stick.

'I must have it tonight!' He struck a vessel violently and the mighty sound echoed up into the tower.

'Calm yourself,' Butterworth cautioned. 'He made a promise.'

'We have eight of the ten pieces,' said the first man. 'You know very well that these are worthless without the other two.'

'He'll be here alright,' said Butterworth bitterly. 'I have risked as much as you, if not more.'

'Good Lord, Holmes,' I whispered, 'so Butterworth is mixed up in this after all.'

'So it seems. Now there're heading this way. We must ascend.'

We clambered up another level, watching our shadows and keeping our heads low. They followed after us.

'Let us take a drink,' said Butterworth. 'An ale would do you the power of good.'

'Whisky,' the man snapped.

'Very well,' he sighed, 'follow me.'

The pair made their way into a small office, lit by a dim light. Beneath the drumming of the rain on the windows, we heard the clink of glasses.

'What now?' I whispered.

'We wait. Not long now, Watson.'

Presently, there was another thud at the door.

'Are you quite certain, Holmes,' I put in, half-seriously, 'this is not a meeting of the Rotary?'

The two men in the office immediately rose and listened intently. Butterworth scuttled down the steps to the outside door. Satisfied he knew his visitor, he opened it.

'Well,' called the man with the stick, leaning over the balcony, 'does he have it?'

'Naturally, I have it,' said the caller. 'Do you suppose I would come here empty-handed?'

'Let me see it then!'

'Give him half a chance,' returned Butterworth. 'The lad's a drowned rat.'

'Show it to me!' At this moment I caught a glimpse of the caller's face. It was Tolwood.

'Not him too!' I cried.

'Hush, Watson!' Holmes hissed.

Evidently alerted by my exclamation, the man with the stick turned towards us. I recoiled in horror: he had no face at all; I saw only my own. In fact, his face was concealed by a mirror; a perfectly smooth, concave mask of polished steel. For a moment, I caught the merest flash of Holmes and me in my reflection. We froze and for the longest time the man stared. Did he even possess the power of sight?

'Here it is,' said Tolwood.

'Bring it to me,' instructed the mirror man,

Butterworth and Tolwood trudged up the steps, the latter wearing a leather satchel on his shoulder. His face looked drawn and he looked at Butterworth with grave concern. Reaching the top of the steps, he reached into the bag and drew out what appeared to be a porcelain or glass jar, with a gold rim and a shimmering turquoise and ochre pattern.

'It belonged,' Tolwood said, 'to the wife of Thutmose III; 1420 BC.'

'What you're looking at,' said Butterworth, 'is the oldest pint glass in the world.'

'So, we have the ninth!' the mirror man exclaimed. 'Leaving only the silver vodka cup! You bunglers lost it on the moor.'

'We believe he has it,' said Tolwood.

'Who?' snapped the mirror man.

'Holmes,' Butterworth affirmed.

'I knew it.' I glanced at my friend who betrayed no emotion.

'Without it,' said Butterworth, 'we receive nothing.'

'The Marquess demands the full set.'

'Then, it is fortunate,' said the mirror man, 'that Mr. Holmes and his amusing assistant are with us this evening.' My eyes widened as Holmes stepped out into the light.

'Naturally,' my friend said calmly, 'I have what you are looking for.'

'Then give it to me,' said the mirror man, 'and you walk free.'

Holmes emitted a thin laugh.

'Butterworth,' he said, ignoring the monster and addressing the head brewer, 'it will go better for you if you assist me in apprehending this man. I will testify that you assisted me.'

'I'm in too deep for that, Mr. Holmes,' he said. 'All the same, I appreciate the sentiment.'

'Help me return these artefacts and I believe the law will look more leniently on you and Tolwood.'

'For once, Mr. Holmes,' Tolwood broke in, 'you have no idea what you're dealing with. Now be a good fellow and hand over the cup.'

'Do you mean this?' Holmes reached into his jacket, and produced a small, bright silver drinking cup.

'Here, Watson, catch!'

Holmes leapt forward and tossed it into the air. Instinctively, I made a grab for it, catching it while my friend lunged for the Egyptian beaker. He seized it and then made for the stairs. I followed at his heels.

'With me, Watson!'

'Not so fast.'

Our way was barred by Tolwood, who levelled a pistol at us.

'Enough,' he said. 'This is a business matter and you have no interest in the deal.' The masked man moved to Tolwood's side. In the reflection, I stared at Holmes and myself, trapped like animals. Instinctively, my hand crept towards the pocket where I kept my service revolver.

'Let us preserve our dignity, my friend,' Holmes remarked calmly. 'It appears that the game is up.'

'So,' hissed the masked man, 'Sherlock Holmes is humbled at last.'

Holmes studied the cup for a moment. 'Magnificent artistry, don't you think, Watson? It is only a shame that it is Philistines who will drink from it.' The masked man stole it from Holmes' hand and stowed it inside his fur coat. 'Oh,' my friend added, 'there is just one more thing. The inspector and four constables are at the entrance. Perhaps you could explain your business interests to them?'

Tolwood turned in alarm, just long enough to discover the fiction and for Holmes to brush the pistol from his grasp. In that moment, he fired directly at a copper tank, hit home, and we heard the sudden gushing of ale.

'A dreadful, bloody waste!' cried Butterworth.

Holmes charged for the front gate. I followed after him, my coat torn from my very shoulders as I pushed past Tolwood.

'A good retreat, Watson,' called Holmes as we burst back into the downpour, 'is better than a hopeless stand.' We sprinted down the lane towards the town.

TWELVE

The Levitating Barrel

Dusk had darkened the edge of the day and a bitter chill had set in. Holmes and I trudged two abreast down the lane towards Brizlingcote Hall, our lengthening shadows venturing ahead of us. We had learned much over the last day and night. Still, the greatest questions remained unanswered. Why had Anaxagoras summoned us to the house, and who had poisoned the regiment?

Untended fields sloped away to each side, gigantically overgrown. 'Holmes,' I began. 'I simply must know. Who is the mirror man?' My friend smiled.

'I am not yet prepared to disclose. Advancing a theory without evidence is not a practice of which I approve.'

'Yet he has the Egyptian vase,' I said. 'Surely, we must attempt to recover it. Or at least report its theft.'

'There will be time enough for that,' said Holmes tersely. A single crow glided above us, as if guiding us toward our destination. Holmes pointed up at it with his cane.

'A remarkable creature,' he remarked. 'You have, no doubt heard how a crow was once witnessed employing the turning wheel of a hansom carriage to break open a chestnut?'

'Naturally,' I confirmed, 'every schoolboy has heard the same yarn.'

'And perfectly true it is too,' Holmes insisted. 'But that is just at the novelty end of their powers. They also have a remarkable memory and a gift for observation that would put most police inspectors to shame. If a man in a crowd were to throw a stone at a crow from thirty feet, the bird would identify the culprit in a moment. What's more, he would still have a clear picture of him in his mind years later. There is a famous instance of a man who lost an eye to a crow that he remembered attacking as a youth. It had the same tattered left wing. What's more, the incident took place exactly ten years on – to the very day.'

'I don't believe it, Holmes,' I laughed, although a trifle unconvincingly. 'What is your inference?'

'That crows hold grudges.'

The singular, concave roof of Brizlingcote Hall rose into view.

'Ah,' said Holmes, 'you will observe the bricked-up windows, on the second and third storeys.

'A result no doubt of the window tax,' I broke in, keen to show that Holmes did not have a monopoly on historical knowledge. 'Unless I'm mistaken, it was the brainchild of William III and led to the coining of the term 'daylight robbery'.'

'Quite so, Watson,' my friend smiled, 'quite so. But I merely wanted to draw your attention to the chalk lettering on the windows.'

'I rather fear,' muttered Holmes, as we approached the great front door of the house, 'that we are not the only visitors this evening.'

I frowned at this, glancing around for fresh footprints. 'What makes you so certain?'

'You will observe the flattened grass to the left of the track where our earlier visitors made their way towards the house. They studiously avoided the wet mud to prevent a trail of footprints. Yet the long grass is clearly set at a thirty-degree angle where it has been trodden down. You will observe the same effect, in reverse, on the right side of the path.'

The door was ajar when we arrived, revealing only a sliver of darkness.

'Let us be on our guard, Watson,' Holmes counselled. 'There is some business afoot.' Standing to one side of the door, he extended an arm then threw the door open to its full extent. We waited a few seconds. Registering nothing but the wind buffeting the glazing of the ancient house, he raised his eyebrows, suggesting no immediate danger, then disappeared inside. A struck match illuminated the gloomy hall while Holmes located a lamp. At once, an imposing portrait of a bewigged man from the last century stared down at us, as if he had been left to guard the house. His stern gaze followed us as we crossed to the drawing room. We set about restoring light to the large but sparsely furnished room. The hearth was stone cold.

Our eyes lit upon on three pewter mugs, set upon a small table between a pair of matching couches. Two of the mugs were brimming with ale, the other proved to be only three-quarters full. In chalk across the table was inscribed the word *Bibe*, which my schoolboy Latin told me meant 'drink.'

'Houghton?' I called, my voice faltering despite myself. The house answered with a hollow echo. An involuntary shiver ran down the length of my spine.

'I don't like this one bit, Holmes.'

'I, on the other hand, find myself pleasantly engaged.' My friend studied the note, then each mug in turn.

'Do you believe they are intended for us?'

'I think not. Come Watson, let us venture upstairs.'

'Not without me.' I leapt a clear foot into the air. Miss Cresswell stood in the doorway with an amused smile, her arms folded. 'Did I make you jump, Doctor?'

'Evidently,' I replied. 'How long have you been lurking there?'

'Barely a minute,' my friend broke in.

'I'm impressed, Mr. Holmes. 'I believed I had covered my tracks well.'

'Reasonably so,' admitted Holmes, 'but your singular brand of fragrance betrayed you. Unless I am entirely mistaken you are wearing a scented oil of musk and civet.'

'Remarkable!' applauded Miss Cresswell. 'It is an indulgence, I admit, but a justifiable one. Even if we spend our time fishing the sewers, there is no need to smell like one.'

'My monograph on women's perfumery,' remarked Holmes, 'was met with some small acclaim in certain circles.

'But,' I stammered. 'We put you on a carriage bound for London. You agreed it would be the safest course...'

'I never had any intention of leaving Burton, Doctor. I merely believed we would be safer apart and that you would fret less if you believed I was in London. Besides, I found a letter waiting for me, no doubt identical to yours.'

'Now,' continued Holmes, 'that only leaves the inspector to show himself. From the other side of the couch, Inspector Hubble rose, somewhat sheepishly.

'It would pay, inspector,' Holmes instructed, 'not to leave a trail of Pontefract cakes from the front door to the drawing room.'

'Upon my word!' I cried, turning in astonishment. 'Anyone else?'

'I most certainly hope so,' said Holmes, glancing upwards. 'Watson and I were instructed to come here. I assume you received a similar message?'

'Indeed,' replied the inspector. Miss Cresswell nodded.

181

'Then, it appears we are here on the same errand. Let us see if Anaxagoras can elucidate us.'

In ragged procession, we bundled up the ancient wooden staircase. Hubble led the way, followed by Holmes, Miss Cresswell, and myself at the rear. More dusty oil paintings lined the walls, each resembling to some degree the ruddy-faced gent who greeted us at the entrance.

'Well, there's certainly a family likeness,' noted Miss Cresswell, holding a candle close to one of the portraits. 'I would also wager that they all enjoyed a drink.' Ahead of us, Hubble and Holmes had disappeared into the darkness, no doubt attempting to locate a lamp.

'Quickly, over here,' called the inspector. 'A light if you will.' Holmes struck a match, his face suddenly ghoulishly lit in its yellow flame. Some words were scrawled across the wall of the landing.

'And when two raging fires meet together,' my friend intoned, 'they do consume the thing that feeds their fury.'

'Let us divide and search the rooms,' instructed the inspector. 'I am becoming increasingly concerned for the safety of Anaxagoras, if indeed he is here. 'If you see anything untoward, summon me at once.'

'By all means,' Holmes demurred.

Bringing a match to a lantern, I followed its soft yellow beam from room to room. Anaxagoras' odd existence revealed itself with each chamber. What were once bedrooms now had a utilitarian function, each one simply part of a larger whole.

Some doors opened stiffly, and only with great effort. On each occasion, I was met with musty clouds of dust. Inside, books lay left open where they fell. Pieces of Roman and Sumerian pottery of indeterminate age lay haphazardly on their sides. I found piles of unsorted stamps from early in the century and tubs of ancient coins, some of which appeared to be of substantial value. Stuffed peacocks, otters and even a bear stood sentinel in the corners of the rooms, guarding the gallimaufry.

Yet, there seemed to be no single theme that bound the collection together. They were many fantastical items, each curious in their own way, but together, they seemed curiously vacuous. To my mind, they pointed towards the questing of a troubled soul. Presently, I abandoned my search and returned to the landing.

'Well?' enquired Hubble as we reconvened.

'He would be a fool,' suggested Miss Cresswell, 'not to charge a sixpence entrance fee. It is a museum of curiosities.'

'No trace at of him?'

'None,' I confirmed. 'It appears several of the rooms have lain undisturbed for years.'

'And you, Mr. Holmes?' Hubble asked. My friend appeared to be in something of a trance, peering intently at the banister. 'Mr. Holmes?' Hubble repeated, a little louder.

'Do you see the damaged banister?'

'Yes,' Hubble replied.

'Half of it is broken away. Odd, don't you think?'

'Not especially,' I said, examining the damage. 'Houghton does not strike me as a man with much interest in home maintenance. Besides it could have happened anytime in the last ten years.'

'It appears rather recent, considering the splintering of the wood. I found the other half in the porch below us.'

'Suggesting recent damage?'

'Precisely,' said Holmes.

'Possibly,' qualified Hubble.

Miss Cresswell was the last to return. Her empty-handed gesture suggesting her search was just as fruitless.

'Then, it appears we have been summoned on false pretences,' I began. 'There is no trace of him.'

'Not quite,' Hubble remarked, then produced from his pocket an envelope, addressed, remarkably, to the four of us. 'I found this, unsealed on his writing desk.' My friend's eyes fell upon the document. 'May I?' he asked. With the dexterity of a spider spinning its web, he extracted the letter and scanned its contents. 'Perhaps I would be as well as to read it aloud.' He glanced around the company, then cleared his throat.

My dear friends,

The world contains a good many mysteries. For me, the most profound of these is the mystery of happiness. I have acquired the world's rarest books, its most exquisite wines, and a goodly many treasures of antiquity. Yet none of these have succeeded in bringing me the contentment which I have long sought. If you have come up to the house and found this letter, then I am grateful for your loyalty and diligence. Alas, you will find me gone, exiting this world by the means that brought me its wealth, but not its fortune.

Remember me, for I remained, your friend,
Anaxagoras Houghton

'Merciful heavens,' I shuddered, 'a suicide.'
'So it appears.'
The wind rattled again at the glass.
'I have no doubt that he is still here,' Hubble declared. 'I propose another search, from the attic to the cellars. If that still yields nothing then I will summon my constables and we can begin going over the grounds. This is a grim business, gentlemen.' Miss Cresswell registered her displeasure at this poor choice of words. 'And naturally, Miss Creswell,' he added hastily, 'we are grateful for your assistance too.'

For an hour, we ransacked the place, pulling open the doors of wardrobes, exploring damp-filled pantries in pairs, for we feared to go in alone – stumbling about in the dank cellar. All manner of paraphernalia was found: ancient flags, part of a cannon from the Napoleonic wars, scores of jars and bottles, each lined with a green mildew, but nothing of the man himself.

My friend and I found ourselves together in the uppermost part of the house by a circular window, where a brass telescope was pointed at the heavens. Holmes appeared deep in thought.
'Something troubling you, Holmes?' I enquired.
'As a matter of fact, yes,' he replied, snapping out of his trance. 'Follow me. He led me back along the corridor, along a threadbare strip of red carpet. 'Do you recall, Watson, that as we approached the house there were five windows on this storey: a small circular window, three large rectangular windows, the second of which was bricked up; and finally, a second small circular window, identical to the first except that it was once again bricked over.' I considered this for a moment.
'Yes,' I returned, 'that is my recollection.'
'Well, now, let us compare our knowledge of the exterior with the interior layout. Here is the door to the first room and its circular window. Here are the doors to the next two rooms and at the end of the corridor is the box room with the blocked circular window. Yet there is no door to the third room with a large rectangular window.'
'By Jupiter, you're right, Holmes.'

'You appear surprised?'

'Only at my own myopia.'

Once again, we entered the adjacent rooms but found no means to access the hidden room. I collected Hubble and Miss Cresswell and presented them with the problem.

'Some hidden panel, perhaps?' suggested Hubble, his hands pressed flat to the wall, 'or a hidden lever?'

'I fear,' smiled Miss Cresswell, 'you have been reading too many penny dreadfuls. This is not a Boys' Own adventure, Inspector.' I failed to conceal a smile.

'Not in the least amusing,' snapped Hubble. 'There must be some means by which we may access the room.'

'Then, why not from the attic?' Miss Cresswell put in.

Duly, we climbed the ancient staircase to the attic and felt the chill of the night air around us. His lamp extended in front of him, Hubble picked his way across a pair of rocking horses, two knotted hammocks and a pair of toy ships, their masts crushed within their tangled rigging. I stumbled over something or other and presently a delicate, haunting melody struck up.

'A child's music box,' Miss Cresswell said.

'Here,' announced Hubble. 'This must be the spot.' He stamped hard, a dull thud emanating from beneath us. The inspector seized a steel bar that may once have belonged to an iron bed and began working at one of the floorboards, attempting to prise it free.

With a fearsome splintering, the board finally came up, only to reveal a beam of solid oak beneath, and further layers under that. He dropped the bar in dismay.

'This can't be it,' he admitted, looking somewhat dejected. 'What about the window?'

'It would require a ladder over twenty-foot long,' I countered. 'Besides, judging from the other rooms, the windows lock on the inside.'

'Then, there is nothing for it,' Miss Cresswell declared, 'we go in through the wall.'

Armed with a sledgehammer salvaged from the cellar, Miss Cresswell stood in front of the plaster wall, where we guessed the door must once have been.

'Are you quite certain,' Hubble asked, 'that you wouldn't prefer one of us to perform this task?'

'Quite certain,' confirmed Miss Cresswell. 'Now, I suggest that you stand well back.' Planting a foot behind her, she took a mighty swing at the wall.

The head of the hammer disappeared cleanly through the plaster, the handle ploughing a fair distance behind it. With magnificent strength, Miss Cresswell wrenched the hammer from the wall, revealing an empty cavity. She took another swing, this time breaking directly through the other side. Shards of plaster lay at our feet and a quantity of pale moonlight seeped through.

'What can you see?' asked Hubble.

'A dark shape,' she pronounced. 'There is a large object at the centre of the room.'

Several more blows succeeded in producing a hole two feet across. Together, we tore at the plaster until it was conceivable we could clamber through.

'What is it?' I asked peering at the object.

'I believe,' Holmes murmured, 'it is a cask, suspended in the air.'

Presently, the four of us stood within the room. It was entirely empty except for an ancient grandfather clock and the barrel, which appeared to levitate before our eyes. We raised our lamps, betraying our astonishment.

'There,' whispered Holmes, 'a length of rope suspended on a miniature pulley system.' For a moment we did little but stare at this phenomenon. The moon shone dull and indistinct through the grimy window. I was the first to speak.

'How long do you suppose it has been here? Since the room was sealed?'

My friend crouched beneath the barrel and felt the bare floorboards. 'Damp,' he said. 'I believe not only that the cask is full, but that a quantity of the ale was spilled when this cask was set into this curious position. This work is no more than a few hours old.' I was dumbfounded.

'But how...?' I began.

Miss Cresswell examined the window. 'Locked from the inside,' she said, 'as we suspected.' My friend joined his fingertips and peered intently at the inspector.

'This is your crime scene, Hubble,' he said. 'I suspect you will want to summon your colleagues before proceeding.'

'Crime scene?' I repeated. 'There is surely no crime in storing a barrel of ale in mid-air.'

'Perhaps,' murmured Miss Cresswell, 'there is still a chance he is alive?' A chill ran up my spine.

'He is inside?' I stuttered. Hubble too seemed to share my surprise.

'Without a doubt,' confirmed Holmes. Hubble and I formed a cradle with our hands into which Holmes stepped, clinging to the cask which swung concentrically on its single wire. Finding his balance, he brought himself level with the top of the barrel.

'The lid is hammered shut,' he informed us, removing a knife from his jacket. He worked for a moment until we heard a snap and the broken blade dropped to the floor.

I returned alone to the cellar and searched until I found a hammer and chisel. I took the stairs two at a time and before long we were all at work on the barrel. It is testament to the craft of the Burton coopers that it took us a full five minutes to break it open. Holmes worked with great precision, attacking the weakened seams, and presently a spout of amber ale poured from a hole we have managed to gouge in the side.

'Stand back,' my friend warned as he drew back the hammer. 'I suspect this shall be the decisive blow.' Gripping the handle of the chisel, he drove the hammer against its base and a great flood burst forth, accompanied by the splintering of wood and the dead weight of Anaxagoras as he dropped to the floor.

Truly, it was a diabolical sight. The poor man wore a look of outrage upon his face, his eyes wide with disbelief, as if he had drowned in a fury of desperation. His body was horribly contorted, a sign no doubt that he had been forced inside, and his face was white and bloated. The palms of his hands were turned upwards and raised above his head, as if he was still trying to push up against the lid.

'You do not require the services of a doctor,' I observed, 'to know there is nothing we can do for him.'

'Look there,' Miss Cresswell pointed, 'around his neck. It is a key on a length of string.'

'This is a dark business,' muttered Holmes, uncommonly moved at the man's plight. 'Let us return to town and send for someone to assist the inspector. No doubt, the county coroner will wish to take a view of such a singular matter. Meanwhile, Watson, Miss Cresswell and I will inform his brothers.' Hubble appeared at a total loss, staring incredulously at the twisted body.

'But it is impossible,' he faltered. 'A locked room and a sealed barrel suspended from the ceiling.'

'An elaborate conceit, I grant you,' my friend admitted.

'And do you not wish to study the crime scene further?'

'I have gathered all the data I need,' murmured Holmes. 'I shall retire to draw my conclusions.'

'Which are?'

'Not yet ready to be presented.'

'Then, at least explain the mystery of the barrel.'

'All that is needed is a little time.'

'You have explained as much,' the inspector said dismissively. 'It is plain you know as little as we do.' Holmes surveyed us all, then shook his head, smiling sadly.

'Forgive me, my friends,' he said. 'These have been troubling days and we do not yet have the upper hand. Perhaps, with a little more haste, Anaxagoras could have been saved. Perhaps not. But at least I should share a little of my thinking.' Miss Cresswell stared intently at Holmes. 'The barrel has been in this room for many years. A moment or two ago I took the liberty of sampling a small quantity of the beer. It tastes slightly of soap due to the effects of oxidation. No doubt, it contained, at one point a highly prized batch. Perhaps even the first experimental pale ale; the ale that built this great empire. So prized in fact, that it was hidden away, most likely by the Houghton brothers' late father. But who would know of its location? Probably only his sons. Yet how would they gain access to this hidden room? Not through the window, the floors, the ceiling or walls. Then, some other way.'

'Impossible,' I muttered.

'Improbable, yes,' cried Holmes, raising a finger, 'impossible, no. Remember my maxim: eliminate the impossible and whatever remains, no matter how improbable, must be the truth. It was a devilish puzzle, but finding its solution was simply a question of time. Miss Cresswell's eyes suddenly widened.

'Of course,' she whispered.

'Watson,' my friend said, 'what time do you have?'

'A quarter to eight.'

'And what time does it show on the grandfather clock?' I held a lantern close to its cobwebbed face.

'The hands are missing,' I noted.

'The hands are missing! Not only the hands,' Holmes returned, 'but its entire mechanism.' He threw open the dark mahogany door beneath the clock face. Inside was nothing but darkness.

'If you would care to follow me,' my friend invited, 'I propose we take a journey through time.' Holmes took a step and disappeared entirely inside the clock. The inspector and I exchanged an astonished glance, then followed suit.

In a matter of moments, we emerged into the next room. I glanced back, barely able to comprehend the ruse, only to find myself stepping out of an identical clock. Once all of us had traversed from one room to the next, Holmes closed the panel.

'Remarkable!' I exclaimed.

'Tsk, Watson,' Holmes admonished, 'little more than a child's magic trick.' He restored his hat to his head. 'Inspector,' he continued. 'I apologise that by necessity we shall have to leave you with the body, but I suspect you have seen equally macabre corpses in your time.'

'Rarely,' he admitted.

I had spent some time lost in my thoughts. 'But, Holmes,' I said, unable to wait until we were alone, 'who is behind all this?'

'Know that and we shall be on a train back to London. More pressing is the smell of smoke.'

'Good God,' growled the inspector. 'Fire!'

Smoke had begun to curl in beneath the door. I tried the handle, but the door appeared to be locked from the outside.

'Back through the clock,' instructed Holmes.

'Once we had returned to the room with the barrel, we could see orange flames already licking the banister.

'A trap,' said Miss Cresswell. 'How could we so easily led?' I ventured forward with a handkerchief across my face, but was soon beaten back by the heat and flames. Miss Cresswell glanced up.

'The rope,' she cried. Holmes was already at work. With the assistance of the inspector, we hoisted him aloft so that he could reach the shorn rope, which hung loose from the pulley that once held the barrel in place. He pulled sharply and it flowed free from the wheel.

With a well-directed kick, we succeeded in removing the glass from the window, then paid out as much of the rope as we could – enough we believed to reach the ground. The inspector was despatched first, followed by Miss Cresswell, then myself. As we descended, the flames seemed to reach for us, like hands bursting through the windows. I could hear the great beams themselves cracking and splintering in the inferno. The heat was overpowering and as I neared the ground floor a great wall of fire seemed to envelop me. I cried out, then dropped six feet to the ground. I coughed and spluttered, emptying my lungs of the acrid smoke. But almost immediately my thoughts were of Holmes. Surely, there was no hope. I stepped back and saw his silhouette against the wall of fire; he was standing perfectly still in the window, his cloak spread wide like wings. For one terrifying moment I believed he would jump; instead, he appeared to swoop like a sparrow-hawk upon its prey, gliding with astonishing speed down the rope, through the flames and into our arms.

'A singular afternoon,' admitted Holmes, as close to rattled as I had seen him. 'Perhaps we ought to alert the local brigade to an incident at Brizlincote Hall.'

We left the great house behind us, a vast funeral pyre, illuminating half the valley, then together stumbled back along the lane. After communicating the evening's events at the police station to the bafflement of the duty sergeant, we made our excuses and returned to our lodgings, much sobered by our experience.

THIRTEEN

Revelations

Once again, we stood at the summit of Waterloo Clump, looking down on the town. From here, it looked like a child's play set, with its factories and houses, horses and railways.

'I cannot help but feel, Holmes,' I confessed, 'that we are chasing our tails.' I shivered as the chill breeze blew through my coat. Autumn was turning to winter and the buffeting wind threatened to cast my hat down the grassy slopes. 'Furthermore, I confess that I find myself utterly bemused by the encounter at the brewery. How did you come to be in possession of the Russian cup? Who was the man with the stick and at what point did our client, Butterworth, whom we have striven so hard to protect, become embroiled in all this?'

'So many questions, Watson!'

'They deserve answers, Holmes. We seem no nearer to finding the poisoner or finding the paymaster of these murderous coopers. What have we got to work with, Holmes?' My friend observed me wryly, then returned his gaze to the town.

'We have accumulated more data,' he attested, 'than you might believe.' I folded my arms.

'Enlighten me.'

'Well, let me first explain the mystery of those drinking vessels, although I imagine you have surmised the salient points for yourself. You will recall mention of the colourful 5th Marquess of Anglesey? He is an individual of unparalleled eccentricity and almost limitless wealth. Precisely two years ago made an outrageous declaration to his bohemian circle: that on the anniversary of that date he would hold a magnificent banquet, like none ever held before. The toast would be served in ten vessels, one from each of the great dynasties of civilisation: the Egyptians, Sumerians, Russians and seven others. All would be represented, or none. His list of demands was specific and seemingly impossible to meet. Until that is, a syndicate was formed – led by the masked man at the brewery. He in turn enlisted, through blackmail or otherwise, the services of Butterworth and Tolwood – and others besides. His fee to supply the vessels is, I have discovered, the sum of one million pounds.

'But, what of the brothers' role in this?'

'Their father, you recall, was a collector of Sumerian antiquity. He was possessed of one of the cups. But there was something else too. A link through the grandfather to the Russian empire.'

'Think again of the brothers, as different from each other as they were alike. From their actions, one might suppose they have nothing in common. Yet they undoubtedly share – or shared – a common secret.'

'Indeed?'

'Did you not notice Michael's cufflinks, Samuel's tiepin and the pendant Anaxagoras wore around his neck?' I didn't need to answer, for my friend knew that all of these details had escaped my attention.

'I remind you, almost daily, Watson, that it is the trifles that matter most. Each in their own way, the brothers wore a pair of black eagles.'

Holmes reached into his pocket and withdrew his notebook. 'Does that look familiar, Watson?' It was a sketch of what appeared to be a two-headed black eagle, the wings splayed, each head bearing a crown. In one claw it clutched an orb, in the other, a sceptre. At the centre was a mounted knight, skewering a dragon. I studied the design.

'It is certainly familiar,' I admitted, 'but I cannot place it exactly.'

'Well, Watson, your heraldry is rusty. It is the coat of arms of the Russian empire.'

'Russian?'

'Certainly,' Holmes declared. I stared at him, quite incredulous.

'I believed we were looking to Africa for our answers.'

'You are at least,' smiled Holmes, 'one continent adrift.' He strode into the wind, stepping through nettles and brambles. 'I have made some enquiries. It transpires that both Peter the Great and Empress Catherine of Russia were both inordinately fond of Burton ale. Its unusual strength and character were both perfectly suited to the Russian temperament.' I followed my friend through the tall grass. 'Now, compare the emblem with that engraved on the side of the silver vodka cup.' He produced the vessel again from his pocket and the silver flashed brilliantly in the moonlight.

'The same,' I agreed. 'But how did you come across it?'

'The tunnel on the moors, dear Watson.'

'What of it?'

'It was in fact no coincidence that we sought shelter there. I had discovered from my eavesdropping at Thor's Cave that it was the hiding place for the Russian cup. It was an elaborate scheme; they could not trust each other. No one person could know too much. When I ventured along the length of the tunnel, I was seeking the cup, and discovered it exactly where it was supposed to be.

'What of the other cups?'

'Some had been found easily: You recall the cup Butterworth was clutching when he arrived at Baker Street in the cask.

'The tin cup?'

'Yes. He was, you recall, inordinately attached to it.'

'Indeed.'

'As well he might have been. It was the personal property of Emperor Marcus Aurelius.'

'Upon my word! How did he come by it?'

'Enough money will loosen the hands of even the most principled curator. A visit to Lucca with a blank cheque was enough to secure the item. When this business of the poisoning came up, quite naturally, he took it with him.'

'But, in heaven's name, why did he not simply hand it to Tolwood?'

'For fear he would be cut from the deal. In the end, my friend, money will rot even the most honest soul.' I threw up my arms.

'And all this, while we pursued another case entirely. How much does Miss Cresswell know?'

'Why, Watson, she knows it all!'

'Her client is none other than the British Museum itself.' Benumbed, I stared into the middle distance. It was as if I had spent the whole week wearing a blindfold. How could I miss so much?

'Do not judge yourself too harshly, my friend. There are worlds within worlds. One reality masks another. Peel them all away and there is nothing.' These words did little to console me.

'Now, by the by, my dear, Watson,' Holmes added more brightly, 'it was inevitable that Miss Cresswell would succeed in seducing you. Possessed of the same qualities as your dearest friend, the same artistic tendencies as yourself and the same attractive figure to which you are so consistently drawn, it was an impossibility that you would not gravitate into each other's orbit. The only question was when.' I was taken aback at this.

'You are wide of the mark, Holmes,' I declared. 'It is you whom she idealises. She is an acolyte of your work and in thrall to your personality. I am merely an adjunct; just a way to get close to you.'

'Pah,' he scoffed, 'it is my methods she wishes to learn. It is immaterial in what vessel they reside. She has an ambition, Watson, to be the greatest consulting detective in London. But she reached an impasse, compelling her to join forces. Only I can give her the insight to break through; to inspire the leap of logic required to solve the case.'

'Holmes,' I cried. 'You still cannot see it! She has complete confidence in her powers. She desires not your mind, but something else.'

'Then, if that is the case,' he remarked, stoking his pipe, 'I fear she will have to live with the disappointment of the unrequited. My passion is brainwork, not the workings of the human heart, much less the body.'

'She desires nothing but your respect. 'She envies only my friendship with you.'

Holmes stared at me with a look of great compassion; as if he could see something in me I could not myself recognise. His hands were joined lightly at the fingertips and he wore that look of supercilious delight I had seen so many times before when he had the advantage. I shook my head.

'I have no more hope,' I confessed, 'of extricating myself from this trap than we have of solving our case.'

'The case?' Holmes repeated, as if it were entirely inconsequential. 'Oh, my dear Watson,' Holmes laughed, 'it is perfectly plain who tampered with the beer supplied to India.' I knitted my brow.

'Is that so?'

'I had that almost from the first day we arrived in Burton.' I stared at my friend, dumbfounded at this extraordinary disclosure.

'Well, go on, Holmes,' I pressed.

'You will recall the formidable Miss Bilton, the former schoolmistress?'

'Impossible!' I cried.

'Patience,' Holmes urged. 'Allow me to present the data. You yourself saw the hatpin by the beer barrel, shortly before we discovered poor Arkwright. A curious object to be found in a place such as a brewery?'

'Holmes, you are forgetting, Tolwood told us he used it to unclog the valve.' My friend's eyes flickered in a moment's impatience.

'Pah,' he scoffed, the man could not lie his way out of a paper bag. He was covering for her.'

'Why?'

'Miss Bilton has half the town in her power. The constable and certainly Mr. Tolwood, for the simple reason that she was their schoolmistress. Besides, Mrs. Tolwood is second only to Miss Bilton in the local suffrage league. Tolwood would no sooner incriminate Bilton than his own mother. Her ability to gain access and pass unreported was effortlessly done. A mere glance could silence them.'

'But the hatpin alone is not enough to incriminate her. A hundred other women use identical pins.'

'Spoken like a true barrister, Watson,' my friend congratulated. 'You have missed your vocation! So let us consider instead why her hatpin may have become dislodged. Have you observed, Watson, that it is Miss Bilton's custom to wear flowers in her hat?'

'Yes,' I mused, 'come to think of it, she does.'

'Do you recall the hat she was wearing on the day we arrived?' I searched my mind, without success.

'Allow me to refresh your memory,' offered Holmes. 'It was navy-blue bonnet with purple, tubular flowers. I am no botanist, but I saw in a moment that they were foxgloves. They are fetching to the eye, but highly toxic if ingested.'

'I have seen the effects myself in general practice,' I added. 'A gardener once accidentally fed them to his wife. She pulled through, but only thanks to an iron constitution and my immediate assistance. I have rarely witnessed such an alarming response. The toxin induces a combination of convulsions and hallucinations, with severe spasms of the heart.'

'Precisely the symptoms shown by the soldiers in India,' added Holmes.

'Then, she did poison them! Yet we have been here over a week? Why have you delayed reporting this?'

'Because, my friend, she is no murderer. I contest that it was not her intention to cause any injury. Did you detect, during our inspection of the brewery, a particular scent that has no association with the brewing process?'

'I recall a hundred intoxicating smells,' I said. 'One did not assert itself over the other.'

195

'Vinegar, Watson. That is what I smelt at the brewery. I enquired of Tolwood whether vinegar was used as some cleaning agent. He confirmed it was not. Yet the smell was unmistakable.'

I felt a sudden and total weariness, as if all life force had left my limbs.

'Holmes,' I sighed, my head slumped forward, rubbing my eyes as if to help them see more clearly, 'I simply cannot keep up!'

'It is my assertion that Miss Bilton contaminated the consignment of beer with a quantity of vinegar. She simply intended to ruin the batch, not render it poisonous. However, she was disturbed. In her haste to cover her tracks, she spilt a quantity of vinegar, concealed the bottle, then feigned to be adjusting her hat. While making the adjustment, it is conceivable that some petals were dislodged and fell into the mash-tun. Thus, the toxin was introduced to the beer. In all probability, she herself would have had no notion of the consequences of her actions.

'Uncomfortably for her,' my friend continued, 'she has a plausible motive. Mr. Houghton is no friend of the women's suffrage; he has opposed it at every turn. It is evident to the most disinterested observer that Miss Bilton has made herself the thorn in his side. Furthermore, Lord Curzon is perhaps the nation's most fervent opponent of the suffrage movement. You told me as much when you shared the extract from *The Times*. It is my belief that her intention was not to poison the regiment, but to simply sour the beer.'

Holmes ventured back to the brow of the hill. 'If she could succeed in her intention to spoil the beer, she might persuade the garrison to change supplier. It would strike a blow at the heart of Houghton's business. You will note from her accent that she is in fact London-born, from the parish of Islington, and not a native of Burton. Her loyalties do not lie with her countrymen, despite the decades she has resided here. If the regiment switched to Everard's ale, the London supplier and the preferred ale of Constable Augustus, that would be a favourable outcome.'

'However, fortunately for Miss Bilton, she was not the poisoner, unwitting or not. The number of petals that fell into the mash-tun was insufficient to create a toxic reaction.' Once again, I struggled to follow. 'Then, how was the regiment poisoned if not by Miss Bilton?'

Holmes rose to his full height and joined his hands behind his back. He reached up, as if to pluck a star from the sky, a trace of a smile forming on his lips. It was a pose I had seen many times before, most often at the denouement of a case. His head was raised in a sort of nobility of thought, his eyes sparkling; it was the aspect of a university lecturer about to elucidate his class with a solution to a problem they had toiled at fruitlessly all afternoon.

'I completed my analysis of the contaminated batch before I left Baker Street. It presented some points of the most intense interest. I would go so far as to say that they baffled me.'

'Sherlock Holmes? Baffled?' queried Miss Cresswell. Our friend emerged cat-like from the shadows. 'I did not think such a thing was possible.'

'On the contrary,' my friend returned without missing a beat, 'it is my happiest state. When one is baffled, there is brainwork to do. Of all my pleasures, none comes close to the mind working at its limit, straining at the edge of its capabilities. You have no doubt heard the entirety of our discourse.'

'Naturally.' I blushed at this, but by now, simply felt compelled to know the cause of the poisoning.

'What did you discover, Holmes?'

'In my analysis of the sample, I found not one contaminant, but three.'

'Three!' I ejaculated.

'Three,' Holmes confirmed.

'The first to reveal itself, he continued, raising a single finger into the air, 'was the *Digitalis purpurea*. It is not easy to conceal and would not be the choice of the discriminating criminal. And as I have alluded, I found this only in trace quantity. The second escaped me for a while longer. However, a series of painstaking experiments finally teased it out.' My friend reached into his pocket, then with the flourish of a magician produced a handful of grey pellets on his palm. 'Zinc Phosphide,' he declared. 'More commonly known as rat poison.'

'Good God,' I murmured, 'the poor devils. It reacts with the acids of the stomach and releases a gas that poisons from within. Extreme nausea follows, then headache, even toothache. In the most extreme cases it can result in spontaneous combustion.'

Holmes listened to this, nodding calmly in agreement. He then selected one of the pellets and dropped it into his mouth.

'Holmes,' I cried, 'no!' Miss Cresswell gasped and pressed her palm to her mouth. My friend chewed briefly, swallowed, then smiled.

'My dear Watson,' he laughed, 'your concerns are entirely without foundation.'

My eyes bulged at my friend's recklessness. 'Holmes,' I protested, 'as a doctor and as your friend, I demand that you at least attempt to bring that up. It is as much a toxin for a man as it is for a rat.'

'It was not entirely unpleasant,' he added, evenly, 'if a little sweet for my taste.' I shook my head, bewildered at my friend's actions.

'Here,' Holmes said, choosing another pellet from the table and offering it to me, 'try one for yourself.'

Miss Cresswell stepped forward wearing an expression of utter gravity, snatched the pellet then bit into it. She burst into laughter.

'You have both lost your minds!' I cried. Both Holmes and Miss Cresswell broke into laughter. 'Forgive us, Watson,' begged Holmes. 'That was uncharitable.'

'This madness must stop!' It was then that I glanced at the remaining half-pellet that Miss Cresswell held between her fingers. I noticed the centre was some sticky, black substance; the outer a broken, grey shell. I stared incredulously.

'Is that..?'

'Yes,' confirmed Holmes, finally collecting himself. 'It is a liquorice comfort.'

'You mean to say...'

'...that Inspector Hubble, whose father died a bitter, penniless alcoholic, is the poisoner of the regiment.'

FOURTEEN

The Chase

It was Inspector Giddings of the neighbouring Leicestershire force who ultimately was responsible for the arrest of Inspector Hubble. A slow, careful and deliberate man, he absorbed the points of the case one by one, nodding his head gravely, finally drawing the same conclusion as Holmes.

'We are in your debt, Mr. Holmes, he declared. 'But it is a heavy blow to the force at large when one of our own is implicated in heavy business such as this.'

Hubble was confined easily in his office by five constables, while Giddings watched sadly from the door. Hubble made no attempt to resist, simply glaring at his colleague as he was led away. For our part, our work was done. My friend and I packed our valises and finally made ready to leave the beguiling town. There was a single knock at the door.

'Our carriage, surely,' I stated. Holmes raised his nib from the page and frowned.

'A pity,' he noted, glancing down at the purple ink drying on the page, 'only a few words more and I would have concluded my monograph. It shall have to wait until we return to London. Please come in, Constable.

Augustus appeared at the door, more than a little perplexed that Holmes had correctly identified him as our caller. He was, I noticed, without his tunic and helmet.

'Ah, Constable,' said Holmes, rising from his chair and extending a hand, 'I barely recognised you in your mufti. But never was a man so truly deserving of a day off. On duty or not, only a policeman knocks with such purpose then waits with such courtesy for a response. We are familiar with the habit from the visitations of our own Inspector Lestrade.

The young constable accepted my friend's hand but was evidently preoccupied with some pressing matter. 'Mr. Holmes,' he began, with some agitation.

'There is no need to thank me,' Holmes broke in, dismissing the man's comment before it arrived. 'It was a trifling matter.'

The constable made another attempt to communicate his purpose. 'It is just that...'

'Loath, as I am,' Holmes continued, still shaking the poor fellow's hand, 'to embroil myself with police matters, I am resolved to jot a note to your district commissioner recommending you for a promotion. No doubt as an expectant father, you would find some use for the additional eight shillings. You are a good and faithful servant of the law.' By now the constable looked almost fit to burst.

'But, Mr. Holmes,' he finally declared, 'Inspector Hubble has escaped.' I leapt to my feet.

'Impossible!' I cried. 'We saw him safely confined with our own eyes.' The constable stared at the floor, his cheeks flushed. Holmes slapped a palm against the table.

'You neglected to remove his set of keys!' Holmes cried. My eyes bulged. 'Watson, we must bend to our endeavours.'

'No,' I said firmly. My friend peered at me as if I was speaking the language of a hitherto undiscovered tribe. 'There must be three hundred policemen in the county of Derbyshire. Let them attend to this. Your business is brainwork, not to engage in games of cat and mouse. It is beneath you.' For a moment Holmes seemed to consider my argument. 'You have done your work,' I added emphatically. Holmes swept to the hat stand and retrieved his ulster and cane. Then he turned and addressed me directly, checking his pocket for his Webley revolver.

'Present company excepted, the only competent policeman north of Watford has just made off with a two-thousand-year-old drinking vessel. We have spent a week disentangling an elaborate web, spun by the greedy, embittered and unscrupulous. And now you wish to deny me the thrill of the chase? No, Watson, the game is afoot.' I seized my hat and followed my friend through the doorway.

'Then Hubble is the mirror man?' I gaped.

'The same!' my friend cried.

'But how?'

'Did you not hear the slight interdental lisp? But enough. We must press on.' I shook my head, knowing full well that further protests were as futile as spitting on a blazing house.

The constable had a four-seater waiting outside. A pair of black mares shook their manes and whinnied in a familiar manner when they heard the policeman's returning footsteps. Presently, we were speeding towards the police station.

'When was the alarm raised?' Holmes demanded.

'A quarter of an hour ago,' Augustus returned. 'The duty constable awoke to discover him gone.' Holmes seized his pocket watch.

'A quarter to nine,' he muttered. 'He has a start on us, but not an unbridgeable one. Were there witnesses?'

'None, sir.'

'No one saw him leave?'

'The streets were busy, sir. It is a Tuesday morning.' Holmes plunged his jaw into the palm of his left hand.

'An elementary mistake!' he exclaimed, an accusation superficially directed towards the constable, but one, I felt, he also levelled at himself.

'Watson,' he snapped, 'your cigarettes.' I fumbled for the silver case in my inside pocket.

'You have three remaining,' Holmes declared, clicking his fingers. 'Please pass them to me.' I reluctantly surrendered my stash.

The carriage wheels had barely stopped turning when Holmes opened the window and let himself out. Instead of entering the police station, however, he crossed directly to the other side of the road, narrowly missing a hansom flying in the other direction. I followed as best I could.

He identified a plump, dishevelled fellow, with unkempt hair, lingering in the shadow of an elm tree. The man was wearing a decaying evening jacket and faded bow tie. Only then did I recognise him as the opera singer we had encountered several days earlier.

'My dear sir,' said Holmes, pressing the cigarettes into his hands, 'a little information if you will.'

'An aria, perhaps?' the man returned, a little hazily, closing his hands on my cigarettes.

'Not this morning,' my friend assured him, 'only your recollections.'

'I regret,' the man confessed, 'that I have not yet penned my memoirs.'

'Listen, man,' urged Holmes, 'did you see Inspector Hubble leave the police station some fifteen minutes ago?'

'Certainly I did,' he replied. 'I sang him a little Puccini as he left. I know he is partial to his early work.'

'And in which direction did he travel?'

'Towards the railway station,' he replied.

'Splendid. Thank you kindly, my friend.'

'Only, he was dressed as a constable, sir,'

Holmes bounded up to the driver's seat; the growler himself had disappeared inside with Augustus, believing himself relieved of his duties. I clambered up alongside my friend while he shook out the reins, turning the horse in a neat half-circle.

'We must be quick with our nets, Watson, if we are to catch our butterfly.'

We sped towards the station, making our way recklessly through the crossing gates as they were closing. 'Surely,' I protested, 'he would not be so dim as to go by train?'

'Why ever not?' Holmes returned. 'It is ten times the speed of a horse and within a few connections he could be anywhere in the country.'

'This is a disaster, Holmes.'

'Nonsense,' my friend replied, his eyes glistening. 'It is a glorious adventure!'

On arriving at the station, Holmes immediately collared the station master, a snow-haired, moustachioed fellow.

'A constable boarded the train,' said Holmes, 'not half an hour ago.' The stationmaster narrowed his eyes.

'That's right, sir,' he confirmed. 'The Buxton train. Left early holidays, has he?' We lost no time and boarded the next train.

'Look alive, Watson,' Holmes exclaimed, catching sight of the sign ahead. He pressed my newspaper back into my hand and sprang to his feet. 'Buxton is upon us and Hubble has a forty-minute start.'

The train slowed and my friend snaked his way along the corridor. Presently, I heard a prim voice in my ear.

'You did catch the train after all.'

'Good Lord, Miss Cresswell,' I chided. 'It is hardly fair to surprise me like that.'

'It is hardly fair for you to head off without me.'

'One step ahead again,' admired Holmes. 'I believe your practice may just prove a success. No doubt you wish to accompany us?'

'No doubt.'

Impatiently, Holmes lowered the window of the carriage door and pulled up the outside handle. Before we had drawn to a standstill, Holmes was away, plunging into a cloud of thick, white smoke. Cresswell and I followed a little distance behind. It was as if a dragon were crouched at the end of the platform, weighing us up as a prospective meal.

'You there!' I heard Holmes cry. He had buttonholed a signalman who appeared like a phantom through the mist.

'Yes, sir?' the man spluttered, blinking through the steam.

'A rake-thin police constable with raven hair,' my friend pressed. 'Did you see him? He was on the last train. He has a livid a scar across his face. The man furrowed his brow drummed a pair of fingers against his lips.

'A constable, you say,' he repeated.

That's right,' my friend confirmed. 'Come on man, quick about it. You were on the platform when it arrived.'

'Of course, sir. Rake-thin, you say?'

'Yes, thinner than me.'

'Thinner than you, sir?'

'Yes,'

'I can't say I did, sir.'

'Confound you!' Holmes scowled. 'How much did he give you, a guinea?'

'I have no idea...' he began, but Holmes was already sprinting through the barrier and away.

'An athletic sort of fellow, isn't he?' remarked Miss Cresswell, tapping the ground with the tip of her yellow umbrella. 'Have you thought about entering him for the Paris Olympic Games? I think he'd do awfully well.'

Clouds were gathering as we mustered outside the station, beneath the great fan window. It was a semicircle of glass, set within an impressive wall of stone, as if a clock face had been sliced neatly in two. My friend was already hectoring a pair of coachmen for information, but it seemed Hubble had bought their silence too. Holmes proffered a coin to one of them, who simply stared at him with his arms folded. It was possible, I conceived, that Hubble had connections in the area and was putting them to good use. The town, it seemed, had closed ranks around him.

'He could be five miles from here by now,' I remarked as Holmes returned to us.

'Or equally, Watson,' he parried, 'he could be five yards. Let us begin a process of elimination. First, let us discount the possibility that he has commissioned the services of a hansom. You will note that each of the growlers are in their bays and that none of the tracks left on the road are fresh. This suggests that he made his way on foot. Now, let us put ourselves in his shoes. You are in flight. Where would you run to?'

'A friend?' I suggested.

'By all means. But that is hardly data we can work with.' I glanced about, somewhat helplessly, as a fair-haired urchin chased a hoop along the pavement with a stick.

'Dash it all, Holmes,' I cried, 'he has slipped into the ether!'

'Perhaps,' my friend cautioned, 'and perhaps not.'

The wind blew up and played at the collars of our jackets. A cloud of dust and litter swept around our ankles. I wiped dust from the corner of my eye.

Presently, Holmes stooped and retrieved a small, striped pink-and-white-striped paper bag that had caught against his shoe. 'Well, well,' he murmured. Holding it between his thumb and first finger, he raised it to eye level, scrutinised it for a moment or two, then sniffed cautiously.

'Suggestive,' he smiled. 'Highly suggestive!' Bewildered, I glanced across at Miss Cresswell, who shared Holmes' inscrutable smile.

'I say,' my friend called to the urchin, 'what would you say to a quarter-pound of humbugs?'

'I would say, yes, sir,' he returned.

'Then lead us to the nearest confectioners, and be quick about it. If you take us there in two minutes, I'll make it a half-pound.'

'Right you are, sir!' the boy cried and, catching his hoop, tore off like a ravenous hound, whipping along the pavement and down the hill towards the town.

Breathlessly, we tumbled along alleyways and down lanes, barely keeping up with the sprite. But within five minutes, we stood outside a garishly painted confectioner's shop. Jars of boiled sweets filled the length and breadth of the window, displaying every conceivable colour, as if someone had somehow fathomed how to bottle a rainbow. Two jars, however, I noted, were entirely empty. My friend fell in through the door and advanced to the counter.

A small, neat, bespectacled fellow stood attentively at the counter. His head was as smooth and white as a mint imperial, his hazel eyes peering out like brandy balls. 'Liquorice,' demanded Holmes, planting a coin on the polished wood. The man's face formed itself into a pained expression, his eyebrows raised like the two halves of Tower Bridge.

'You're right out of luck, sir,' he confessed. 'I have just sold my entire supply of comfits, sticks and wheels not half an hour ago.'

'All of them?' I queried.

'There has been something of a run on them. Perhaps I could interest you in some chocolate limes?'

'A thin man,' Holmes broke in, 'with jet black hair and a scar across his left cheek.'

'And who might you be to make such enquiries?'

'Sherlock Holmes of 221b Baker Street.' The shopkeeper stared at my friend for a moment, then burst into a peal of high-pitched laughter

'And I'm the Emperor of China!' He dabbed at his eyes.

'Well,' urged Holmes.

'Yes, that's the fellow,' the man confirmed. 'He seemed in an awful hurry.'

'As well he might be,' noted Miss Cresswell. 'Perhaps it is as well for you to learn that you have just received a visit from a murderer.'

The man blanched and felt for his handkerchief.

'A murderer?' he dabbed at the beads of sweat gathering on his brow.

'A murderer, my friend clarified, 'with an addiction to liquorice, one might add, and in need of a month's supply. You have just abetted a known felon.' The hapless shopkeeper pulled a lever on his cash register and the drawer sprang open. Collecting a handful of coins, he flung them on the counter.

'Blood money!' he cried. The coins clattered to a standstill, a single sixpence left spinning.

'May I ask,' Holmes enquired coolly, inspecting the coin, 'in which of your upper rooms I would find Mr. Hubble?' He peered intently at the shopkeeper, fixing him with that cold, steely stare I have seen him deploy at such moments.

'I'm sorry?' the man spluttered. His cheeks flushed the same deep shade as the cherry drops that stood in the jar by a large set of scales.

'Is it the front,' pressed Holmes, 'or the back bedroom?' The man appeared dumbfounded, his lower jaw agape, in a manner I fancied somewhat akin to a whale, as it prepared to consume a shoal of plankton. 'There is a trail of footprints belonging to Mr. Hubble,' Holmes noted, 'leading to your counter, but which do not appear to have returned to the front door. Do you see the small indentation at the heel of the left foot? It is a singular aberration and entirely unique to

Inspector Hubble.' The man glanced down at the floor, then back at my friend, a wild look in his eye. In an instant, he pushed past Holmes, reached over for the brass service bell and struck it repeatedly with the flat of his hand.

'Run, Mr. Hubble, run!' he blurted. My friend leapt up and over the counter in a single smooth movement, an athletic display only marred by catching his shoe against a jar, sending it hurtling to the floor, the sweets shattering in a cloud of sugar. Holmes disappeared up a set of stairs. The shopkeeper, meanwhile, had crumpled into a corner, flailing, his hands covering his eyes. I flipped open the counter and dashed after my friend, pulling my service revolver from my pocket.

There was a stamp of boots on the floorboard above us as someone ran from the back to the front of the premises. I was only halfway up the stairs when I heard the crash of glass and a wild cry, I identified as Hubble's. Scrambling up the remaining stairs, I flew to the front bedroom to find a morass of broken glass and a gaping hole in the bay window. I was just in time to see Hubble's lanky figure below, his jacket torn, his hair dishevelled, and bloodied about the face, his own revolver pointing towards my friend who stood with him, utterly defenceless in the street. My soldiering instincts took command; I felt a curious detachment from my actions and sensed my heart rate slowing. I took careful aim and prepared to despatch Hubble there and then.

Two shots cracked in quick succession. There was a polyphony of cries and screams as pedestrians bolted for cover and the entire shop window caved in. For one terrifying moment, I believed he had murdered my friend in cold blood. Hubble stood with a smoking gun, as aniseed balls, gobstoppers and tom thumbs cascaded from their shattered jars and into the gutters around his feet.

'Kindly tell your friend,' Hubble warned, evidently referring to me, 'to return his revolver to his left pocket. Dr. Watson, you are not only dim-witted, but your reactions are those of an old man. I took a gamble that your nerves were shot to pieces, and my assumption was correct.' It was only then that I saw Holmes' own Webley 45 lying on a faded ochre rug that meanly furnished the floor of the bedroom. Evidently, the revolver had slipped from his grasp as he followed Hubble through the window.

A hansom, I perceived, was clattering along the street at some velocity, a black mare at its head. For a moment, I believed the case would be resolved in an instant, but, at the critical moment, Hubble took a pace backwards and watched as the horse reared up, almost unseating the driver. With the carriage now between Holmes and himself, Hubble brusquely ordered down the confused growler and frogmarched the passengers onto the pavement.

'I say,' said a woman in a pink frock and elaborate hat, peering at him through her pince-nez, 'are you a highwayman?'

'I am,' he hissed at her, 'the very devil himself.' She shrieked and dropped her eyeglass. Taking up the reins, he continued to train his gun on my friend. 'Attempt to follow me,' he cautioned, 'and I will shoot a member of the public. If I so much as glimpse one of your faces, I will not hesitate to kill a man.'

'Do not attempt to follow me, Holmes,' he warned. 'This is not your business; this is not even your case.' With that, he shook out the reins and then took off, all the while his arm outstretched, with the barrel of his gun directly on Holmes, who stood perfectly still in the street.

At once, Holmes dropped to one knee in the gutter; for an appalling moment I believed he was shot. Then, relief and no little curiosity, I saw him scoop up a handful of pineapple cubes. In one fluid movement, he flung them onto the roof of the departing Hansom. Hubble glanced back with a look of irritation, then finally, lowering his gun, took the corner at speed and disappeared.

I took the stairs two at a time, and presently, I was standing with Miss Cresswell at Holmes' side.

'Ah, Watson,' said Holmes brightly. 'You missed all the fun.'

'Your revolver,' I frowned, pressing it into my friend's hand.

'Most grateful,' he remarked, returning it to a pocket inside his coat. 'We must have parted company in all the excitement. Just like you and me.' The sound of the hansom's wheels died away.

'Not hurt I hope?' I enquired. 'It must have been a ten-foot drop.'

'You forget the Reichenbach Falls, Doctor,' returned Holmes, flashing a boyish smile. 'I survived a drop of 360 feet, at least.'

'You did no such thing!' I demurred.

'It depends whom you choose to believe,' he said. 'Let us only hope Moriarty did not pull off the same trick. A crash of glass came from behind us, and, as we turned, the shopkeeper came staggering out into the street. The last unbroken window pane had succumbed to gravity. The man stared at the shattered remains of his shop; not a single piece of glazing intact and two great holes blasted in the brickwork.

'Perhaps, Mr. Barniston,' advised Holmes, surveying the devastation, 'you will think twice before harbouring a villain again, no matter how sweet his tooth.'

Dejected, I kicked at an assortment of sweets.

'Now, now, Doctor,' chastened Miss Cresswell. 'There's no need to lose one's temper.'

'Well,' I said, my hands plunged deep into my pockets, 'we are no better off than we were a half hour ago. Pursuit would be an act of madness. And yet, if we don't give chase, we will have lost the trail entirely. By breakfast he could be halfway to Kathmandu.'

My friend essayed that thin smile I knew so well. 'My dear Watson! Such a noble spirit. Disappointment ill suits you. We have a line-life yet.' I glanced up.

'Which is?'

'The pineapple cubes.' I cocked my head in enquiry.

'You will have observed I cast a handful of them upon the roof of the Hansom as it departed. It stands to reason that, one by one, they will topple off the roof as it makes its way across town. All that remains for us to do is to follow the trail at a safe distance and it will lead us directly to him. Now, let us make haste before the town's children devour our wayfinders.'

I noticed how my friend's eye suddenly caught the colourful miscellany of fondants and bonbons that carpeted the pavement.

'If I may,' Holmes said, turning to the shopkeeper, 'perhaps I could make a suggestion?'

'Yes?' the man stuttered, squinting through his cracked spectacles.

'Have you considered throwing together a mixture of sweets, rather than selling them along strictly partisan lines?'

'No,' he said, 'I don't believe I have.'

'For instance,' proposed Holmes, warming to his theme, 'there are those who enjoy coconut ice, aniseed jellies, liquorice plugs and twists. Why sell them separately? You are imposing a decision on your customer he may not wish to make. Look at what an attractive mishmash they make together. Sell them as a merry jumble and you will make a fortune!'

'They would need a name,' complained the shopkeeper. 'Whatever would I write on the jar?'

'Call them 'Liquorice Allsorts'.'

A thin mist of rain swept in off the moors and Buxton was enveloped in its damp veil. Nonetheless, the town retained enough nobility from its handsome architecture and bustling, respectable folk to prevent this from dampening its spirits. The shops were laden with brightly coloured trinkets for the tourists and delicatessens glowed, their displays brimming with pickles, scotched eggs and sweetmeats. It occurred to me we had not eaten since breakfast, and I felt a momentary dizziness – a sensation I had often experienced on my adventures with Holmes. As I have frequently related, he is more machine than man in his methods and, when in thrall to a case, his bodily needs become a triviality. Sleep and sustenance cease to interest him entirely.

My friend led the way, his hawkish nose to the ground, his eyes lighting on each golden cube that lay in the gutter or half crushed under a brougham's wheel in the centre of the road. Occasionally, he would venture across to a newspaper hawker or boot shiner and enquire after the hansom, on each occasion being met with shrugs and furtive glances, as if they knew but would not tell.

Presently, I heard an aria; it was the same glorious voice I had heard in Burton – another matchless melody from Puccini. I barely had time to doff my cap at the itinerant maestro and fling a shilling in his hat as I passed. He peered at me with a strange intensity as if he could read my very thoughts.

I had long wished to visit the town and sample the waters. I could not count the number of patients I had referred here with a prescription to clear their heads and air their lungs; to escape the prison of London's sulphurous skies. Mary too had spoken of it several times, gaily suggesting that I close my practice early on a Friday, board a train and spend the weekend drinking wine and taking in the opera. As we hurried through its streets, I felt that sharp pang of loss that can ambush the widower and leave him utterly bereft.

The tenor continued to stare as I looked back, and in my distraction, I collided directly with the solid, brass-buttoned chest of a policeman. It was akin to running into the side of a house at full tilt. I reeled sideways and would, no doubt, have toppled over, had he not caught me with both arms and steadied me.

'You'd best watch where you're going, sir,' he warned. 'If I had been an omnibus instead of a servant of the law, you would have been flattened like a slice of mutton.' He wore a door-knocker, a laconic look and carried at least a third of his body weight in reserve. He levelled his gaze at me, no doubt to ascertain whether I was two sheets to the wind. Satisfied that I was sober, he released me and even dusted my shoulders. I was still too winded to gather my thoughts into a coherent reply. He took the opportunity to fill in my part of the conversation.

'You appear to be a respectable-looking gentleman, sir, albeit in an awful hurry. If I were you, I would take a little extra care, and a little extra time too, especially if your sport is to walk blindly down the middle of the road. We are not mayflies, sir. Our mortal coil extends longer than a day. Take some time to smell the roses, that's my advice, sir. All this rushing about does you no good at all. I've already had cause to remind your friend here. The same goes for you, madam, if you wish to preserve your dress, I'd suggest the pavement would be your preferred path.' Holmes appeared at my side.

'Constable,' he broke in. 'Preposterous though it sounds, we are pursuing Inspector Hubble of the Burton Constabulary.' The constable frowned at what he evidently perceived to be the utterance of a madman.

'Inspector Hubble?' the constable responded, incredulously. 'He's the straightest lace there is.'

'Have you not heard,' my friend continued, 'he is responsible for the attempted murder of fifty of the Queen's men in the Punjab? Moreover, he has threatened to murder others in this very town. Would you be able to offer your assistance, operating under my direction?'

'Operating under your direction?' the constable returned, ushering us to the side of the road. 'You'd make a stuffed bird laugh. Now, I think the appropriate course of action would be for you three theatrical birds to follow me to the station where you can explain all this to my superior. He is a sensible man of even temper. Let's see if he can make some sense of you, even if I can't.'

I was suddenly aware of a commotion building behind us. Glancing back, I could see a crowd moving towards us with the momentum of a locomotive, elbows and knees pumping like pistons. At the head of the crowd was small, bald man I recognised instantly as Mr. Barniston, the confectioner.

'There they are!' one of the mob shouted.

'Now, what's all this,' frowned the constable, reaching for his baton. One of the crowd jabbed a finger towards us.

'They're the vandals who destroyed Mr. Barniston's shop. I saw them with my own eyes.'

'I suppose,' the constable growled, 'that this is also Inspector Hubble's work too, isn't it?'

'As a matter of fact, it is,' I offered, a little weakly.

Holmes shot me a look. 'Thank you, Constable,' he offered, 'but perhaps we will be able to manage on our own after all.'

'Now, you just wait,' he began, but before he could conclude his thought, we were away again, our hands pressed to our hats, weaving through the crowds.

'It is perhaps fortunate,' Miss Cresswell suggested, 'that I have been in late summer training ahead of the winter snow season. 'I was led to believe that Sherlock Holmes led a largely sedentary existence. On the contrary, I think we should enter him into the Cheltenham cup!'

At full gallop, we had succeeded in putting some distance between ourselves and our pursuers. However, as we neared the north-western edge of the town, where the red-brick houses gave way to sloping fields and trees, I knew that I could not maintain this pace. Already the day's exertions had winded me; a dull throb in my old war wound had become a burning ache, and I felt my frame weaken with every step.

'Here!' my friend declared. 'The trail ends here.' It was a blessed reprieve. 'I threw fourteen pineapple cubes onto the roof of the hansom.' He held up a cube between his thumb and forefinger. 'This is the fourteenth.'

'With respect, Mr. Holmes,' Miss Cresswell put in, not a little sceptically, 'all that tells us is that fourteen sweets fell from the cab. Hubble could well have continued for another five miles.'

'As well as he might,' agreed Holmes, 'but not in that conveyance at least.' He gestured towards a hansom, abandoned and lop-sided on the edge of the hill. Beside it, a black mare nibbled contentedly at the cud.

Quick as a whip, my friend was next to the carriage, crouched next to its right-hand side. He then made his way around to the other side and examined the ground, meticulously, clearly inspecting some footprints.

'Most singular,' I heard him mutter. Suitably intrigued, Miss Cresswell soon joined him.

'Two sets of footprints,' she observed.

'Precisely so,' my friend concurred.

'Then, he has an accomplice,' I deduced.

'Perhaps,' said Holmes, somewhat doubtfully. I stepped a little way forward, keen, I admit, to show Miss Cresswell my own aptitude in this area.

'There!' I declared with triumph. I pointed towards a set of footprints leading back into town, neatly printed into the mud at the edge of the road. 'Those are Hubble's and no mistake. Look at the small indentation at the heel.'

'Bravo, Watson,' Holmes returned, inspecting them for himself and brushing away a flurry of golden leaves that had caught against his ulster. 'I agree that they are Hubble's shoes.'

'Then, let us waste no time.'

'I am of the same view,' Holmes replied. 'However, I would make one further observation. Hubble was not wearing his shoes at the time.' I stared at him.

'What? Holmes, this is hardly the moment...'

'My dear fellow,' my friend smiled, straightening up, 'I don't mean to suggest they became somehow enchanted. I am merely inferring that Hubble persuaded a passer-by to exchange his boots for his own.'

'Who would agree to such a bizarre request?'

'Someone,' he replied, 'with a gun pressed to his temple?' Holmes cast about, then uncovered a small, thin object from the leaf litter.

'The broken stem,' he announced, 'of an old briar pipe; and here, a tattered handkerchief. Ah, yes, and the ancient pipe bowl itself. These belong to a man with few possessions. He has accosted a gentleman tramp and forcibly removed his boots, then sent him into town.'

'Unless, of course,' Miss Cresswell broke in, 'it is a double bluff? This inspector is no fool and perfectly familiar with your methods.' I registered a flicker of irritation on my friend's part, followed by a rare moment of indecision. He recovered himself in an instant.

'Do you see,' he indicated with a long, white finger, 'the deep impression in each boot-print two-thirds of the way along the length of those heading into town? The man wearing Hubble's boots indisputably has smaller feet. His toes, rather than the boot heels themselves have made the indentation.'

Miss Cresswell shrugged. 'I could produce the same effect by curling my toes within my shoes.' She flashed me a mischievous look. 'While my theory is improbable, it is not impossible.' If Holmes were annoyed, this time he managed to disguise it better.

'There are three of us,' I put in, attempting to broker a peace. 'Perhaps we would be best advised to divide our party?'

'No,' my friend pronounced, his eyes fixed on the invisible summit, 'he is up on the hill.'

Moments later, we were ascending a steep bank, thickly lined with ash and birch. Wending our way through the trees, it was impossible to see far ahead and I could not help but feel exposed if Hubble fancied taking a pot shot. Once more, I felt myself weakened, if not from fear for the day was far too strange for such a hum-drum emotion – then at least from lack of food and exertion.

'If you don't mind my saying, Doctor,' Miss Cresswell noted, trudging at my side, 'you look a little pale. In my experience, it is doctors who neglect themselves most. Are you feeling quite well?'

'Never better,' I muttered, unconvincingly. She reached into her pocket and produced a handful of unclaimed babies, those jelly sweets favoured by children and the aged. 'I took the precaution of swiping a handful before we left the shop.' I nodded my acknowledgement and devoured them gratefully.

Within ten minutes, we were met with a dry-stone wall that ran along the length of a field. Sheep stared at us with their alien, rectangular pupils.

'Ah,' said Miss Cresswell brightly, 'the even-toed ungulate. Perhaps we ought to ask if they have seen anything.' Miss Cresswell's discourse had assumed a facetious note. Holmes glanced about him.

'The footprints lead east, along the length of stone wall. Let us keep our heads low and use the cover of the wall. Be on your guard, it is quite possible he is watching us at this moment.'

'Holmes!' I cried suddenly, pointing to the earth. 'Two has become three.' My heart pounded as Cresswell and Holmes stooped to inspect the footprints.

'Well, well,' said Holmes, 'so our friend, the three-legged man, is with us here on the hill. He appears as if from nowhere.' He scanned the horizon. 'This way.' We stumbled onwards, the prints leading us to a gap in the wall, then across an open field.

Navigating through the sheep-droppings, we crossed as quickly and cautiously as we could. Without the trees for shelter, we found ourselves utterly exposed, with the wind and rain conspiring to create a hellish gale - what my friend always referred to as 'hat-losing weather.' The terrain had grown positively volcanic, with large, grey boulders breaking through the thin, wind-blown grass, attempting to trip us at every step.

Finally, we reached the wall of sheer rock that led to the summit. 'Listen,' cried Holmes. 'Do you hear that?' I listened for a moment, hearing nothing but the wind playing through the gaps in the stone wall, followed by the caw of a distant crow. Holmes held himself perfectly still, his fingers raised as if conducting nature itself.

'There!' he cried. 'There it is again.' Sure enough, I could hear a faint voice intoning an ancient melody.

'Yes, I think I hear it.' It seemed eerily familiar, a child's ballad perhaps. Holmes' eyes gleamed in the most peculiar way.

'After me,' he called, then skipped nimbly along the path in the direction of the singer. He held up a hand to silence me, then gestured to the figure of a man crouched on a hill. Keeping our heads below the wall, we saw the figure through the loose rocks, his face hidden in shadow. He was singing random snatches of verse.

'Then, up spoke the cook of our gallant ship,' he croaked, 'and a greasy old butcher was he.'

'The Mermaid!' said Miss Cresswell. 'A hoary old tune.' Now where did I hear that before?

'Brizlincote Hall,' muttered Holmes. 'Do you remember the music box?'

Presently, my friend rose to his full height. I seized his coat, attempting to hold him back.

'Have you lost your wits, Holmes?'

'We are coming towards you,' he called over to the man.

'Come! Come!' the man called back. 'All of you.' Miss Cresswell peered at me with a look of strange serenity, then laid a hand on mine. 'There is nothing to fear, Doctor.' She too got to her feet and walked towards him, as if held in a spell or hypnosis. There was nothing for it but to follow. A few steps further, and I saw his face.

'By great Gordon's ghost,' I cried, 'it is Anaxagoras!' The man stared at me with the face of a ghoul. He looked ten years older, his hair pure white, his face utterly drained of colour. He clutched his side, as if recovering from a stitch.

'But...' I started. It was unfathomable. 'I saw your lifeless body myself in the hidden room at the hall.'

'You mistake me,' the man said, in a hoarse whisper, for my brother. My name is Claudius. Claudius Houghton.'

'A twin,' I whispered. The man winced and allowed himself a hollow laugh.

'We shared a face, but not our father's favour.'

'Did you not see, Watson,' said Holmes. 'In the attic at the hall. There were two of everything: two rocking horses; two cots.'

'No doubt,' the man said, 'you remember from your schoolbooks, Claudius, Emperor of Rome. The crippled god! He was born with a limp and deafness to boot. I was the one they hid away. Our father, Charles Houghton, the great Founder himself, how could he admit to any weakness? I saw only a handful of people in my whole childhood. My brother Anaxagoras was my closest friend. When I was all of ten years of age, they sent me away. To Canada. But they could not hide me forever. I came to claim my birth-right, but my brothers turned me away. They disowned me – even Anaxagoras!' He buckled up in pain.

'Where are you hurt?' I asked.

'Keep away!' he barked.

'They were brainwashed by my father. When he died, I took this.' He reached down and lifted a walking cane at the base of which, was an ancient leather boot.

'My father's foot,' he cried. 'May he suffer in death what I suffered in life!' I stared in horror.

'Hubble knew of me. He approached me with the scheme: to raid my father's antiquities; bring the trinkets to the Marquess, and restore my fortune. He promised he would help me destroy my father's legacy and avenge me of my brothers.'

'But,' I began, 'why are you telling us this?'

'Because...' He lifted his hand to reveal a palm, painted in blood. 'Because the game is up. Naturally,' he added with a bitter smile, 'there is no honour among thieves.'

I sank to my knees, righting to compress the bullet wound, but it was too late. He was gone. His glassy eyes stared at the heavens. In that moment, I saw the reflection of a crow passing overhead, as if his very soul were leaving him.

The sky shook with thunder. Great dark billows of cloud stacked upon themselves like a fortress, towering into the heavens. There was a whistle-crack and a bullet passed between Holmes and myself. We exchanged a glance, then glimpsed Hubble's silhouette on the brow of the hill.

We scrambled after him, higher up the path, the grass yielding to bare patches of loose scree. Hubble's boots struggled for grip as he staggered back, his revolver still pointing towards us. In the distance, a small, stone tower crowned the summit of the ridge. We edged closer until we were within earshot, sheltered now by a large boulder just feet from the tower.

'I have been conducting some investigations of my own,' growled Hubble, walking backwards, a wild look in his eye. 'Your clever Miss Cresswell is an agent for a London museum.'

'Nothing we did not know ourselves,' my friend said evenly. 'Now it will go better for you if you end this now.' Hubble shook his head, a shank of wet, dark hair plastered to his brow.

A pair of constables in glistening capes were climbing the path behind us, both with a hand affixed to their custodians.

'Those buffoons,' sneered Hubble.

I stole a quick glance over the rock. My foolhardiness was rewarded with the crack of Hubble's pistol. The shot glanced away, not three inches from my cheek, scoring the stone and sending up a cloud of dust.

'For pity's sake, Watson,' scolded Holmes, 'yours is not a handsome face, but I prefer it in its current arrangement.' We lapsed into silence. 'Do you hear that?'

Holmes put a finger to his lips and we listened intently.

Sure enough, there was a sound beyond the wind whipping around the cold, grey tower. It was the sound of horses: hooves sucking at the mud and drumming against the grass. They were approaching and building to a furious gallop.

Holmes' brow was knitted in concentration. 'Two mounts,' he pronounced, 'only one with a rider.' I dropped down a few steps and peered through the narrow window.

Sure enough a figure was approaching on a magnificent chestnut stallion.

'It's him,' shuddered Miss Cresswell, 'the man with the mirrored face.'

'But Holmes said it was Hubble.'

'Well Sherlock Holmes was wrong.' The words clung to the air.

'So it appears,' he confessed.

I looked again and, sure enough, the man's features were curiously blank – one moment sky, the next earth. He gripped the reins and rifle in one hand, and with the other, held a length of rope which was tethered to a white mare. It was fitted with a saddle and bridle in readiness for a rider. Plainly, he was heading towards us.

'I believe,' said Holmes. 'This man is effecting a rescue.' The horses reared up at the base of the tower.

'Go with him,' shouted Holmes after Hubble, 'and you are as good as dead. Give yourself up and things may go better for you. I shall do what I can.' Hubble gave his answer in gunpowder and lead shot. Holmes flung himself forward and through the doorway. We followed as best we could, watching Holmes' heels disappear up the stone steps. We arrived at the top only to see Hubble drop down from the ramparts onto the waiting horse. He landed heavily, sprawling over the beast's neck but managed to grip the harness and right himself. I stood at my friend's side as Hubble and the mirror man tore down the hillside and away.

'Confound it!' I cried. 'So close and yet he escapes.'

'Not quite,' Miss Cresswell declared. 'I have a notion.'

Such was the strange and luminous world of my friend, Sherlock Holmes, that I had long ceased to be surprised at the seemingly impossible turn of events.

Follow me,' she instructed. With an impish grin, Miss Cresswell turned on her heels and bolted down the steps.

'We can't very well outrun a horse,' I protested, clattering after her.

'I have no intention of outrunning anything, Doctor,' she called back. We arrived at the top of the slope, which gave us a perfect vantage point of the escaping riders. They were already half-way down the valley.

'Do you know,' she said, surveying the vast hill below, 'give or take a little snow, this isn't so different from the slopes of St. Moritz.' I had still not yet fathomed her plan. 'Now, ideally, a length of elastic would be useful to stop my skirts gathering up, but needs must.'

'A capital idea!' declared Holmes, evidently ahead of me.

'Now, would you mind, lending a hand, Doctor?' She gestured towards what appeared to be a rusted water trough, almost entirely hidden in the long grass.

Stamping down the undergrowth, we discovered the trough owned a pair of large, rusted wheels, which stood upon an even rustier set of steel rails. Evidently, it was some abandoned contraption from the lime works that once prospered on the hillside.

'You can't possibly...' I began.

'Not just me,' she replied. 'It will take all three of us to generate enough momentum.' I glanced desperately at Holmes in the hope he could dissuade her.

'There must be some other way,' I urged.

'Not that I can see,' shrugged Holmes. 'I'm game if you are.'

Hauling out a bird's nest, a quantity of rocks and a single ancient leather shoe, we carved out just about enough room for the three of us. With the end of her brolly, Miss Cresswell hacked away at the largest of the shrubs and weeds that tethered the cart to the track and for the first time it seemed conceivable it could in fact move.

'Given my experience on the Cresta Run,' declared Miss Cresswell, 'I rather think it's best that I drive, don't you, gentlemen?' With that she clambered in at the front, leaving us little choice but to join her, with Holmes at the rear and myself sandwiched in between.

'Well, Watson,' my friend put in, adjusting his position a little, 'this has a singular advantage over a hansom: no fare!' I leaned out and peered down, now able to make out the trajectory of the rails that appeared to put us on a collision course with the riders.

'I suppose,' I said, without a great deal of conviction, 'there is always the brake.' With the three of us aboard, the cart began to move forward, imperceptibly at first, then slowly gaining momentum as it broke free from the remaining grasses and vines that snared the axles and wheels. I heard the grinding of the ancient mechanisms, a whine from somewhere below us, and finally the snap of something – important or otherwise – and we were unquestionably on the move. Within seconds it felt as if we were inside a speeding brougham; a few seconds more and it was as if we were piloting a cannonball.

218

'Hold tight back there,' Miss Cresswell warned, her hat flying off and away. She gripped the sides of the cart. A wild, joyous note had entered her voice.

'Perhaps a moment to apply the brakes?' I suggested.

'Nonsense!' she cried. 'We reached sixty miles an hour out on the Cresta Run. This is nothing, Doctor!'

The hillside became a blur of green light and the cart shook so violently that I felt certain my teeth and bones had become permanently rearranged.

'Most efficient!' chortled Holmes, clearly enjoying the ride. 'I say, perhaps a little to the left, if we can manage it?'

It seems likely that as we approached critical velocity, I blacked out for a moment or two. Even now, I can recall only fragments of the final stages of that terrifying descent. There was the frantic whinnying of a horse; the spectacle of my friend, Sherlock Holmes, staring quizzically at the brake wheel that had sheared away in his hand; the giddy whoop of Miss Cresswell as we left the rails and shot into the air. I was only faintly aware of the rider who was thrown from his horse, although I am entertained now by the thought of us all in the air at the same time, not unlike a set of juggling balls.

Like a mighty slap across the face, I was met with the full force of the earth as it rose up to meet me. This was as nothing compared with the sensation that followed. My chest compressed like a concertina. In an instant, I was lying utterly winded in the quagmire. Quite calmly, despite the acute pain, I counted my cracked ribs: two for certain, and possibly a third. With a huge effort, I succeeded in raising my head to discover I was lying prostrate beside Hubble. He lay on his back, stunned and insensible, a livid gash drawn across his forehead. I studied his chest a moment. Satisfied he was not in mortal danger, I glanced to my right to see the other horse and rider galloping away into the distance. As a man whose life was saved by a horse in Afghanistan, I have always maintained a solemn respect for our equine friends.

'Look alive, Watson!'

The familiar voice shook me from my reverie. In a moment, I perceived the dark shape of the inspector standing over me. He had recovered his wits. Instinctively, I rolled to one side, in time to hear his gun discharge into the shallow pit I had just vacated. Forgetting my pain, I leapt to my feet and faced him, my hands coiled into fists. He seemed now more beast than man. Abandoned by his masked conspirator, his face was grotesquely distorted with pain and rage. Yet this time, I stood no chance. The barrel of the gun was aimed directly at my chest. I closed my eyes.

The next moment, I felt a blunt instrument strike my face, sending a lightning bolt of pain through every tooth and bone. I crumpled again to the ground, conscious only that his gun had not fired, and that instead I had been struck by the handle. By this time, Holmes was upon him. His own stick raised in Bartitsu, after which all went dark.

I came to, I am told, some five minutes later. Surveying my friends, I admitted an involuntary laugh. Each of us was daubed from nose to knee in mud. Indeed, Miss Cresswell, who was the first to be thrown from the cart, appeared to have stepped directly from the primordial ooze.

'A perfectly good bit of tweed ruined,' she remarked, fingering the collar of her jacket.

Holmes, who had somehow managed to retrieve his pipe, miraculously unbroken in the spill, was now, it seemed, having trouble locating his mouth.

'You have no cause to snigger, Watson,' my friend warned as he snapped one damp match after another, 'given your perfect impersonation of a hippopotamus at bathing time.'

'God's teeth,' put in Miss Cresswell at the mention of this, 'what would I give for a hot bath and a long, cool glass of gin.'

'I doubt,' I remarked, rubbing my face and passing my handkerchief to her, 'that we would gain admittance to any local hostelry of decent standing.'

'I would settle,' my friend opined, 'for a bucket of water in a workhouse.'

It was only then that I noticed Hubble lying quite still on the grass. 'He will have plenty of time,' opined Holmes, 'to nurse his wounds at Her Majesty's pleasure.'

For the first time that day, a seam of golden light glowed at the edge of a cloud. Presently, one or two rays shot through and lit the corners of distant fields.

'It is time,' Holmes announced, succeeding at last in locating his lips, 'to illuminate the dark corners of this case and to be on our way.'

We made our statements to Inspector Giddings, while the two constables stood watchfully over Hubble, who quietly seethed as Holmes explained the events as if telling a simple tale to a young child. Orders were given to arrest Butterworth and Tolwood, but Holmes asked for leniency. They were, he said, good men led astray.

Throughout the account, Hubble glared at him, his cheeks livid, his eyes blank with rage. We watched as the pitiful figure was led away from that dark, Derbyshire hillside, his hands bound behind him, his head raised defiantly still.

'Proud to the last,' I mused.

'A pitiable sight,' remarked Holmes. 'To his unbalanced mind, a sort of crooked justice was served.'

'And what of the mirror man,' I asked.

'We shall see him again, I fear,' he mused. 'But that is not for today. Once again, my powers are called into question. How could I not see that a greater force was at work? I must restore my strength and return to the chambers of my mind.'

'And the antiquities?'

'They will return with Miss Cresswell to the British Museum and a grateful nation.'

'And finally, the coopers?'

'Mere hired thugs,' explained Holmes, 'in the pay of Hubble, to scare us away.'

The inspector shook our hands, lingering I noticed as he thanked Holmes, a little star-struck and deferential in his manner. 'I shall arrange for a carriage to meet you at the bottom of the hill,' he informed us, then, nodding at our muddied attire: 'I should imagine, if you tip your driver well enough, he may forgive the mud on his seat leather.'

Soon enough, we were left alone on the hillside.

'There,' said Holmes, 'do you see the crow flying into the sun? He returns to his tree, another day of butchery and cruelty behind him. It is time we returned to the comforts of our own nest. My supply of Persian tobacco grows dangerously short and the soft cushions of my chaise longue at Baker Street beckon. Now, if you would be so good, Watson, as to step three paces to your left.'

I furrowed my brow at this obtuse request, at the same time dimly aware of a lengthening shadow gaining upon us.

Presently, three Penny Farthings descended gently from the heavens, bounced lightly on the grasslands, then rose gracefully back into the air, their wheels spinning slowly. I craned my neck, peering up as a hot-air balloon hovered not ten feet above us.

I was greeted by the unmistakable face of our old friend Crabtree, a pair of monocles affixed to his face, sporting that same idiotic grin. Ten years on from our first encounter, he was greyer about the whiskers, but no less ebullient in his manner.

'Would you care,' he offered, raising his topper, 'for a lift back to London?' My friend returned the gesture, raising the brim of his own hat.

'How very kind,' he replied, as if the balloon's arrival were no less surprising than that of an omnibus.

Despite my reservations, I was too tired to protest. We each clambered aboard the appliances, which were suspended on wires from the basket.

'You will find a slice of ox tongue and a pint of pale ale in the pannier,' Crabtree called down.

'We are very much obliged,' said Miss Cresswell gamely, already astride her contraption. 'Up, up and away!'

'There is urgent business afoot,' warned Crabtree. 'Captain Solomon Birdwhistle has returned and is wreaking havoc in the capital. Lestrade seeks your earliest assistance.'

Crabtree fired a burst of flame and we rose giddily into the air, our feet involuntarily turning the pedals as if we were powering our own flight. The greys and browns of the earth fell away until the hillside became little more than a table cover and the tower a coffee pot below us. To our left, the town receded too as we cycled, the three of us, into the salmon-pink sunset, yet another adventure behind us, following a murder of crows back to London.

Acknowledgements

Thank you to Sir Arthur Conan Doyle for creating these wonderful characters, and to Eleanor Davison for her meticulous copy editing. All mistakes that remain are my own. Thanks also to my partner in crime, Maria, and to her family in Burton-upon-Trent, particularly Toni Walsh, for their kind hospitality during our many visits to the town.

Also by Christopher James and published by MX Publishing:

Sherlock Holmes and the Adventure of the Ruby Elephants
Sherlock Holmes and the Jeweller of Florence